The Sea Is Coming

(A NOVEL)

BY
JACK D. WHELAN

THE SEA IS COMING

OLD HEAD MEDIA
Republic of Ireland

First published in 2021
ISBN: 978-1-9993045-1-5

Cover Art: Basya Rose Kilcoyne

DEDICATION

For family

It began in a brief and dizzy spell of possibilities,
and ended on a sea of shattered dreams.

CHAPTER ONE

I have a dream. In my dream I see a man on fire, falling from an almost cloudless sky. He is flailing madly and trying to put out the flames, which have engulfed him, unaware that the earth is rushing up to meet him. An unseen entity whispers, he believes there is still such a thing as hope in the world. A parachute huffs and puffs but can no longer resist gravity's merciless pull. Like a puppet of crimson red and orange and black, he dangles there, tethered to the finest of strings. Beyond the flaming torch, a distant aircraft blows pitch-black smoke as it coughs and spits and spins towards the earth. The man, still patting madly at the little fires all over his body, falls through a green canopy and disappears, and somewhere in the distance, the aircraft disappears out of sight.

There is a second part of my dream where I see the man again. He is burned black, his limbs splayed haphazardly across white sand, lying motionless. The sound of water gurgling and splashing echoes throughout this part of my dream, and as I conjure up the image a fast flowing chocolate brown river reveals itself. A mottled green landscape surrounds it and completes it. Sounds echo loudly. Animals and birds calling out to each other in panic. An invisible hand reaches forward and turns the man about. It is in that moment before all is revealed, that I wake drenched in sweat, shaking and unnerved. I reach out my arm to feel for Henry's reassuring presence, realising as the wakefulness comes upon me that he isn't there. He is gone and I am alone, with just my memories for company.

CHAPTER TWO

The day, which began with the news that would change everything, was like every other day. I remember I sat at the kitchen table for breakfast, eating a bowl of porridge, and listening to the BBC Home Service on the wireless set. It was going a little crackle and pop and snap as the announcer's voice faded in and out, but I could just about make out that the man was telling his audience about some minor breakthrough regarding supply ships getting to Liverpool and Glasgow, and reminding the listener that the danger of submarines still existed.

I stirred my porridge and added a little honey and stirred it again as I listened intently, feeling the waft of steam on my face, and let the announcer's words resonate a little longer.

The outlook looks rather glum, I thought to myself. Status-quo, blockades, submarines, made it all seem impossible for anything at all to be done. There was bombing at that time, of course. London had endured most of those terrible early days and nights. Liverpool and Birmingham had their share too. A part of me felt glad to be out of the city because of the siege mentality and constant worry about the menace overhead. It was the random nature of it all, which filled me with a terrible dread. I had known people for example who, when the air raid sirens began to wail, had chosen to remain in place, perhaps enjoying a simple chat or a cup of tea, and watched in awe and horror as the very place in which they would normally have sought shelter, was obliterated in a flash. Such strange twists of fate erode the very foundations on which we place our trust; those tried and true rules and regulations built to protect us from all harm. Yet nothing is indestructible. Not faith in foundations, concrete and otherwise, or faith in God, if one chooses to believe in such things.

I was thankful that I had somewhere to go, to escape the city, when it was urgently required. A place so far away from death and destruction, that the events happening elsewhere, in places such as London and Birmingham and Liverpool seemed as if they were on a completely different, and far away continent.

Yet, when I listened to the programmes on the wireless, it was with a certain amount of nostalgia and longing for a different time. You see, I still longed for just a hint of the hustle and bustle, the music recitals and theatre, stolen afternoons at the Provincial.

Even the run-down boarding houses of peeling wallpaper and shattered window panes, Henry and I sometimes found ourselves in, still held a strange allure. In the moments when I allowed myself those memories it was also with a sense of bittersweet regret for all the sacrifices made, and choices, which had turned my world upside down.

The goings and comings of the folk of Rashleigh continued, I imagined, cocooned in their own world, as if nothing at all was the matter, to-ing and fro-ing to the daily rhythms of uninterrupted potential. Dogs still yelped in the night, and rain continued on tin roofs, pitter-patter. Shopkeepers still opened their shops. Farmers still milked their cows. Post-men still delivered letters. People still listened to wireless programmes.

Rashleigh seemed like it existed in a world of its very own, sequestered as it was in that tiny corner of England where the sun nearly always shone, where cakes were baked for fetes, and croquet was played by geriatric generals and gentlemen alike. On Sunday, after church, veterans gathered at the war memorial and saluted fallen comrades, and a band of greying spinsters, in their Salvation Army uniforms, played spit-shined brass instruments to loud and sustained applause. I describe it that way to myself. What I remember of it.

Perhaps that is the way with memory. It is just like the needle on the record, which becomes stuck in the groove, repeating that old nostalgic tune, until it becomes a background accompaniment to the rest of one's life. The unusual circumstances in which one finds oneself, together and all at once, is terribly confusing. It surrounds you like a sea mist until you cannot tell the difference from one day to the next, where the sun rises and sets, even to the point where you no longer care. It seems so unnerving now, at this remove, to have a memory of such complacency, like consoling music to lull you to wakeful sleep, as the maelstrom descends.

I remember that very morning so very well you see, because I had a feeling of being out of sorts, like just such an all-encompassing mist had crept in, and I had become stranded, alone on a little rock, far out to sea, with no one to hear my calls for help. I have always thought that mists and memories are like that. The boundaries of both become so very hard to describe without an anchor of some sort. The anchor must be something both recognisable and steadfast to resist the torment of a world suddenly unhinged and adrift.

Anchors such as the lighthouse at the Old Head forever flashing its bright warning to those blessed to see it, or the rough-stone marker at the crossroads to Rashleigh, a reminder of different paths and possibilities. There was the wireless set too, and its precious but monotonous hum, a reminder that an outside world still existed in some faraway place, or that old grandfather clock going tick-tock towards the quickening hour. There was the notch in the kitchen table where the breadknife missed its mark and cut deep, or the daily routine of spooning honey into porridge to make it less gruelling.

I was daydreaming and thinking about such things, when I heard Father return from his morning chores. The wireless set still hummed away like an industrious bee in the background and I remember that Father grunted his dissatisfaction with whatever tune was playing. He went to the stove and poured himself a cup of tea.

Then with a booming voice, nearly as loud as the swell in the cove below the Old Head he said, 'You're needed at the Big House. You're needed at Millrace.'

'Millrace?' I said.

'Didn't you hear me?'

He stirred his tea and came to the table to sit down.

'Whatever for?' I replied.

'There's a vacancy of some sort. That was all the messenger would say. There's a letter here for you. It has a monogram at the top, and a note at the bottom,' he said, pulling out a chair to sit down.

I could smell the season from the scents that wafted towards me. The animals fed. I could smell sour milk and fresh dung. Honey gathered. Pollen tickled my nose. Spring was surely upon us.

'Read it to me.'

'*Master of Millrace*,' he read.

'That's all?'

'The Master of Millrace seeks to retain your services for the sum of three pounds, ten shillings per week. A driver will be sent tomorrow it seems.'

'That's a small fortune in times like this.'

'A girl like you could do with work. Make hay while the sun shines, I say.'

A girl like me, I thought. Damaged and unwanted. Father didn't mean to be cruel of course. His words, like the fresh country air, came freely to him. When I returned home, after those years away Father reminded me that what had happened was all part of God's plan. He couldn't know everything that I had lost in the war. He would never know, because it would have broken his heart to know such things.

He moved his chair and I heard the slow drag of his foot along the flagstones, then the drone of the wireless powering down, and the familiar sound of that useless limb slapping off the stone floor resumed as he made his way back to his seat.

'Your leg is acting up again. Isn't it?'

'It's nothing. No more and no less than any other day.'

'Perhaps it's the weather,' I said.

He mumbled a reply and shifted his position.

'I know it's bothering you. I can tell. Shall I ask Dr White to pay a visit?'

'Dr White has better things to do than examining a gammy leg.'

'I'm sure he wouldn't mind. If it's money, I can …'

'Stop right there, girl. You know we can well afford a doctor's fee. I know what ails me. I have known what it ails me since nineteen-eighteen. A bloody souvenir from the Kaiser. That's what it is. And no amount of doctoring will fix that.'

The bullet which ended my father's military career, lodged in his left knee and never left. It was making its way towards his heart and eventually it would do for him, he would say. The Kaiser's final revenge.

'If you insist, Father.'

'I do,' he replied.

'Have you been to the Big House of late?' I asked, swiftly changing the subject to avoid an argument of the sort, which usually occurs early in the morning and lasts all day.

'Not in some time,' Father said. 'I wouldn't have much cause to be up there.'

'No ... no, I don't expect you would.'

'I've heard that the property is in a bit of disrepair,' he added, 'but that might just be idle gossip. What with a war going on they can't be doing too badly to have staff waiting hand and foot on their every whim. And pay for your services into the bargain.'

'Yes, I suppose that's true.'

I ate a spoonful of porridge and thought about the world outside the farm, where people were busy getting things done, helping out with the war effort and the like. In a way, I felt a little useless, secluded as we were in Rashleigh.

It was as if I was adrift at the edge of the world, remote from important things, with only memories and dreams to cling to for any semblance of my former life.

My chest grew tight if I thought about my circumstances for too long. You see, Rashleigh was such an isolated place, on the outer fringes of a peninsula, bordered as it was on one side by sloping hills and on the other by treacherous cliffs and the unpredictable sea. The closest town, several hours away by car. The village, an accident of geography, known in pre-war years for its quaint, idyllic, coastal life of fishing and farming, and little cottage enterprises. Those activities continued during the war of course, but tourists and day-trippers had mostly evaporated from the landscape of the local economy. It was a mixed blessing. While belts had to be tightened to economise in straightened times and to support the war effort, the vacuum left through absence of outsiders allowed squinting windows to squint even more, and navel gazers to gaze more intently. Such preoccupations for the occupants of a small village emboldened the sense of being under a different type of siege. A self-inflicted one.

Rashleigh had known its share of tragedies. The sea had claimed many of the village's men-folk over the years; men who had ventured out to fish. Some joined the navy and were swept away by one war, or another. In addition, there were the other brave souls who risked their lives to rescue them both from boiling seas. They had a monument for seafarers at the harbour point. It was an anchor reclaimed from the seabed, which had belonged to a ship cast upon the rocks, and lost eventually to the waves. The monument had a little brass plaque with names and each year they would add a few more, a reminder of the impermanence of life itself.

I remember that I thought of Henry that morning and wondered where he might be. Henry always said that an effective officer needed to be in the thick of it, not thousands of miles away in some backwater fixing typing fonts for some pernickety general, or minor politician.

I perked up when the news came on the wireless set. There had been mention of Rangoon. Just a little item snuggled in between a notification on soap rationing. *Soap rationing. No Registration required*, and a reminder to, *Dig for Victory*. How ridiculous and inconsequential the broadcaster had made it seem, the fall of a city against the dirt of a nation. How far away and forgotten that part of the war had become in everyone's minds. People seemed more concerned with the immediacy of their own circumstances, I suppose, with worries about what might be rationed next, or speculation on when the enemy would invade.

Didn't anyone realise what happened over there, in those hot and tropical lands, out of sight, was as important as the rest of it? The enemy over there was just as relevant as the one closer to home, I always said, but I expect people didn't pay me much heed. The people on the wireless never voiced concern about places like Singapore, Hong Kong, or Rangoon. They seemed even less concerned than the people of Rashleigh and more concerned with margarine and *Maris Pipers* of all things. I was concerned, however. Rangoon might well have been over the crest of the hill or just down the road because Henry could be there.

*

A heavy rain was falling as I raced along Milford Street, hoping in my quiet desperation to make the last bus home. As I rounded the corner and hurried across the busy intersection, I watched as the tail lights of the bus faded into the distance.

'Blast it,' I said under my breath, then embarrassed I looked around to see if anyone might be standing close by, or watching me; to witness the rain-soaked mess standing there.

'It's a terrible night,' he said, stepping from the shadows and lighting a cigarette.

'Yes,' I replied then went to move away.

'There's always the tube,' he quickly added.

'Yes.'

'Do you normally agree with everything a stranger says?'

'Yes,' I replied rather nervously, and tilted my head back to feel the steady beat of raindrops on my face.

'Care for a cigarette?'

I turned towards him and stared for a few moments in that unfocused sort of way you might do when thinking deeply about something, or daydreaming, but then he stepped a little closer and stood underneath the dim, yellow-hued gaslight. I wondered for the briefest of moments if this might be the very opportunity I needed to use my unused umbrella.

'Those things can be dangerous,' he said, eyeing the flimsy weapon in my hand.

I laughed then and felt the tension of my grip around the umbrella slacken a little.

'Well, you never can tell,' I said sheepishly.

I remembered that moment later, and how it made me smile. Standing there, wondering what I should do next, I heard a car speeding by. There was that usual sound of rubber licking a slick surface then the car slowed a little before the front wheel dropped into a pothole and splashed dirty water across the back of my legs. As a sort of instinctual reflex, I jumped out of the way and threw myself into the path of the stranger, causing him at that very moment to react by raising his arms, I thought, in a sort of defensive posture. Perhaps he believed I was going to attack him. I managed to trip and fall forward, and as luck might have it, he caught me in his arms instead.

'I'm truly sorry,' I said breathlessly.

'I'm Henry,' he replied. 'Henry Morton.'

*

'What is it you do?' he said, leaning on the table with one hand clasped around the glass of whiskey he had barely touched. In his other hand he held a cigarette. It seemed like he had an endless supply of *Pall Malls*. He smoked one after the other in quick succession, barely pausing to stub one out, before lighting another.

He studied me and waited for an answer, but I was busily stirring my ginger ale with my finger in a sort of nervous fidgeting action, lost in whatever thoughts were racing around in my head, and too distracted to reply.

Then,

'Butter,' I blurted out.

'Butter?'

'Yes, butter. Mrs Simpson asked me to get a few ounces of butter on my way home.'

'Did she?' he said, half-smiling and nudging his ashtray with the back of his hand. '*Mrs Simpson* …?'

'Mrs Simpson is my landlady. I have my coupons, and she … Oh, never mind. There I go just blabbering on. Doris says I'm always blabbering on, about this and that.'

'Doris Simpson…?'

'They're two separate people you see. Mrs Simpson my landlady and Doris my flat mate.'

'Ah! I see.'

'Doris is always saying that I twiddle my fingers when I'm nervous.'

'Are you?'

'I don't know. Do I appear nervous to you?'

'You're twiddling your fingers again.'

I laughed and said, 'Yes, I am. Must stop doing that.'

'It's rather endearing, if you ask me.'

'Really?'

He smiled and sipped his drink and cast a glance towards the door.

'You must think I'm a complete idiot.'

'You're a secretary then?' he said, stubbing out his cigarette and swirling the amber liquid around in his glass then rested it on the table again without drinking any of its contents. I watched his gaze casually scanning the room as if he was expecting someone to arrive at any moment.

'Why do you say that?'

'Fingers,' he said, raising his cigarette hand and making a twiddling motion.

I shook my head side to side, smiled, lifted the glass to my mouth, and sipped my ginger ale without giving a reply.

I wondered why he had taken me to the Savoy, of all places. I wondered too how daring I had been to accept. You are so very bold, I told myself. I turned my head and studied him a moment longer, then looked about in a sort of never-a-care way, whilst trying to conceal the fact that my nerves were a little on edge throughout.

Every so often, he adjusted the cufflinks, which pinned together the sleeves of, what appeared to be, an expensively tailored shirt. He wore an appropriately tailored tweed jacket, which bore a barely discernible red and green argyle pattern. The fit was snug across his shoulders. How old was he? I asked myself. Forty perhaps? One could never tell, though his dress sense was suitably middle-aged, or the attire of a man dressed by someone else.

There was something about his sad eyes that betrayed a sense of world-weariness, or was it disappointment? Perhaps it was the dreadful weather, or the whispered rumours of another war, or the rather plain-featured specimen sitting opposite him. Yes, perhaps that was it. I blushed at the thought and ran my hand along the sleeves of my jumper in a nervous, fidgeting sort of action.

If that was indeed the case, and I was just a convenient ornamentation for a wet and dreary evening in London, then I thought it better that I left, there and then, thanking him for the drink and leaving him with my own sense of what might have been. I didn't leave however. Instead, I sat there studying him. It was a trait that I found sometimes useful in awkward social situations. Situations such as the one in which I then found myself.

I watched, for instance, the movement of his cigarette hand as he flicked ash into the tray in front of him, or the way he puckered his cheeks together every so often and made a sighing noise. I watched too as he furrowed his brow as if he was deep in thought then stared into the distance, his eyes widening to a glare, when a realisation suddenly came to him. I saw these things and felt a sudden frisson of excitement that I found him, in a strange way, so very attractive. A rush of blood coursed through my body at the thought, and then something else popped into my head. I wondered, at that very moment, if he would be a tender lover.

I remembered my first time, you see. One always remembers their first; or rather, one might disremember and choose instead some imaginary reconstruction. Bertrand Du Pont. That was the chap. I would rather have chosen to forget Bertrand, but his name and singular passion in life, which was playing the tuba, kept the memory alive. The tuba of all things.

'Doesn't anyone have a drink anymore?' he said, disturbing me from my thoughts.

'Why do you say that?' I replied, perking up in my seat.

'Well, there's no one here. A few months ago the place was

14

heaving, full of politicians and journalists, and their mistresses. Now, well … There's not a damned soul in sight.'

'You seem disappointed. Do you come here often?'

'Yes,' he said, and left it at that.

'Oh!'

'It's not what you think. I don't pick up young women at random.'

'I beg your pardon.'

'I mean to say, I come here to have a drink, to be by myself to think, and to become anonymous in a crowd. Is that too much to ask?'

'I'm sorry, I didn't mean …'

'It's like this … I might run into someone I know if I went elsewhere. Perhaps someone from the office, or an old army chum, and the conversation would be a repetition of subjects I try desperately to avoid. At least here … well, it's not my typical circle,' he said sharply.

'Nor mine,' I said and smiled, trying to disarm the rather serious look he had suddenly adopted. 'You were in the army then? The last war?'

I noticed how his facial features contorted a little more. It was as if someone had inflicted an invisible blow and it made him wince in pain.

'Yes, that's it,' he said, swirling the whiskey around the glass.

'I'm sorry I didn't mean to pry. My father was in the war too.'

'Is that so?' he said and his features contorted even more.

Perhaps I sounded naïve but the truth was quite the opposite. I had lived the aftermath of war in my father's shouted nightmares and drunken stupors. Those were the terrible days of my youth, but then it stopped. Rather suddenly it has to be said, and without any particular rhyme or reason.

15

'He used to drink, to forget I think. He was a bad drunk or perhaps it was because I was very young then and it just seemed that was the case.'

'Used to drink—?'

'He stopped for a while. Perhaps it was my mother's influence or the fact that he needed to earn a living. Then my mother died quite suddenly and he started it up again. Fortunately, he abstains now. I suppose he replaced one vice with a virtue. My father found God, you see.'

'God?'

'Yes. Is it so hard to believe?'

'I'm afraid I'm quite the opposite in that regard. When I went looking for him it seemed God had decided not to make the journey to France.'

'You don't mean that.'

'I'm afraid I do,' he said, and swirled his whiskey again without pausing to drink. 'What God would allow such terror and destruction? No, a little amber nectar soothes my soul now, more than any prayers ever could,' he said, and gave a wry smile before bringing the glass to his face and taking a mouthful of whiskey.

It was difficult to give an adequate answer to any of what he said, so I didn't try. Instead, I searched the room for a reason to change the subject.

'I've never been here before.'

'Does it disappoint?'

In one corner of the cavernous lounge, a man sat playing piano. He was dressed in evening wear with bow tie and tails. He had narrow, gaunt-like features and slicked-back dark hair. He reminded me a little of Mr Fred Astaire in one of those films, with music and dance, and romance.

He was playing something rather upbeat and energetic and I

wondered if he was about to launch himself out of his seat, but at the last moment he thought the better of it and remained seated for the rest of the performance. I noticed that the piano was a little out of tune, but if he knew that then he was doing a jolly fine job of covering it up.

There was a small rectangular dance floor situated in front of the piano. It was suitable perhaps for three or four couples, if they all moved in the same direction, at the same time.

A crystal chandelier hung from a long chain attached to the ceiling somewhere out of view. The glass from the chandelier sparkled, glistened, and threw narrow beams of light onto the dancefloor below.

'You asked me what I do. Well, that is what I do,' I said and made a nodding gesture in the direction of the music man.

My companion followed my gaze. 'You mean you play piano?'

'Yes,' I said and took the proffered cigarette from his outstretched hand. 'Actually, to be more precise, I teach music.'

He shook his lighter a few times and thumbed the lever, but it refused to produce a flame. 'Darned thing,' he said, and shook it a few more times. 'Must buy myself a new one.'

click-click

Eventually, after a few attempts, it worked. He brought the lighter towards me and almost brazenly I wrapped my hands around his, as if some imagined wind had blown in and was about to extinguish the flame again. He was suddenly nervous, or embarrassed, I couldn't quite tell, as his gaze went hurriedly all about the room again.

'Is something the matter, Mr Morton?' I asked, releasing my grip.

'Whatever do you mean? And *do* call me, Henry,' he said defensively, folding his arms one over the other, to where the sleeves of the snug-fitting jacket climbed up his forearms.

The moment gave me an opportunity to study the gold-coloured heart-shaped cufflinks which brought the shirt together at the end. Self-consciously he unfolded his arms and extinguished the cigarette he had been smoking.

'It's just you seemed a little unnerved there.'

'It's nothing. Nothing at all, Miss *Truly Sorry*. That's my name for you, you know. *Truly Sorry*,' he said and a thin smile passed his lips.

'If you like,' I said, rather nonchalantly.

'So you teach music.'

'I teach at St George. It's a preparatory school.'

'It's just that—' he looked away then, as if remembering something.

'Yes.'

'Well you seem quite young to be a teacher, don't you think?'

'I'm nearly twenty-three,' I said.

'Oh!' he said, and there was a hint of disappointment in his voice.

Perhaps it was this new information that caused the conversation to become a little forced on my behalf, and a little more hesitant on his.

'And you Mr Morton … I mean, Henry. What do you do?'

'Oh, I don't want to bore you,' he said in reply and lit another cigarette, then pushed the ashtray towards me.

'Please …' I said, blowing a cloud of smoke over my shoulder, as I'd seen one of those fashionable ladies do. 'Do go on.'

'Do go on,' I said.

Do go on. Who said things like that? I thought. Do go on indeed. I felt myself go absolutely beetroot at the thought that those exact words had come from my lips. It added to the flush I was already feeling as I smoked the cigarette. It brought to mind an embarrassing memory of the first time I smoked a cigarette. It was at a Woolworth's Christmas party. Doris worked there as a perfume girl and had asked me along as her plus one. Oh, I regretted it almost immediately. Not the cigarette so much as that pest, Mr West, from the accounts department. What a creepy fellow he was. Doris had warned me of course. Watch out for Mr West, she whispered, as we stood at the mini-bar waiting for our drinks. And when he had wormed his way my direction I had no idea who Doris had been talking about until he started working his hand along my shoulder, and down my back, in a sort of overly-friendly way, before he summoned up enough courage to pinch my bottom.

I should have slapped him there and then, but I think I was so taken aback that I was frozen to the spot instead. So he pinched my bottom again, and gave a little titter of playfulness and self-congratulation, and took another bite from the egg sandwich he was clenching in his fist. Doris, poor sweet Doris, catching that rabbit-in-the-headlights look I had in my eyes, eventually came to my rescue. So you've met Mr West, she said, as she dragged me away, chuckling to herself.

'I want to know a little more about you,' my companion said.

'My life will probably sound rather boring,' I replied. 'School five days per week then I volunteer at an orphanage on Saturday. I have air warden duty too.'

'Sounds action-packed,' he said shortly. 'Another?'

He made a waving motion with his hand and tried to attract the attention of the rather ancient and doddery-looking waiter who was standing in another corner of the room. The poor man appeared to be almost on the point of sleep. When my companion failed to get satisfaction, he took a swig from his drink, swallowed the remainder in one gulp, and pointed a finger at my unfinished ginger ale. Then he rose from his seat and walked towards the bar without waiting for my reply. I watched him go and studied his upright bearing and his long, confident stride. The jacket that had appeared a little tight now seemed to fit him quite well as he walked away. I thought then how he was so unlike those frisky boys at the Friday night community dance, with their talk of war and bravado. When he returned to the table, he was carrying another ginger ale and a glass of whiskey for himself.

It was only as he retook his seat that the waiter suddenly perked up again and made his way in our direction. Then another couple came to sit at one of the empty tables nearby. They were older. The woman observed me studiously for a few moments then moved her chair so that her back was to me. When she had made herself comfortable she leaned across the table and said something to her companion, then she sat upright again and turned her head to look over her shoulder. She tut-tutted and shook her head from side to side.

Her companion followed her gaze. I blew a cloud of smoke brazenly in their direction then turned away. My companion didn't seem to notice; or perhaps he did, but didn't care one way or the other.

'Where are you from?' he said. 'You're not a city girl. I know that for certain.'

'Cornwall,' I said meekly.

'Cornwall. Fine country, Cornwall.'

'Have you been?'

'Yes,' he replied, without any further explanation.

'I studied at the London School of Drama and Music,' I said rather hurriedly.

'Did you? A very fine school indeed.' He looked away then, disinterested or bored, I couldn't quite tell.

'I was wondering why you asked me to come for a drink with you. Do I look like the type of girl you'd just pick up with a quick line?'

'You missed your bus, then that passing car splashed you, and you sort of fell into my arms.'

'Is that it?'

'And you looked like a drenched little monkey in need of a drink,' he replied.

'Drenched little monkey?'

'Truly sorry,' he said and gave a wry smile.

'What were you doing standing there in the shadows anyway?' I asked, boldly.

'As a matter of fact I was making my way home. Just like you I suppose.'

'Home?'

'Doesn't everyone have one?'

'I don't know. I mean there are the homeless of course.'

'Anyway,' he said, 'the conversation has turned rather dull, don't you think? Would you care to dance? Give it a twirl, so to speak.'

His request seemed rather forced and I could discern no genuine interest on his behalf, apart perhaps from his growing discomfort with something. He was already standing, forcing a smile, when he offered me his hand. Almost on cue, the piano player struck a tune, a slow number, but one which almost demanded attention.

'I won't embarrass you, if that's what you're thinking,' he said.

It wasn't what I was thinking at all. I was more concerned with how quickly the evening had progressed, from the mini-disaster, which was a missed bus home, to the invitation of a total stranger, to drinks, and dancing into the bargain. I pushed my chair away from the table and stood facing the bandstand, and then I placed my hand in his.

When we reached the dance floor, he drew me close, in the manner of someone who was trying to regain control of a situation that had been slowly spiralling out of control.

'Do you know this one?' he asked, and nodded in the direction of the piano.

I shook my head and said, 'No.'

'*Underneath the Arches*,' he whispered.

'It's nice,' I replied, and placed my hand on his shoulder and got that faint hint of cologne masked by a stronger tobacco smell.

In truth, the music, much like my companion's cologne, seemed a little old-fashioned. I turned my head to look across the room and saw the couple at the table next to ours get up and leave. We were alone again, with the exception of the bartender polishing already-polished glasses, the piano player tinkling away as if he was in another world, and the waiter who was suddenly alert and making his way in our direction; his face full of a sort of sullen determination.

'Excuse me, *sah*,' he said, his arms wrapped tightly around his back. 'I regret to inform you that you must be properly attired to dance. We require evening wear.'

My companion loosened his grip and un-wrapped his arm from around my waist, and I let my hand drop limply from his shoulder. We stood there, neither one of us moving, as if we were the only two people left in the world, listening to the end of the tune.

'Of course you do,' he eventually said in reply.

'Yes, *sah*,' the man said, bowing his head and retreating back to the same spot he had been standing in a few moments before.

'I really must be getting home,' I said to break the silence.

He looked away and said, 'I should have remembered the damned dress code. How absent minded of me.' His face reddened as the words spilled from his lips.

'It doesn't matter,' I told him.

'Should have remembered it all the same.'

'It has been rather lovely,' I said.

He stared at me, his eyes glazing over as if he was lost in thought. Perhaps the moment had rekindled a lost memory of something, or someone, but I suddenly felt very out of place.

'Thank you,' I said, 'for rescuing me from the rain and puddles, and for the ginger ale.'

He continued to stand there, frozen to the spot, staring. How strange, I thought.

'Are you all right?'

'Perfectly,' he mumbled.

I returned to where we had been sitting and put on my coat. As I was readying myself to leave I turned to see where my companion was, but he was nowhere to be seen. I waited for him to return, but when he didn't I made the decision to leave.

'Well, goodbye to you too,' I said under my breath.

I left then, passing firstly through the hotel lobby at a hurried pace, then through the revolving doors and into the foyer. It was raining still, only heavier now, and suddenly remembered I had left my umbrella behind.

'Oh, fiddle-sticks,' I said to no one in particular.

'Is this what you're looking for?'

I turned and Henry Morton was standing there with his arm outstretched and in his hand, he held the umbrella, still tightly bundled. I thought at that moment that perhaps he had resolved whatever conundrum he was mulling over and having suddenly come to his senses realised he was alone, and that he was letting the opportunity slip from his grasp.

'Yes,' I said, and I took the umbrella from his grip.

'Can I see you again?' he asked.

His voice was almost a whisper against the din of the passing traffic and plink-plink patter of rain on our coats.

'Yes,' I said, and felt that frisson of excitement at the thought.

I watched his mouth soften a little into that half-smile of his as I hurriedly scratched my telephone number into the notebook he procured from the inside pocket of his coat. Then he called for the parked taxi that was across the road.

'The young lady will tell you where to go,' he explained to the driver as the taxi idled. 'Two shillings should cover it.'

'Well that'd take you to Dover and back,' the driver said. 'We're not going to Dover, are we luv?' he said jokingly.

'Spitalfields,' I said.

'Well that's right kind of you, sir. I'll make sure the young lady gets home safe and well.'

'Thank you,' Henry said, and opened the passenger door to allow me to climb in.

I slid across the leather seats and waited while he closed the passenger door behind me then rolled down the window to thank him but the taxi was already pulling away. I looked out the rear window just in time and watched as Henry, for he was Henry in my mind then, pulled the collar of his coat around his ears, turned and disappeared into the night.

I remember I felt another rush of excitement. I turned around in my seat and through the side window, I watched huge beams of light illuminating the night sky; searching for the threat, which had not yet manifested itself. It was an ominous sign for what was to come because the very next day the prime minister announced that Germany had ignored Britain's ultimatum and that we were at war again. I remember that as I sat listening to Mr Chamberlain's address I had this feeling that it was the end of innocence, and the beginning of the end of the world.

CHAPTER THREE

I rose that morning, to go to Millrace for the very first time, filled with feelings of excitement, and a slight trepidation at what was to come. I remembered that I performed my usual routine: washing my face in cold water, then running a damp cloth around my torso to clean myself. Then I dressed myself in the order to which I had become accustomed.

There were one, two, three buttons to fasten my blouse, a clasp to tighten my skirt and long woollen stockings to roll above my knees. My shoes were to my right, beside the bedside locker. A cardigan brought the ensemble together. I rested my hand on the bible for good fortune, or out of superstition, and gave the looking glass a frustrated nudge to remind myself of all that had been lost.

There were seven paces to the door. So practiced was I that I did not give it a second thought. Placing my hand on the doorknob, I twisted it right and pulled. Four paces then a banister to my left. I slid my hand along its polished surface and climbed down the stairs, twelve steps in all, listening as the wooden floorboards creaked with my presence.

Along the passage, I went until I reached the grandfather clock. I pulled the little glass door and ran my fingers over the hands of the clock. I wound it seven times and returned the key to its place, closed the little door, then ran my hand over the wooden case and smelt its timelessness. My daily task completed, I stepped ten paces to the kitchen door and placed my right hand on the doorframe. The chair was there to greet me, where it always was, by the kitchen table, that strong, sturdy, high-backed chair with its long armrests and washboard seat. I pulled it towards me and sat. A place was already set. I felt the waft of steam on my face and took a spoon and the first taste of porridge, food to warm my insides, and turned my face to the light of that new and extraordinary day.

*

As soon as the car rumbled through the gates, over that noisy metal cattle grid, and onto the gravel driveway I could discern its former splendour. Like an unseen pressure it closed in on me from every side. I rolled my window down to get a better sense of the place and felt the marginally cooler air on my face. There was the smell of azaleas to greet my arrival, and the sound of large trees creaking and swaying in the breeze, like sentries marking time. There was a smell of freshly cut grass, early for the time of year, as we entered the part of the driveway, which gave way to what was once described to me, as the long meadow. I heard the sound of men's voices in the distance calling out to each other. Teasing, I should think, as they worked their scythes.

I conjured up the images I remembered of the place from my younger days. I knew that a river ran under a stone bridge, tumbling in turmoil from a height and gathering in a pool before continuing its journey to the sea beyond the boundaries of the great estate. The bridge marked the point where the road turned to match the course of the river and then turned again to carve a

27

kind-of-straight section for a while, and in my mind's eye I pictured the house appearing briefly, then disappearing out of view once more, just like in a game of hide and seek.

'Here we are now,' the driver said half-heartedly, before growing silent again, perhaps reminded of the redundancy of his commentary.

I was still distracted, my face turned to the sun, basking a little in the warmth of its rays.

Millrace, they called it.

The mill was long gone by that time of course, and in its stead stood a crumbling ruin, overgrown with bush and bramble, and no longer used. To this day, the river runs through it. I expect it always will. Even when we are all long gone, the river will chart its course to the sea, searching for a new path, turning back to its natural course. The family who owned Millrace were mostly dead by then, and their ill-gotten fortune made and spent. There was a sole heir, about my age, but I expect there was not very much for him to inherit, even if he had had the desire to.

'Almost there,' the driver said.

I heard a dog barking; barking and running alongside us as we drove towards the house, and when the car did eventually come to a stop, it was with the sound of gravel being pushed aside and the noise of a squeaky hand brake to hold us in place, and the excited barking of the dog that greeted us. There was a smell of burning too, that acrid smell of fresh-cut grass atop an open fire. For those first few moments, it catches the back of the throat, until you become more accustomed to it. I heard him get out and walk around to the opposite side, then the car door opened and I reached out for his hand. I could feel the roughness of the skin, and those gnarly, knot-like calluses on the palm of his hand, like the exposed roots of a great tree, weathered and worked by nature's forces. My hand, by contrast, was such a delicate, necessary thing, that I wondered for a moment what impression it might make on him. Perhaps he thought me soft, pampered, cosseted even. I thought these things at that moment because I had known such an assumption in myself. It was a judgement of someone else, a man who had arrived at the house one day selling bibles.

When he offered his hand in salutation, I remember I took it in mine, and thought how soft and pillow-like, and unmanly it felt to the touch. Such a simple action yet such a complicated set of conclusions one draws in that instant. I was not such a creature, of course. I had known hard days and more. Days of working in the fields, gathering hay and the like, then hours spent learning my scales, until such a time as one labour became the thing that consumed me the most and those once callused hands became soft and supple, but no less determined.

'Thank you,' I replied, stepping from the comfort of the car and placing my feet on the ground. The dog moved around me. I could feel its long tail hitting my leg repeatedly with excitement, until I eventually put my hand down to pat his head.

'That's Tramp. Away with you, Tramp. It's this way, miss. Just some steps to navigate. *Tramp,*' the driver said.

He had hardly said a word, this man, this driver of mine. For the whole, long journey, he had kept his counsel, and I had dutifully kept mine. It all seemed rather quaint, like a sense of Edwardian old-worldliness existed between us, two people in the service of another, unable to speak our own minds for fear some lordly, invisible presence would be listening in to our idle chatter. As he gave Tramp a telling-off, I could discern his west-country accent.

'He's fine,' I said, grabbing Tramp's collar.

He was an energetic dog. A Labrador, I believe, given free run of the estate, and was known I later learned, to disappear for hours on end, returning as the light began to fade, or the hunger overcame his desire to continue his wanderings. I crouched down to let him smell me some more and felt his hot breath on my face. He had a wet dog smell about him, as if he might have been swimming, caught in a shower, or perhaps he had been rolling in wet grass.

'You're a friendly one,' I said and stroked his head.

'Careful, miss or he'll knock you over, that one. Let me take you in,' the driver announced, and I followed as he guided me towards the steps.

We climbed each step pausing for just a moment with each success, before we arrived at the top and a flat area. I remember it was hot and humid that day, not like now of course, but muggy just the same and I perspired with the effort. I stood there for a moment to recover and while I did, a door opened and someone stepped out to greet us. I waited for something to happen or for someone to say something, to guide me onwards or command me to stay.

Instead there was this moment, like you imagine being caught in a vacuum might feel like, where nothing was said, and no movement took place, even the swaying trees stood still and the blades of grass stood sentry-like, and the birds stopped flapping their wings and calling out to each other. I had felt that way once before, in those terrible moments just before the darkness descended upon me and I was condemned to my preternatural existence.

It was like that moment, a fraction before the burning light, when it seemed like time itself stood still and all the air in the world had suddenly disappeared. Then bang! Events rushed in to fill the vacuum once again. A door opened noisily on its hinges and someone stepped out to greet us.

'Welcome to Millrace,' she said.

CHAPTER FOUR

Her voice had that sort of gravelly quality that one might associate with lifelong smokers of tobacco, or stage actors past their prime.

We stepped into the main hall, a cavernous, damp place of dulled noises and smells of mould and rot. It reminded me of places I had once read about, or which were described to me in books by Dickens and Brontë and the like, with shadows I could not see but could only perceive, and mystery I might allow myself to imagine quite vividly.

I heard another door open to my left; a creaky, heavy thing, and then a bell rang, as if to summon a servant. The clanging-banging noise was coming from somewhere else, somewhere above me. Then it rang out again, more shrill this time, and with a certain urgency to it. I gripped the driver's hand a little tighter.

'That will be the Master needing my services. I shall return shortly,' the woman said. 'If you would be so good as to take our guest into the drawing room.'

'Yes, Mrs Butler,' the driver replied.

He led me from where we were standing to another part of the house a short distance away. Unused to such exotic things as I was, I almost tripped on the thick rug which mostly covered the wooden floor as we entered the drawing room. I would surely have fallen if it were not the help of the driver's strong grip.

'Thank you,' I said.

'My pleasure,' he replied. 'By the way, I'm Mr Burrows,' he continued. 'Alfie,' he said rather familiarly.

'Thank you, Mr Burrows,' I replied, untangling my arm from his.

I got a whiff of cologne, a spicy aroma, and sweat as Mr Burrows came a little closer. The cologne reminded me of Henry. I had purchased a small bottle of a similar-smelling concoction, in Wickham's on the Mile End Road. It had cost a pretty penny, I remembered, and the thought came to me at that moment, that it was an unusual item for a servant to possess.

'It's over here, it is,' he said, a little more animatedly.

I took off my wax raincoat and folded it over my arm, and removed the flat cap I was wearing.

'I'll take those for you, miss. There isn't much need for them today, though you never can tell. This weather seems to change on a penny, it does.'

I held out my coat and cap and waited as Mr Burrows went to store them away.

When he returned he said, 'Would you like me to ring down for some tea, miss?'

'That would be nice,' I said.

'Well, why don't we get you comfortable and I'll see about those refreshments then,' Mr Burrows said.

I felt his hand on my arm again.

'I can manage,' I said. 'It will just take me a little while to get accustomed.'

'Well, if you're sure, miss?'

'Yes. I'm sure.'

Mr Burrows left me then, and I remained standing in the same position for some time, listening for sounds, like the sightless animal that I had become, sending out signals and waiting for one to bounce back.

A fire was crackling away, working hard to keep the damp air at bay. I imagined little streams of water running down the walls in places and pooling in spots out of sight, growing an army of black mould and rot. Not for all the money in China would I have swapped homely comforts for Millrace's musty splendour, but it had a strange appeal; the sort of nostalgia for former glories and gentler times one sometimes conjures up to immunise oneself against the darkness of one's present circumstances.

I held out my cane and swung it rhythmically side-side until it made contact with the nearest object. I ran my hand over the back of a chair, which was covered in a rough and tattered material. I smiled to myself. It seemed rather cheap for such a luxurious dwelling but confirmed for me a feeling I had of something once beautiful, now in decay, like a once beautiful corpse whose deathly make-up had begun to drip and wax and wane. I conjured up brighter images too, of days of leisure and evenings of decadence, the dances and balls, Strauss' *Blue Danube* played by an orchestra, loud voices and ladies fanning themselves with free abandon, tittering and whispering, the noise of clinking glasses and the silent, watchfulness of a myriad of servants waiting on an every whimsy. I imagined the coming outs of young women and the going out of tweed-jacketed men in their plus fours marching across the gravel courtyard to join shooting parties.

All these things echoed around the halls of Millrace; ghostly remembrances of a life that was eroding away even then, like a scrappy wallpaper long past its prime. The first War had signalled its decline. The second War had merely confirmed how far it had fallen.

I swung the cane again and found a low table, a coffee table perhaps, a few feet away, and next to it, something mounted on a pedestal, a bust of someone important, I assumed, perhaps a member of the family held in high regard, or some distant relative, a political leader or philosopher. I ran my fingers over the features. It was a marble bust of a man, I concluded. The proportions of the face, the outline of the jaw line and the prominent nose and forehead were all clues to its identity. The baldness of the head was my final clue. An ugly creature I determined. Suddenly a voice stirred me from my thoughts.

'I see you have found great-Aunt Juliet.'

I almost knocked the bust off its pedestal such was the fright I got. 'I am sorry,' I replied. 'I didn't realise there was anyone else here.'

'I was hidden away in the big armchair facing the window. Do you know I have been hiding in this exact spot since I was a child? I used to find a sort of solace here, in this chair, with a view of the gardens, and the sea beyond. Old habits and all that. Don't you agree?'

I had become more alert to these things in the months since my drama, but he must have remained quite still, this man, this stranger, when I came into the room.

Was he staring at me the whole time?

The thought made me feel a little uncomfortable. My handicap, for that was what some had assumed me to possess, was not for entertainment. Nor was I a specimen in a human zoo. I should have told him so but instead I said,

'If you say so.'

'I do. Mr Burrows has gone to fetch you some tea has he?'

'Yes,' I replied, and waited.

I was trying to ascertain the provenance of his accent, but it was too hard to tell. Wounded was my first impression. Yes, a wounded voice was the best conclusion I could arrive at; constructed to mask some terrible injury. I noticed a catch at the end of every sentence he uttered, as he struggled to take an inhale of breath before continuing with whatever he was saying. It was a rasping sound, like a smoker's rattle, and just as the thought crossed my mind, he said,

'Do you mind if I light up? It's my pipe—'

In truth I did. Henry smoked and I found the habit a little irritating. He laughed at me that time I remembered. Laughed that deep, manly laugh of his and I laughed too and smoked one of his cigarettes, trying deep down to act older than I was. A filthy habit, he would say. Don't ever take it up. Yes, I would reply and put the cigarette to my lips, and wait, wait for him to lean across and kiss me on the mouth just as I knew he would. I found myself touching my lips with the tips of my fingers as if he had just been there a moment before and in that instant a faint ripple of melancholy ran through the very fibre of my being. I heard a dull, mechanical sound: *click-click*

At least it's the pipe, I thought to myself. I can bear the pipe. Father smoked a pipe, I remembered. Occasionally, in the evening, or sometimes when the weather was too inclement to go outside, he might sit by the fire in contemplation and smoke. He might also have occasion to go to the stables, where he kept the draught mare, Nell, and between mucking out, he would light the pipe and whisper to Nell. She didn't seem to mind, he would say. The only woman who never talked back to him.

'I said, do you mind if I—'

'No, of course not,' I replied.

36

'You don't sound so sure,' he said and made the puffing sound again.

'I find it affects the voice, don't you think?'

'Yes, that,' he said. 'I'm afraid matters can't get any worse for yours truly. I find I get very irritable if I don't have my daily ration of contemplative medicine.'

I wasn't quite sure what he meant and was tempted to ask but then he cleared his throat and I heard the sound of a match being struck and a strange smell. Not pipe-smoke exactly. It was unlike any pipe-smoke I had ever encountered. It wafted towards me like a serpent, and coiled its way up my nostrils to lodge its aroma in my mind.

click-click

'Ah! That *choo-choo* train.'

'Are you quite alright?'

'The dream of dreams,' the Pipe-smoker said. 'Jolly hard to come by though. Mrs Butler has her ways. A bit of this and a bit of that, that's good old Maggie for you.'

'Shall I call for one of the servants?'

'They know to leave me be. Play something.'

'Shouldn't I wait until the Master comes down?

'Are you hard of hearing too? Sit, sit, play...' he said rather shortly.

'What would you like to hear?'

'There's a piece by a chap called Satie.'

'*Gymnopédie?*'

'That's the one. The piano is right behind you. There, there … over there.'

I imagined he was pointing towards it, assuming I could follow his direction. I turned around and found the back of a chair. Round edged, with a lace material. I ran my hand along it to the end and pushed my cane ahead of me.

'That's it,' he said. 'A few more steps. One step, two steps, three steps more…'

His words had a sort of nursery rhyme quality, as if this was all just a game.

'You know,' I said. 'I don't think I'll play for you after all.'

'Don't be a silly little thing,' he mumbled. 'Damned voice gets so dry. Ah well, more puff-puff will sort that. A perfect remedy for ghosts and demons of all shapes and sizes.'

click-click

I had heard stories about Millrace, idle gossip and the like. I never paid those stories much heed before then. Life was full enough of real dramas without the need to create imaginary ones, but as I stood there, in that place, and without an explanation for its cause, the palms of my hands grew clammy and a slight chill ran along my spine.

'Is it me, or are you still standing where I left you? Mrs Butler will take care of everything,' he yawned.

'Are you quite all right?'

'Never better,' he replied. 'Never better.'

'Would you mind if I sat down? The air is quite stuffy.'

'Puff-puff gone to your head too?'

'Puff-puff? Oh, you mean the pipe-smoke. Yes, that's it. The pipe-smoke.'

click-click

'You look a little peaked, if you don't mind me saying.'

'You've already said it.'

'What?'

'I don't mind you saying it, but you had already said it in any case. So what does it matter that you ask me if you mind that you say it?' I said a little giddily.

'That is a jumble. I am sorry. I didn't mean to—'

'It's nothing,' I said. 'I get like that sometimes. It's the unfamiliar smells and sounds, the strangeness of a place, or people. People mostly. People can be ghastly sometimes.'

'People can be ghastly a lot of the time,' he said, his voice cracking a little. 'Anyway, what do you think of our little pile then?'

'It seems like a very fine place indeed.'

'Oh, come now,' he teased. 'I know what you're thinking.'

'What am I thinking?' I said.

'You are thinking that the place could do with an airing. The furniture has seen better days and this room could do with a good dusting.'

'Well, I—'

'Admit it. I have you rumbled,' he said jokingly and I heard the sound of leather creaking as he shifted his position. 'Do you want to know what else you're thinking?'

'Are you a mind reader?' and without allowing him to answer I said, 'Well, if you insist.'

'I'll tell you,' he said. 'You are wishing that you had never accepted the invitation in the first place.'

'Really! Do you find me so predictable?'

'I've already got you sized up to a tee. Right at this very moment, you are wondering how you can escape this strange pipe-smoke and my father's clanging bells, and this decrepit old house, and all its ghosts. Isn't that right?'

'It's perfectly—'

'I'll move over here. Is that better?'

'Much,' I said, and realised he had been closer to me than I had thought.

'Good. I can't do anything about the bells and the ghosts, I'm afraid. I had thought of having a séance and purging the place, but séances are so passé, don't you think? Whatever one might think about the spirit world, charlatans are a completely different matter altogether.'

click-click

'You mean the people who run séances then? Psychics and the like?'

'Psychics, *pfff!* Psychics are like canned air merchants.'

'Perhaps some people would buy a product like that.'

'Really? Canned air! It's everywhere, and all at once, and free. Why on earth, would you pay for it? That's what psychics do. They put air in cans and sell it to the gullible.'

'Don't you think that in the future ... if the air was really bad or full of noxious gases there could be a market for canned air, just as there is a market for mystics? Do you know that after the last war there was a thriving business in the type of séance you describe. People were so desperate to talk to their loved ones that they paid vast sums to mediums to make a connection with the other world.'

'Let's hope we won't need the type of canned air you speak of. As for the other world ... My dear girl, it's all a fallacy. I've been as close as you can be to the other world you're speaking of. I touched the void. There's nothing there. Just one big, dark space.'

'Yes, well, I—'

'Shall I tell you what you're missing?' he said.

*

'It's mostly reproductions here. For the real thing you'd have to go to the National Gallery, but I'm afraid there's nothing to see there now that they've hidden them all away.'

We had arranged to meet at a small, out of the way art gallery close to Trafalgar Square.

'I suppose it won't be long before they move these ones too,' he said.

'Do you like art?' I asked, scrutinising a rather abstract piece which had drawn my attention.

'I thought *you* might.'

'How kind of you,' I said, and ambled on, allowing him to follow in my wake.

'Do you, then?'

'As a matter of fact, I do. I know nothing about it though … except that is, for the usual suspects, Da Vinci, Constable, Rembrandt.'

'There's one that caught my eye. May I?' he said, and took my arm to lead me in a different direction.

'Yes, of course.'

He had left it a full week before making contact. I counted those days. I could think of little else. Then when Doris came running up the stairs, announcing at the top of her voice that my fancy man was calling, I could feel the ground opening up and swallowing me whole. Yes, of course, I had said. Of course I'll meet you. Where? An art gallery. Splendid.

'Do you find it warm? Or is it just me?'

He gave me a quizzical look and said, 'Perhaps if you open the top buttons of your coat. That might make it a little better.'

I don't know what possessed me, perhaps nervousness or excitement, but I had worn a heavy overcoat, which I had buttoned right up to my chin, and beneath that I wore a thick, sheep's wool jumper, and several more layers.

'It's just that it was cold when I came out, and now …'

'Yes,' he said. 'It's a bit stuffy. Shall we go elsewhere?'

'No. No. I'll do like you've suggested,' I replied, and went to open the top buttons of my coat. 'Oh dear, I'm all thumbs.'

'Here, allow me.'

I turned to face him, my nerves jangling like loose change in a too-wide trouser pocket. He looked directly at me as he worked his fingers around the buttons of my coat. I smiled back up at him and met his gaze. I studied those sad brown eyes to get an indication of what he might be thinking, but he averted his gaze and focused on the job at hand, then he said,

'Well, that should do it.'

I felt a little more air circulating around my neck and face. 'That's better. Thank you!'

'Shall we find that painting I mentioned?'

'Yes, let's do that,' I replied, and followed him around one corner and into a different part of the gallery.

A number of paintings were hanging from three of the walls, and several more were mounted on easels and positioned such that they faced towards a large bay window with a view of the street.

'This is the one I wanted to show you.'

'It's very beautiful,' I said, lost for anything more perceptive to say.

'*A Dance to the Music of Time*. It's not my favourite, but there is something about this painting that draws me back.'

'I suppose we all dance to the music of time,' I said, coming to stand beside him.

I watched him, as he studied the painting, a sometimes frown appearing on his forehead as he moved a little closer, to scrutinise some minor detail.

'I suppose we do,' he said, without looking in my direction.

'Would you like me to tell you more about it?'

'Yes, of course.'

'Then, come to dinner with me.' he said, turning towards me. I would like that very much.'

'I don't know if …'

'I'll pay, if that's what you're worried about.'

'It's just that, Doris …'

I had made a promise to Doris that I would go to the cinema that evening. There was a half-price show at the Odeon.

'Good old Doris again,' he said.

'I'll go, but only if you promise that I'll be home by eight.'

'Cross my heart.'

CHAPTER FIVE

'Missing?'

'About the room I mean … The other world will have to wait for another time.'

'Oh! Yes, that—'

'With the possible exception of Aunt Juliet I think this room is quite splendid, decorous even. There's the footstool brought all the way from China. The cloth has this wonderfully vibrant shade of blue. In fact, it's more azure than blue. What do you think of the Chinese, then?'

'I—'

The conversation jumped about from one topic to the next without very much rhyme or reason. It seemed to me that he was following a stream of consciousness, sometimes lucid, and at other times completely bonkers.

'They think long term,' he said.

'What do you mean?'

'Most people can't think beyond today. Most governments don't plan beyond the next election. The Chinese, they plan generations ahead. Some day they might even take over the world. Take this for instance. This little pipe of dreams.'

'It's Chinese, is it?'

'In a circuitous sort of way.'

'And that's why you think they will take over the world.'

'I didn't say that … though with enough of—'

'Well, what are you saying then?'

'I don't think it will happen today or tomorrow. No, I think it will happen when we are long gone.'

'Then you appear to have answered your own question.'

'You are the funny one. I believe I'm going to like having you around. Now, where is Mrs Butler? I have the most pressing business to discuss with her.'

'Shall I call out? Perhaps one of the servants is close by…'

'No, no, no need,' he stammered. 'Now, where was I? Yes. I was drawing a picture of your surroundings. In that corner of the room, there's a suit of armour,' he said.

I imagined he was off on one of his pointing adventures again and I was somewhat at a loss.

'I'm sorry,' I said, 'but I'm afraid I can't see. They did explain that, didn't they?'

'Yes, yes, damned foolish of me. It's behind you. It's a suit of armour worn by Oliver Cromwell. A rather diminutive sort of chap, don't you think?'

I shrugged my shoulders.

'Take my word for it, will you? Small hands, small feet. You get the picture. The accoutrement of every tin-pot dictator that ever was.'

'Small mindedness!'

'That too. Now, the fireplace, at ten o'clock.'

'What?'

'Aviation term. Ten o'clock.'

'Ah!'

'There are five paintings. All of them landscapes of one sort, or another. Would you like me to describe them to you?'

'Yes,' I replied. 'If you don't mind, that is.'

'Just a quick puff and we'll get on with it. Let's see if I can remember. Yes, here is the first one. It's above, and to the left of the fireplace. The artist is Cole. Have you heard of him?'

'Yes, I think I might have.'

'Good. No need to go into detail, other than to say, he was an American chap, inspired by Byron of all people. You know, *Lord Byron*?'

'Yes.'

'Well, I'm not an expert on these things but it seems to me that it's rather well painted. It's oil on canvas. Full of the wildness of nature. The sun appears to be rising and there are several semi-naked hunters in the scene. They appear to be pointing towards a settlement in the distance. There are trees too, and a mountain surrounded by what appears to be gathering storm clouds. What do you understand by that then?'

'I don't know really, though it has a sense of foreboding. Doesn't it?'

'Are you hungry?'

'No.'

'I'm famished. Where's Mrs Butler I wonder? Never mind. The second painting depicts man's attempts to harness nature. Trees have been cleared and a temple has been built. There's a fire burning. In the distance, there are ships. A man sketches a geometric pattern, a boy paints a figure of a warrior as his mother looks on.'

'She's showing concern,' I said.

'What makes you say that?'

'I don't know. I suppose all mothers worry about their boys … and war.' I said.

'This third one. The painting that sits directly over the

fireplace, depicts a scene of decadence. There's a river with a stone-built bridge, on which a crowd has gathered. An emperor or general appears to be returning triumphant to the city. Nature seems like an afterthought, replaced instead by grand columns. A little like Millrace, what! Yes, well …'

click-click

'In the fourth painting an army has invaded and everything is in a state of collapse. The city's inhabitants are being put to the sword. Off with their heads,' he said. 'In the final painting old ruins are shown overgrown. A river is choked. It is a less vibrant scene than in the first painting. It's as if nature itself has given up. Well, that's the story of Millrace just about summed up, isn't it?'

'I don't know what you mean. I think this place is perfectly lovely.'

'Oh dear have they got you under their spell already? What else shall I tell you about? Oh, yes, over here—'

His voice faded away and I was left standing there, wondering, and picturing the scene in my head, until my thoughts were disturbed by a loud knocking noise, then the sound of a door opening and closing again, followed by approaching footsteps.

'Your tea, miss.'

I recognised Mr Burrows' voice and I heard the rattle of silverware on a tray then the sound of footsteps grew silent.

'Just put it down there,' Mr Burrows said.

I heard another set of footsteps approach, and the tray was placed on the low table in front of me.

'Shall I pour, miss?' a girlish voice asked, sheepishly.

'That won't be necessary,' Mr Burrows interjected.

'Very good, Mr Burrows,' she replied.

'I'll call for you Daisy, when we're finished here,' Mr Burrows said.

Footsteps retreated towards the door again.

'Has she gone?' Pipe-smoker asked.

'Yes, sir,' Mr Burrows replied.

'Good. I see you've brought tea for the young lady.'

'Yes, sir. Shall I get a second setting, sir?'

'Could you ask Mrs Butler to prepare my special tea like a good man?'

'Yes, sir. Of course.'

'And Burrows, I'm absolutely famished. Can you bring some sandwiches?'

'Sandwiches, sir?'

'Whatever you can muster up.'

'Very good, sir. I'll ask Mrs Butler to see to it right away. Shall I pour, miss?' Mr Burrows asked then.

'Yes, please.'

'Very good. I'm afraid it's just powdered milk,' Mr Burrows said.

'I prefer it black.'

'We're like peas in a pod, you and I. Can't tolerate the stuff. All tea should be black. I could never fathom why the English would ruin a perfectly good tradition. Do we have to ruin everything? What do you think, Burrows?'

'My thoughts exactly, sir.'

'Are you not going to offer the young lady something to sit on, Burrows?'

'Yes, sir. Of course. There's a chair right behind you, miss. If you'd please.'

I heard the sound of something heavy being moved about and then Mr Burrow's hand came to rest lightly on my arm.

'Thank you.'

'Will that be all, sir?' Mr Burrows asked.

48

'Yes, yes. Very good, Burrows. Sandwiches. And Mrs Butler's special tea.'

'Of course, sir.'

I heard footsteps again; a creaking floorboard and the door opening and closing gently this time.

'Your tea will get cold,' Pipe-smoker said, '… though I think that cold tea can be even more refreshing on days like today, days when it's hot and muggy. Wouldn't you agree? What a drag it has become. Hot one day, cold the next. It's hard to know what to do with oneself in such circumstances. Is it spring, or winter, or something else entirely?'

'Yes, very strange indeed.' I reached out my hand and lifted the cup to my face. For the briefest of moments, I thought I detected a smell of gasoline. 'Thank you. I'm afraid I'm still at a bit of a loss,' I said, and blew gently across the surface of the hot liquid.

'How's your tea?'

'Oh, it's lovely, thank you,' and took my first sip. 'You see, I—'

'Can I let you in on a little secret?'

I held the cup to my face and said, 'Yes, please do.'

'I failed to point out some unique features of this house.'

'What are they?' I asked and sipped my tea again.

'Secret doors.'

'Secret doors?'

'Nothing demonstrates intrigue more than secret doors, sliding panels and hidden passageways.'

I tried to imagine what those passageways might look like and where they might lead and found my mind suddenly filled with endless possibilities.

'Perhaps one of the days I'll give you the grand tour,' Pipe-smoker said.

'That would be quite interesting.'

'I used them as a child, you see. I used to flit between rooms and hide out of sight. I am sure I drove the servants demented. There's a passage leading to an underground tunnel. It runs all the way to the boathouse. Can you keep a secret?' he said.

'We don't know each other very well,' I replied.

'That's not the point. Can you keep a secret?'

Secrets, it seemed to me, were the only things I still possessed.

'Yes,' I said.

'I sneak out sometimes. Down into the long tunnel and to the boathouse. I go mostly at night, confident that I will never encounter another soul. I am sure they would get quite a shock to see a ghoulish spectre disgorging itself from the earth that they would turn on their heels and run for all they were worth. *He-heh!*'

'Don't say that when you know it isn't true.'

'But it is, you see … so very true.'

'What do you do when you get to the boathouse?'

'I sit there and watch it all unfold before me, light and shadows, the moon glistening off the water, the bats emerging from their nests to feast on insects, the occasional fox might happen by, an unlucky rabbit between its jaws. I listen too, because you can hear a pin drop. Sometimes you can hear the drone of distant bombers or the sputtering of an engine somewhere, but it is rarer than you think, and sometimes it is so dark you cannot see your hand in front of your face without some sort of lamp or lantern. I like those nights the best.'

If only he knew, I thought silently, what it felt like to be in a perpetual state of darkness.

'It is soul destroying,' I said.

'What is?'

'The darkness when I once knew the light.'

'Yes, of course … I didn't mean to offend. Can I offer you a smoke? I've already asked you, haven't I?'

'Yes,' I said, and left it at that.

He cleared his throat and said, 'I suppose you're wondering why you're here then?'

'Why, yes. I suppose I am.'

'We'll get to that,' Pipe-smoker replied.

'Biscuit? They're right in front of you and a little to your left,' he said. 'You can eat it, or use it as a weapon. Might have one myself. Do you mind?'

I heard the rattle of china and then a crunching sound. 'Famished. Absolutely famished.'

I smiled and reached out my free hand. I found the edge of the table, then the tray, and next the plate on which was stacked several hard-tack biscuits. I pinched one between two fingers and placed it on my saucer. I sipped my tea again, holding the cup aloft with two fingers outstretched as I had seen someone do once. I think it was in a magazine on etiquette, or perhaps I had seen one of those society women at the Provincial do it. Yes, that was it, the Provincial, I remembered. Such seemingly insignificant things reminded me of Henry. We danced at the Provincial. We—

I nibbled on the biscuit, and conscious that I might let crumbs fall, I placed my cup and saucer underneath.

'It must be difficult,' he said, in a sympathetic voice.

'Difficult?' I replied.

'You know, with your affliction.'

'We're back to that again.'

'I'm sorry …'

'I've grown used to it, though I am known to be a little accident prone. I also have a terrible sense of dress, don't you think?'

'I think you look very nice,' he replied.

I could tell that he was being sincere by the very gentle way he said it.

I heard that mechanical noise again, *click-click*, and smelled the unusual pipe-smoke, stronger now that he had come closer. I gave a little cough.

'I'll go to the window. Is that any better then? I like the view from here. I like looking out the window to the sea. It is one of the only other constants in my life now. The view of the sea. I watch it, you know. I watch it come and go, ebbing and flowing. There is nothing we can do except bow to its tremendous will. Shall I tell you a story? I promise, it's quite a short one.'

'Yes, do go on.'

'I remember as a young boy ... I might have been ten or eleven, making my way through the tunnel I have described to the boathouse. We keep a rowing boat there, a wide, cumbersome craft for one man to handle, but I thought of myself as a capable enough sailor even at that age. I stole out one morning, quite early, just as the tide was turning. The mist was rising and I remember the sun was just a dim saucer behind the clouds. It was summer, the air clean and fresh, and life and the day itself seemed so full of possibilities. I untied the boat and rowed out into the bay, to the point where I could still hear the church bell chiming the hour. I hung up the oars and lay back in the boat to listen to the sounds of the sea. Gulls swooped and called to each other. In the distance, I heard the sound of an engine sputtering away. The water lapped at the sides of the boat, lulling me with its gentle waving motion. I lay there, my face to the sky, closed my eyes, and allowed myself a sigh of contentment. I don't know how long I was asleep, hours perhaps, but I woke up again with a start when the boat was rocked suddenly and violently by a wave.

Another one followed soon after the first. I sat up and looked around. All I could see was water and realised with a quickly rising level of dread that I must have drifted far from the shore. The sun was blazing down at that point and there wasn't a cloud in the sky, and I, in my enthusiasm for the venture, had packed neither water nor food. I was alone, with just the sea for company.'

'What did you do?'

'What could you do? I had no idea which way to go, even if I had the inclination to let out the oars and row.'

'You survived and lived to tell the tale.'

'Yes.'

'But, how?'

'The sea gave me up.'

'What do you mean … gave you up?'

'Just as the tide goes out, it must also come in again.'

'It pushed you back to the shore.'

'Yes. About two miles from where I had started my journey. The sea is my saviour, always.'

'Was there no search party?'

'I don't think *they* even knew I was gone.'

'Surely not?'

'I'm afraid so. I rowed back to the boat house, tied up the boat and scampered back through the tunnel to this very room, if memory serves me.'

'You must have been exhausted?'

'I slipped up the stairs to my room and went to bed. I didn't wake until someone knocked on the door to tell me that supper was being served. Can you imagine?'

'Yes, all very *Boy's Own* …'

'I suppose it was,' he said, rather mournfully.

'*The sea, the sea, the beguiling sea, carrying all before it, of love and loss in the main.*'

How very sad, I thought.

'That's quite beautiful.'

'It's just something I'm tinkering around with. It's quite depressing really.'

'Is it a poem …?'

'You could say that. It's a stream of consciousness.'

'You should try to finish it. See where it brings you.'

'Perhaps I will.'

He changed the subject then, 'Some days I catch a glimpse of the dogfights taking place far out to sea and think how wonderful it would be to be free like that again … like that day I was cast adrift with the sun on my face and the wind in my hair.'

'Did you say dogfights?'

'Oh, yes, out there a constant drama unfolds?'

I imagined him sweeping his arm rather dramatically in a big swooping arc to illustrate the immenseness of the sky.

'I can see them, like little birds swooping and diving, but then you see smoke and fire, and you know that they are mechanical after all. It sends a shudder down my spine to see that happen.' He seemed lost in his thoughts for a few moments then he said, 'It's a horrible, bloody great tragedy playing out thousands of feet above us, day after day, night after night, and most people never notice. Most people never look up. Perhaps they are too busy wondering about their own personal perils. I can't say I blame them. I mean we must get on with it. Bread must be buttered, tea must be drunk, and cakes must be baked. In a time of pandemonium, the small things count the most. There I go rambling on again.'

'No, you … I mean to say, you're not rambling on.'

He sucked a rasping breath and said,

'Intrigue, the very life blood of Millrace itself. You have heard the gossip and scandal I assume. Perhaps, by revealing secret passageways and tunnels I have merely confirmed what you've suspected all along.'

'No more than any other. Houses such as Millrace should have secrets, don't you think? It's fodder for active imaginations, idleness, and writers of fiction.'

'Aren't they the same thing?'

I laughed and said, 'I didn't think of it like that, but yes … I suppose they are.'

'Well, let me just put your mind at ease. We don't have any ghosts at Millrace, not the imaginary ones in any case.'

'What other types of ghosts are there?'

'Real ones,' he said.

I remembered thinking for the briefest of moments that I was such a ghost, caught in a world of imaginings.

'I can sometimes hear the drone of the bombers overhead. All I can think of is death and destruction happening somewhere else. Not little old Rashleigh.'

'Because we're insignificant, is that your rationale?'

'I suppose it is.'

'We must drive them back into the sea. Isn't that what the prime minister says?'

'I don't know.'

'Haven't you heard any of his speeches?'

'I'm afraid not recently in any case.'

'Shame. Damned patriotic, they are. One must always keep a stiff upper lip. Isn't that so?'

His voice had taken on a bitter tone, as if something had upset him, or he had been slighted in some way.

'Father is not terribly fond of our Prime Minister, I'm afraid. He calls him a warmonger. I'm not sure he agrees with the whole stiff upper lip sentiment. He saw too much war, I expect.'

'Your father sounds like a sensible man.'

'You must watch the sea for hours,' I said, changing the subject and taking another sip of tea. 'I wish—'

'You wish you too could see the drama of the sea unfold.'

'Yes.'

'I think I like it better that you can't see it.'

'Why?'

'Because I can describe it to you instead.'

'You like that, then? Painting a picture with words.'

'Yes,' he sighed, '... It's the small things in life that make it so bearable. A pleasing view and a little puff- puff, and off we go. Sometimes it's one and the same. I am sorry for being so rude. Filling your head with tales and melodramas. You probably think I'm a proper cad.'

I shook my head and said, 'Could you describe the rest of the room to me? It helps you see, when I find myself in an unfamiliar place, to orientate myself to my surroundings.'

'All right, then,' he said, rather assuredly. 'You've met Burrows. He's part of the furniture, and Mrs Butler, her too. She can be a bit sharp around the edges but she's a good old sort. I don't really know what I might have done without her. It was her idea to … never mind, there I go again. Let me see, this room is the drawing room. You entered through the main entrance. If you had continued straight ahead, you would have entered the main ballroom. They held dances there in the old days. It's quite ornate, with lots of chandeliers and mirrors, don't you know. I detest it myself. Reflections everywhere. I suppose neither of us need reminders. Do we?'

I remembered the mirror hanging on the wall. I paused each day to check my appearance in it. A habit I suppose. It no longer served its intended purpose of course. At least not for me.

'Now the room we're currently in is a little more casual. I've mentioned the secret doors. We'll get to that again. There is a floor-to-ceiling bookcase over there, full of dusty old tomes I'm afraid. There is one I like. It's a book by Ford Maddox-Ford I rather like.'

'*The Good Soldier* …?'

'Yes. That's the one. You've heard of him then?'

'Yes,' I said. 'Someone I once knew liked that novel very much. He claimed to know the author as it happens. Actually, he had a signed copy of … gosh, there I go rambling on.'

'Ramble away. This chap you mention, was he a sweetheart? Has he gone away to the war, or …?'

'The truth is, you see, I haven't heard from him in quite some time. I believe he may be somewhere in the Far East. I've imagined that he might have been in Rangoon. Whatever possessed me to believe such a thing I don't know. Perhaps it's because I heard it through the wireless.'

'Army is he?'

'He's in Royal Naval Intelligence.'

'I see. Now, where was I? There's a piano, of course. I used to play the very same one, when I was young. Watch out for *E sharp*. It can be a little tricky.'

Pipe-smoker's voice trailed away again and I was lost in my thoughts a little longer.

For just that moment, when he had asked about Henry, I felt that perhaps here was someone who might sympathise in some way. It was right before he continued on describing the room's décor that I felt I might unburden myself, to him, a perfect stranger, but then the moment passed and we were on to other things. 'I will,' I said, without really hearing what he had said and in response to some remark he made.

'What else can I describe for you? Apart from the paintings around the fireplace, there are several more hanging from the walls. Reproductions, I'm afraid. Portraits mostly. There's one of Admiral Nelson, posing proudly in uniform. It's mounted so that he is looking out to sea. Nelson is squinting, as if he sees something in the distance. He seems to be wearing an element of recognition on his face though. It's almost like the image is slowly forming in his mind like a wave rolling towards him. Strange, don't you think?'

'The sun and sea will do that to you.'

'I never thought of that before. Yes, yes, now that I examine his features in more detail I think you might be right. Well, I'll be … the sun and the sea.'

Just then, there were two loud knocks on the door, followed a few moments later by two more.

'Ah, that's my signal. Coast is clear. No need to dash off.'

The door opened then and I heard the march of determined footsteps, and something else, a squeaking noise, rhythmic, grating on the ear, like something metallic was in need of oiling. Then I heard another noise, very much like someone blowing up a balloon.

'The Master is here now,' a voice announced. It was Mrs Butler who had returned to stamp her authority on the proceedings again.

'Father,' Pipe-smoker said, in a low and careful voice.

Someone made a yawning noise.

'Yes, quite beautiful,' Pipe-smoker said out of nowhere.

I felt heat rising in my cheeks for no other reason than I

thought that all eyes were suddenly upon me. However, before I could become too distracted Mrs Butler said,

'Quite plain and much too thin I should think. Some weight on her bones would suit the girl. No bosom, no bottom, no hips of burden. I've seen meatier waifs in my time. Are you quite finished with your tea?'

'Now, now, Mrs Butler. You always were a tough old bird to please. You've brought my special tea, I see,' Pipe-smoker said.

'Of course, sir.'

'... And sandwiches too. What do we have today?'

'Rabbit, sir'

'Rabbit sandwiches! Are we at that point now, Mrs Butler?'

'Rabbits are plentiful, sir. Mr Broom has shot a few recently.'

'I thought you might bring me one of those corned beef ones.'

'*Where* would we get corned beef, sir?'

'Oh! Of course, Mrs Butler. I don't know what made me think of corned beef.'

'How is your tea, sir?'

'Just the ticket, Mrs Butler. Let's see ... and down the rabbit hole we go. Hmm! Delightful. There is nothing like a rabbit with a little relish, and I am *weally welishing* the *wabbit*. Bravo Mrs Butler!' he said, and laughed at his own humour.

'I'm very happy to hear that, sir.'

A second yawning sound made me sit upright. I placed the cup and saucer in front of me and nervously brushed invisible crumbs from my skirt.

'The tea was lovely,' I interjected.

'Yes, and our fine china too. Daisy should know better.'

The cup had little chips in it. If it was fine china then it surely would have seen better days.

'The Chinese again ...' Pipe-smoker said. 'They're going to

59

take over the world, father. Our guest believes so. Don't you?'

'I didn't actually say that …'

'Do you know why you've been summoned to Millrace?' Mrs Butler said.

'I'm to play piano.'

'It seems you have quite the reputation.'

I have played piano since I was quite young. My parent's squirrelled money away to ensure I got only the best in life, from dresses to music lessons, until I won a scholarship to the prestigious London School of Music. It was almost unheard of in Rashleigh where many girls went into service at places such as Millrace. I expect Mrs Butler was such a girl once.

'That's rather kind, miss—'

'Mrs Butler,' she added. 'You can call me, Mrs Butler.'

I noticed that mechanical noise again, slightly different on my ear, more like a bellows. Yes, that was it. Air sucked in and out. The pipe-smoke became a background smell, overwhelmed by a more clinical and hygienic odour, like detergent or bleach.

'It's to your left,' Mrs Butler snapped, drawing my attention quickly back to present matters.

I placed my hands on the armrests of my chair and rose to standing then I searched with my cane for nearby objects.

'Right in front of you now,' Mrs Butler instructed.

I found a low bench and made my way around it to take my seat and make myself comfortable. I placed my cane to one side, and let my fingers do the walking along the various surfaces until I could feel the smooth and polished piano cover.

I lifted it and pushed it carefully out of the way, and rested my fingertips lightly on the keys.

'You see, the young sir was somewhat of a prodigy too, you know. Yes, he was—'

Someone blew their nose loudly several times.

'Now, now, Mrs Butler. I still have at least one ear for music,' Pipe-smoker said.

'Master Charles likes the works of Mozart and Beethoven mostly, and Chopin, amongst others. I believe you'll find the piano is in tune,' Mrs Butler said. 'I don't expect you'll need sheet music, given … given your predicament, that is.'

'No, sheet music won't be necessary.'

I ran my fingers gently along the keyboard, feeling the polished ivories for inconsistencies, chips or gaps, and then I moved my seat a little closer to find the foot pedals.

I waited to allow my ear to become more accustomed to the bellows sound, to let it fade into the background, and then I began the piece I had intended to play that day. It was a piece Pipe-smoker had reminded me of, and one Henry would ask me to play repeatedly.

I remembered how he used to sit and watch me play, his eyes closed, concentrating on every note, as if each one carried a message, just for him. I loved him for that. I placed my fingers on the keys and played the first movement of Erik Satie's *Gymnopédie*.

CHAPTER SIX

Later, as we made the long journey home Mr Burrows chatted about this and that. I was otherwise distracted by my thoughts and apart from the cursory acknowledgment of this or that, I kept my counsel, lost instead in mulling through the fog of confusion that lay over the day's events.

I had played constantly for one hour, Satie, Chopin, Bach, Beethoven without stopping, as agreed, and at the end, I felt Mrs Butler's spindly fingers upon my shoulder.

'You can stop now,' she said. 'Master Charles is tired.'

I stopped playing and stood to stretch my aching limbs. I found my cane and waited.

'Bravo,' Pipe-smoker said. 'I was just sitting here entranced, my stomach full of relished-rabbit and Mrs Butler's herbal tea and felt, for the first time in quite some time, lulled into a wonderful contentment. Don't you wish it was like this all of the time, Father? Relished-rabbit and recitals!'

Someone moaned loudly.

click-click

'Thank you,' I replied and my words were quickly followed by that moaning noise again.

'I once knew a man who loved that Satie piece so much that he would hum it all day long, as if it reminded him of something.

Father seemed to enjoy it too. Didn't you Father?'

I heard the sound of the bellows again, then that mechanical squeak I had noticed an hour before. It receded into the distance and I heard instead the sound of Mrs Butler's voice in the corridor. She was barking orders. The next voice I heard was that of Mr Burrows.

'I have your hat and coat, miss. It's turned chilly out there. Don't want you getting a cold. Not with such important work to do.'

'Important work?'

'Mr Burrows means to say that you are bringing great joy to a man who has very little else in life to be joyful about. Isn't that right, Burrows?'

'That's very true, sir. Very true indeed. The Master loves his music, he does.'

I felt the heaviness of the coat about my shoulders and Mr Burrows held my cane while I fixed my hat in place.

'That was right wonderful music, miss, he said then. Right wonderful, it was. I was listening from just outside the door, I was. It was just me and the servant girl, Daisy, and Mr Broom, the horses' groom, but don't tell Mrs Butler if you wouldn't mind. She would have our guts for garters, she would. I hope you don't mind, sir.'

'I won't tell, if you don't,' Pipe-smoker replied.

'Nor shall I Mr Burrows, and thank you for your kind words,' I replied, taking the cane from his hand.

Later, as we drove down the gravel driveway I tried to imagine the house and all its windows. In each one, a person stood watching as we got further and further away. I imagined Pipe-smoker standing at the drawing room window, looking forlornly out to sea and the Master in his wheelchair silently praying for an end to his torment. I saw Mrs Butler too, the curtains parted just enough for her to catch a glimpse of the car receding into the distance, her eyes narrowed in determined suspicion. I must admit that the image sent a slight chill down my spine and I chastised myself for having such childish thoughts.

It was true, however, that the house and all its inhabitants were possessed of a strange melancholy. I felt it in the small things, like Pipe-smoker's tortured voice, and Mrs Butler's icy demeanour. It was there too in the Master's confinement and Mr Burrows somewhat sorrowful ways. As if there wasn't enough to be sorrowful about in life, Millrace it seemed was determined to add to the woes of the world.

I was thinking about such things when we rounded the bend in the road before the bridge. Mr Burrows was busily explaining the topography and I was paying just enough attention to what he was saying when there was a squeal of brakes and I felt a little bump, then the car came to a sudden stop.

*

'I really must be going.'

'Yes, of course.'

'Did you enjoy your meal?'

'Yes. It was lovely. Thank you.'

'It wasn't much but I enjoyed our chat.'

'So did I,' I said.

We'd sat for more than two hours chatting our way through our meal of potatoes and cabbage, and something resembling custard for dessert, explaining our likes and dislikes, without once mentioning the war. It felt like such a relief.

All anyone ever seemed to talk about was the war.

'You didn't keep your promise,' I said. 'You were supposed to have me home by eight.'

'Oh, dear, is that the time,' he said, glancing at his watch. 'How did you know?'

I pointed in the direction of the clock which was mounted at an awkward angle on one of the dining room walls.

'Quarter past nine,' I said.

'Yet, you didn't leave.'

'I was enjoying the conversation.'

'Won't Doris be annoyed?'

'I'll expect she'll get over it.'

He smiled in return and took a cigarette from a battered cigarette case. 'Care for one?'

'I better not. They make me a little light-headed.'

'I don't blame you. I've been trying to give them up for years,' he said, striking a match.

'Lost your lighter?'

'It has given up the ghost,' he said, and blew a cloud of smoke over his shoulder. 'I must buy another one.'

'I've really enjoyed myself,' I said.

'Oh, yes, the hour, I …'

'It's not that, though I do really have to go. I was wondering if you would like to come to a recital. It's a small affair, in aid of wounded servicemen.'

'I'd love to,' he said.

'But I haven't finished telling you the details,' I replied.

'Will you be playing?'

'Yes.'

'Then that's all I need to know,' he said, and blew another cloud of smoke.

At that moment, he reached across the table and took my

65

hand. I let him. He ran his thumb along the palm of my hand, applying gentle pressure.

'Mr Morton, I …'

'Henry.'

'Henry, I—'

'May I kiss you?' he said.

*

'Oh my,' Mr Burrows said.

'What is it?' I asked.

I heard the car door open and Mr Burrows' footsteps passing by.

'Oh my,' I heard him say again.

Then I heard the car boot open and the sound of rummaging. Something gave a little squeal then I heard a dull thud and crack. A few moments later Mr Burrows returned and I heard the car boot close and the squeak of leather as Mr Burrows returned to the driver's seat. The door closed behind him and the engine started up again. I heard Mr Burrows sniffle a few times, as if he was crying, then he cleared his throat, and blew his nose.

'Everything is all right now, miss,' he said.

The car lurched forward then and not another word was said of the incident until we arrived at the cottage, Mr Burrows choosing instead to talk about the change in the weather, and such things, but the incident and the day's unusual events continued to plague me.

My inquisitiveness overcame me then. I just had to know. I heard his driver's side door open and close, then the passenger door opened and I felt for his hand.

'Watch your step there, miss,' he cautioned.

'What happened at the bridge?' I asked.

'It's nothing to be worrying your head about, miss.'

'But I want to know,' I persisted.

'Well, if you insist, miss. It was a little rabbit, miss. I'm afraid I had to put it out of its misery,' he said, as he closed the passenger door behind me. 'It's just as well you didn't have to see me do it.'

I thought back to the sounds I had heard, the car boot and the dull thump and crack, and Mr Burrows' regretful utterances. I felt a knot in my stomach.

'Oh,' I replied, 'what a terrible thing to happen.'

'Aye, miss. It was. There are a lot of rabbits these days. You know … those poor little blind ones. They just run around in circles. You would think they might learn, but they never seem to. Around in circles, miss. It's the times we live in if you don't mind me saying. Everything and everyone is going around in circles. Isn't that what they say, miss? History repeating itself. Very well then, miss. If that will be all I'll be bidding you farewell. I'll see you again at the same time in the morrow,' Mr Burrows said.

I heard the sound of his footsteps receding, the car door banging shut then the engine starting up again. I remained where I was standing, thinking about what Mr Burrows had told me, and listened as the car pulled away, leaving me in the lingering exhaust fumes. I thought about little rabbits, and how the world can turn on the toss of a coin, or the spin of a bottle, or a crack on the head, and a fall into darkness.

*

'Is that you?' Father said.

'Who else would it be? It's not like we get many visitors about these parts,' I said, jokingly.

'Aye, true. Well, come inside, or you will catch your death. The weather has turned a little. It's a cold snap and the flowers are only coming into bloom. They'll all be killed off,' he said.

I noticed the chill then, and followed Father's voice to the threshold of the front door and felt the warmth of the house on my face, drawing me into its comforting embrace. I heard the grandfather clock marking time and the wireless crackling out of tune. He must get so lonely, I thought then, being there in the cottage, without her for company. He loved her too much for God to burden him with such loneliness. Oh Freya, he would sometimes mutter, exasperated with some minor task he might have set himself. Why did you have to go?

Then, as if she had answered back, he would say. It should have been me.

I wondered what he meant by that. I wondered too if he realised that I might be standing there all the while. How odd it might have looked to someone else, a stranger, to come upon such a scene, and witness a blind woman watching her father conversing with a ghost.

'Where's Jess?' I said, returning from my thoughts and stepping into the narrow hallway that led to the kitchen.

'She might be up in the field,' Father replied, referring to one of the sheepdogs who was heavily pregnant.

'Isn't it better if she was kept close to fire? She's nearly ready to birth those pups I should think.'

'Aye, I'll go and see about her,' Father said. 'There's a vegetable stew on the stove. Be careful. It's very hot. You can tell me all about your day when I return. I won't be long.'

I removed my hat and placed it on the waist-height table by the door. Then I took off my coat and hung it on a hook by the hall mirror. I studied myself unconsciously, arranging an unseen strand of hair, here and there, a loose thread, an invisible blemish on my face. I was lost in this peculiarly redundant act when I heard Father switch off the wireless, then the back door creaked open and closed again.

I hummed a melody in my head and made my way to the kitchen. A pot simmered away on the range. I found a bowl and lifted the cover of the pot with a tea cloth. Steam wafted up to bathe my face as I filled the bowl then I made my way to the table and sat down, and allowed myself a deep sigh. Rain danced across the windowpane and a bitter wind whistled under the door and lulled me into contemplation.

Life had come full circle, I thought, returned as I was to the place of my birth. Still it was different of course from my childhood. Circumstances meant that I could only imagine and sense the things I once took for granted, through hearing, touch, and smell. Every now and then, a dim, grey light streamed in front of me like a benign spectre, teasing me with possibilities, before disappearing again. The curse was in knowing that beyond the limitations of my affliction there existed a beautiful garden, a place where, as a child, I had once played without a care.

Sometimes, in my daydreams, the garden would come to me again in all its splendour. Sights, such as the old oak tree, leafless and weather beaten, bent sideways by one storm after another, its roots clinging on for dear life. I marvelled at how its branches reached like spindly fingers to point towards a full moon, and how in summer the dogs still went to lie there, in its shade, moving around its trunk already stripped free of bark, and bleached white from the elements, as a blazing sun moved across the sky. And how, despite its age and precarious existence, Father insisted that he would never cut it down, not while there was still breath in his lungs, for that tree symbolised everything he had lost, the tree under which Father had laid my mother, and my brother, to rest. The little wrought iron fence, no higher than my knee, which ringed the spot where they lay side by side, separated by years but together in the afterlife. There were other things too. Like the rose bush, Mother's favourite yellow, planted so that when in flower it would adorn the place with its sweet scent and cover the grave like a quilt with its wilted flower when it went into decline. There was a little fountain too, fed with water from the well, where birds would come to drink and bathe. All these unusual ornaments surrounded her in life and were part of her in death too.

She was a cabaret singer who had travelled the world before marrying my father, and he had been a writer who received a commission to the Yeomanry. He became an insurance salesman after the war, before becoming a sort of gentleman farmer and occasional writer for trade magazines and scientific journals. I believed Father never quite liked that sort of writing. Drudgery, I once heard him call it. Something done to pay the bills. I believe he thought of himself as a serious writer, someone who might one day produce a thing of consequence, a novel to transcend the generations. Writing for *Town & Countryside,* that was the short-term solution to the pressing problem of expenses. The real money, he would say, lay in a best-selling novel. Just one. He wasn't greedy, he would say. As the years went by the dream of writing a novel of substance seemed to dim, increasingly replaced by articles on growing your own fruit and vegetables, or how mechanisation was changing agricultural practices, or choosing the right draft horse to pull a plough. I quite enjoyed those. Father tended to inject a little humour into every piece. Perhaps that was why the magazine continued to commission him, albeit irregularly.

As the world about them spun, through one crisis after another, the first war, the death of little Thomas to the Spanish flu, and Mother's depression which followed, it always seemed like they managed to trundle on. Then, to add to their woes an economic winter descended. Just when they believed they were on their uppers, a few shillings would magically manifest themselves. An envelope would arrive with a new commission, or payment for a previous article.

It was only after I had gone away to music school that a greater darkness fell. Perhaps it was the unpredictability of their financial situation, which eventually led to my mother's worsening depression. One day she went to the lake and walked into its cold waters, leaving nothing but the silver necklace she wore on the shore, and a short note: I am sorry but I must go, she wrote.

I tried to imagine what she was thinking in those final moments, as the last of the air left her lungs. Did she think of baby Thomas? Did she meet his shadow in the depths? When they found her body some days later she was clutching a yellow rose tight in one hand. Rose Cottage had had its share of tragedy that was true. Father found consolation at the bottom of a bottle. When he had drained the last of it, he found God.

I was lost in my thoughts when suddenly disturbed by a noise. It was the latch on the door and the sound of paw steps on the flagstones.

'Is that you, Jess?' I said, and pushed my plate away.

I reached down and found a furry head and a cold nose.

'You need to stay indoors, you do.'

'Aye, she needs to stay put now. She's not long off,' Father added.

'Where did you find her?'

'Where you said of course … up the field there, lying down,

71

and too tired to make the trek back. I had to carry her most of the way.'

'Poor, Jess.'

'She has my back broken. How was your dinner?' Father inquired.

'It was very tasty, Father.' He tried so hard.

'Well, that's good then. Would you like a cup of tea? I'll put the kettle on, and you can tell me all about your day.'

'There's not much to tell,' I said.

In truth, I was unsure where I should start. I was still trying to untangle the strangeness of it all. Should I tell him about the mysterious Pipe-smoker, or Mr Burrows, or the chilly Mrs Butler, or the journey, or my sore fingers and tired hands? In the end I told him as much as I was sure of.

'Mr Burrows ran over a rabbit,' I said.

There was a moment's silence before Father replied.

'Is that so?'

I suddenly felt like a child recounting a tale.

'It was as we were driving down the avenue from the Big House. We felt a little bump and Mr Burrows swore under his breath. He was out of the motor and onto the road in a matter of moments.'

'These things happen, my dear. There are more and more blind rabbits every day. The government will have to do something about it. You would think the Land Ministry would have taken care of it somehow. They like to take care of everything else. Perhaps I could send a proposal to *Town & Countryside*. What to do with blind rabbits! Do you think they would go for it?'

Father hadn't written an article for Town & Countryside for many years but instead of reminding him I simply said,

'I don't see why not, Father. It's quite topical.'

'Yes, rabbits. Crepuscular. Did you know that?'

'No, I …'

'Mr Burrows, you say?'

'Yes. Mr Burrows.'

'I met a Burrows chap once. It was when I went away to the War. But it couldn't be the same man.'

'Why is that?' I asked.

'Well, to the best of my knowledge, Mr Burrows is dead. Unless, it is some relation of his, which is very possible of course. The name is quite unusual for these parts though. In fact, I don't know any other families in the valley with that name.'

'I'll ask him tomorrow then.'

'People don't like to be bothered with talk of the last War, my dear. You know that. And now we're in another one …'

'I meant only to ask if Mr Burrows was from these parts.'

'Certain things never leave you,' Father began, 'like the smells of life and death, or how you felt when standing in a trench half-full of freezing water. It makes me shudder to think about it, even after all these years.'

'I'm sorry, Father. I didn't mean to bring it up.'

'There was a tunnel. *Gladstone* they called it. They looked for volunteers, you know, from amongst the ranks, men who had worked the coal and tin, and copper mines. A voice would call out in a sort of singsong way, *Volunteers for Gladstone*, as if they were advertising a newspaper headline. Volunteers for Gladstone indeed. Volunteers for certain deaths were more like it. Nevertheless, a few souls would raise their hands, knowing that there might just be a chance that they would survive a little longer underground than above it. It was like that you know. When all the volunteers had come forward, an officer would come through and pick a man at random. In such a way, a squad was formed to work on a section of the tunnel. Poor sods.'

'Father, you really don't have to ...'

'Every now and again,' he interrupted, 'you might hear an almighty bang. It would sound different to the rest, because it came from underground, and it was *their* tunnel, or ours going up, and with it a dozen men or more. I remember the man with the name of Burrows being amongst a group of Volunteers for Gladstone. I remember reading his name from the list of missing-in-action. You see, one of the tunnels had flooded and collapsed. Who bought it? Someone would ask. This fella or that fella. A chap from Liverpool, or London. Perhaps a Yorkshireman or some poor lad from Devon. You would have time to know a man by his whereabouts. You would know a Cornish man, maybe his family, or his family's family and you would think to yourself that you must pay a visit, you know, to say a few words to his next of kin when it was all over. I never did, of course. I had intentions but then we needed to leave it all behind and to get back to the business of living. That's all you can do.'

'What about this Mr Burrows?'

'News came back that a group of men had been trapped by an explosion further down a tunnel shaft. You might have an image of men, buried alive or drowned, never much matters when the result is the same, then you would shake that image from your head and focus on what mattered, getting through another day. I remember though that there were twelve of them in all. Twelve apostles, they called them. That is why, when you mentioned Mr Burrows, I thought of the twelve apostles and it brought back those terrible times. You know, the Germans blew up the whole tunnel network the next day. Could see the explosion from half a mile away. It was like a great big mushroom cloud in No-man's land, it was. A great big mushroom.'

I took a little intake of breath. It was almost too dreadful to think about. Those poor faceless men, trapped underground, buried forever, and yet, if they had been rabbits, they could have dug their way out again. It is so strange the way the world works, men dying underground and blind rabbits everywhere.

'That's enough tragedy for now. The only good thing to come from all of it was that I met your mother, God bless her soul,' Father sighed, interrupting my thoughts. 'Anyway, you haven't told me about your day. Did you do what was required of you?'

'Yes, Father. I played piano, mostly classical pieces,' I said.

'A strange request from strange people, there's no doubt about it, but you are the best in the valley, and beyond, I might add. It must be nice to have such work. There's not much call for … There's none the like of you is what I mean to say.'

'*Father.*'

'Mother would have been proud.'

He always called her Mother. It seemed like such an old-fashioned thing.

'Tell me again how you met her,' I asked.

I heard him sigh then, 'Haven't I told you before?' he said mockingly. 'I have, you know. Well I suppose there is no harm in telling it again. Mother had come to sing for the troops, you see. Aye, she was a wonder. Brought a kindness with her everywhere she went. I was assigned as her liaison officer. My job was to drive her here or there, up the line and down again. I would organise for a small stage to be set up and a little piano brought out, and there she would sit, singing the same old songs, night after night, and all those faces staring back at her. I expect they looked like every mother's son, faces in the crowd, but I will say this, she made them all feel special. It was just as if she was singing for them alone. There was never a dry eye. Those men, young and old alike, hardened by death and destruction, brought to tears by a song, or a tinkle on the piano, and your mother's gentle smile. You have her ways too,' Father said sadly.

There was silence between us then, lost as we were in our own thoughts and inner torments.

'You must be tired,' Father said then, to break the silence.

'Yes. Now that you mention it … I am feeling a little …'

'And I dare say you'll be needing to prepare for tomorrow.'

'I'll take my tea to my room,' I said.

'Of course, dear,' Father said.

I pushed my chair away from the table and stood. Jess made herself more comfortable in her creaky wicker basket by the fire. She moaned a contented sigh when she eventually found her place.

'Don't worry about her,' Father said. 'I'll make sure she keeps warm, and dry. No need to worry about the dishes, my dear. I'll clear them away.'

I smiled to hide my melancholy and held the teacup in a tight grip. With my free hand I felt for Father's gnarly hands and found them, clutched tight around his cup, as if he was praying, or in deep contemplation. I patted them a time or two, then I reached for my cane.

'Goodnight, Father, and thank you for making supper.'

'Goodnight, dear,' he said, placing his hands on mine and kissing me lightly on the forehead.

'You know, you remind me so much of your mother. Have I told you that?'

'Yes, Father. You've said that already,' I replied.

'I did. Didn't I?'

I made my way around the edge of the table, passing by the

76

cupboard, and felt for the door jam, before stepping into the hallway.

'Your mother was—' Father said.

I turned my head, 'Yes, Father. What is it?'

'She was the best of them, is all I'll say.'

I heard the sound of furniture being moved about and Father's footsteps. I heard the kitchen door open then and close quickly again. I took Father's words to mean that he had been lucky. He had been lucky to meet her, and lucky to have had the time he had with her. I turned to find my way along the passage letting my own memories of my mother swim around in my head. I found the grandfather clock, and the little glass door. I pried it open with my fingertips and ran my fingers over the hands of the clock. I took the key from its perch and wound it, replaced the key, and closed the door then I made my way upstairs. I crossed the landing to my room, each step a cruel reminder of the burden I now bore. Even after all the years of treading those same steps my mind played tricks on me, taunting me with fear of the unknown crevices of the darkness which still remained unexplored.

In my room, I undressed, slowly and a little clumsily, thinking still about Mother. I thought too about the brother I had never really had, buried beside her underneath the old oak tree. I wondered, not for the first time, if that had brought on the melancholia.

As if to wake me from my thoughts, a cold breeze blew in from the open window. I hurried to finish undressing then climbed into bed. On my bedside table sat the Bible, a special Braille edition, which Father purchased especially for me. With the best of wills it was hard to imagine how God had not abandoned me to my dark and lonely existence, but I took the bible in my hands nonetheless and let my fingertips roll over the little bumps and spaces. I suppose old habits die hardest; like the repetition of prayer and the self-flagellation of the soul. Was this my purgatory? I often thought as much. If only I had done this, or that, things could have worked out differently. If only I had given Henry my answer there and then, in that room, as we stood watching the snow falling outside.

Perhaps if I knew the whole truth then everything would have been resolved, and everything would have been in its place, just as it was meant to be. Another thought came to me then, that I would probably still have gone to wave him off, and the same terrible sequence of events would have had no different result.

What were the chances that I could have made the bus that night?

Could I have walked a little faster, just a pace or two, and never have encountered the stranger standing in the shadows?

The possibilities were endless but always came to the same conclusion. It was meant to be. I propped myself upright with two pillows and fidgeted, thinking and remembering, moments and actions that could have made the difference, but each iteration brought me back to the same conclusion. Everything is preordained.

There were no such things as random acts. From that very first breath, our course is determined. These thoughts were swimming around in my head when the tiredness crept over me, willing me to accept it. I let it in, slowly, like the draught through the crack beneath the door, drawing me into its deep embrace.

I felt the book slip from my grasp and drowsily I placed it on the bedside table. I had no sooner placed my head on the pillow than I was asleep.

*

'Get that into you.'

'I'm frozen,' I said, and wrapped my fingers around the mug.

'Well—'

'Well, what?'

'Tell me everything,' she said.

'There's not much to tell,' I said. 'We went to a gallery, then for something to eat.'

'Food. Dish everything. What did you have?'

'Pork chop.'

'Pork chop! You lucky beggar. What I wouldn't give for pork chop. What else? Go on. I'm green with envy.'

'Oh, please, Doris. I'm tired.'

'All right. Tell me about your fancy man then.'

I drummed my fingers on the side of the mug then took a sip of tea.

Perhaps it was the damp cold, or a nervous excitement that caused little goose bumps to rise along my skin. I placed the mug on the sideboard and ran my hands quickly along the length of both arms, and made a burring noise with my lips, and then I pulled a blanket about me and cupped the mug in both hands again.

'I bet he's married. All the good ones are these days.'

'*Doris*,' I said, and felt a slight pang at the thought. 'That wouldn't be right.'

'You find me a good man and I'll find you a woman who's already staked her claim on him. You still haven't told me his name. Come on, name please.'

'His name is Henry Morton, if you must know.'

'Henry Morton. I'm going to commit that to my little black book.'

'You don't have a little black book.'

'And how would you know? I don't tell you everything I do. A gallery too?'

'Yes. Henry wanted to show me something.'

'I bet he did.'

'Doris, *please*! It was an art gallery ... very public and proper. There was no hanky-panky I'll have you know. Mr Morton is a perfect gentleman.'

I neglected to mention that we had kissed.

'Mr Morton! You're falling, you are.'

Doris' eyes widened with delight. A hint of scandal, that was all it took, and off they went hither and thither, like little dancing faeries.

'I'm not.'

Oh, how she made me laugh.

'What would your father say?'

'He wouldn't say anything at all ... because there's nothing to tell. There's no scandal in that.'

'A country girl like you swanning about town with a man. God only knows who might have seen you. And you with your position.'

'Oh Doris, please, you are making me feel so terribly guilty. I—'

'I'm only pulling your leg. You know that. Don't you?' she said, giving my free hand a shake.

'Yes. Yes, of course I knew that.'

All the same, Doris' words had had an effect. Someone might have seen me. What would I do then? Headmistress would not be pleased. I could hear her already. What sort of example are you setting for the girls? The girls. If only she knew what antics *her* girls got up to she might have something altogether different to worry about. Suddenly the silence was broken by the whine of an air raid siren.

'Drills. Drills. And more drills,' Doris complained.

'It might come in handy someday,' I replied and jumped from my seat to find my coat and gas mask.

'Do you really think they will bomb cities like London?'

'I shouldn't think so,' I said.

I remembered what Father had said about the previous war. The Germans had dropped bombs on London before, and there was nothing to say they wouldn't do it again.

'No, I shouldn't think they'd be bothered,' Doris added.

As if to prove us wrong the noise of the anti-aircraft batteries fought to drown out the screech of the air-raid sirens, and new and terrifying noises were added to the mix. Whistling noises. Thousands of whistling noises to accompany the metal rain falling from the night sky.

CHAPTER SEVEN

The noisy crowing of a cockerel disturbed me and I woke from my dream with a start. I was suddenly frightened and searching for something familiar to hold on to, and found the bedside table and the bible in its place. I allowed myself a deep breath before pulling the blankets back and placing my feet on the wooden floorboards. I rose and performed my daily ablutions, and went downstairs. Father had already left for the morning.

I checked on Jess. She sighed as I laid my hand across her head to comfort her. I placed a bowl of milk beside her. After I had finished my breakfast, I rubbed my hand along her swollen body and felt her head loll back into her bed. Father had forgotten to switch off the wireless set that morning and the sound of music was echoing throughout the house. I had lost myself in some tune or other when a man's voice suddenly announced:

This is the news from the BBC Home Service. Rationing on all goods remains in force throughout the land. There have been reports of long queues forming at soup kitchens but the public is reminded that there will be no increase in the daily ration. A reminder that Land Ministry inspections are to be increased in the coming days. If you know of any person, or persons, operating illegally you are encouraged to contact your local constabulary, without delay. In other news, the Eight Army under Field Marshal Montgomery continues to harass Rommel's Afrika Korps. Well done you chaps. Keep up the good work. We are returning now to your scheduled programme.

An uplifting and patriotic tune signalled the end of the announcement. I turned off the wireless set, listening as the valves hissed and whined, and then I went into the front hallway. I put on my woollen coat and hat, and for good measure, I pulled a scarf about my neck. It was an unseasonably cold day. I could feel it as soon as I stood to dress that morning, the chill and goose-bumps rising like little anthills on my bare skin. I fixed my hat in place, and redundantly checked my appearance in the mirror and wondered, not for the first time, what might be staring back at me. I shuddered a little at the thought, remembering that I once considered myself moderately attractive; slim, and reasonably well proportioned. I smoothed the front of my coat with my hands and felt the hard bony bits where my hips protruded. I had lost weight, I thought. As if to confirm this observation, I pulled at my face and felt the thin layer of skin hanging on my cheekbones. I walked the tips of fingers along the scar line just below my left eye and followed the ridgeline to where it met my hairline. How many times had I done that before? Too many. There was no escaping it. It existed as a feature on a mountain might exist, hard and sharp, with only time to erode it away. I sighed, and pulled a strand of hair from my face then pulled on my sheepskin gloves to keep my fingers warm.

'You'll have to do,' I said aloud. 'You'll just have to do.'

Mr Burrows arrived at the hour of nine. I know this because the grandfather clock chimed nine times. Nine, for every hour passed in a new day. I could hear the car idling outside. It was an uncommon sound, the noise of a car's engine, as so few people possessed one. With petrol so severely rationed, I knew at once that it could only be Mr Burrows coming to collect me. I pulled my cane to me and opened the front door to greet the day.

'Good morning, miss,' Mr Burrows said in greeting.

'We are blessed with another day, Mr Burrows. We should be thankful.'

'And that we should, miss. A little colder than what we might expect though,' he said jauntily.

I pulled the front door behind me and tapped my way along the little gravel path to the garden gate, lifted the latch and pulled it towards me, then bent forward to close it again.

'I should get that, miss.'

'I'm perfectly fine, Mr Burrows. I've been opening and closing this gate for many years. It only takes a little determination.'

'If you insist, miss,' he said.

'You have to keep a stiff upper lip even when the chips are down.'

'Yes, miss,' he replied. 'Let me get the door there for you instead.'

I walked to the car and slid on to the back seat, not without some effort, for the seats were deep and spacious. I imagined it was one of those older, plush vehicles, like a Rolls Royce, or some such thing.

When eventually I righted myself I heard the door close behind me and the sounds of Mr Burrow's footsteps as he walked around to the driver's side. The motor was still idling. I heard Mr Burrows get behind the wheel. He must have turned to see if I was all right and noticed the look of concern on my face.

'You're probably wondering why I kept the motor running,'

Mr Burrows said. 'It's because of the cold, miss. This old thing struggles a little in the cold weather, you see.'

'Of course,' I replied.

'It's very unlike the weather to be as cold this time of the year,' Mr Burrows said.

I heard him huffing and puffing, and struggling with the gears. He pressed the clutch then he lifted his foot and tried again, with more success the second time around. I know this because the grinding noise stopped and the motor gave a little lurch forward. When Mr Burrows searched for another gear I slid forward in my seat, then back again when he found it. It was then that a sort of decaying smell pinched my nostrils.

'I'm sorry, miss. It's been acting up a little today.'

'The cold, I assume.'

'Yes, the cold, no doubt. Are you warm enough? There's a blanket beside you.'

I placed the heavy woollen blanket over my legs. It took the chill away, but I could still feel the draught through the window to my right. Was it an old car? I wondered.

We were some time into our journey when I remembered to ask Mr Burrows about his relatives, or whether he had gone away to war, or if he knew of the Mr Burrows that Father had spoken of.

'Mr Burrows,' I said, and waited for him to reply.

'Yes, miss. Is anything the matter?'

'It's nothing really. You see, I mentioned you to Father and he told me that he had known a man with your surname once. It couldn't be you, of course. It must have been someone else.'

'Your father, miss—'

'Yes. He was in the War ... not the most recent one. He is a little too old for that. He was in the first War.'

'Was he now?' Mr Burrows said, and slowed the motor with a change of gears.

I felt the mechanics of the spinning world as I was pulled to the right. Then we hit a straight patch of road again, before I felt myself being pulled to the left. We must be going around the mountain now, I thought to myself. The lake was to our left. I remembered how bone-chillingly cold it was. Even in summer, with the heat of the day at its most intense, the water remained ice-cold, dark and foreboding. Uninviting for even the hardiest of souls. I remembered that I fell from the jetty once, as a child, distracted by something, and sank all the way to the bottom, before Father's long arm reached down to me, his fingers gripping my long hair, to pull me to safety. I remembered that I couldn't move my limbs, such was the shock of it. My teeth chattered uncontrollably and if it wasn't for a thick, woollen blanket, and several hours in front of the open fire, I think I might have died.

I tried not to think of Mother then and that day they pulled her body from its depths, but the images came to me anyway. You see, I was in Manchester to visit Aunt Mildred, Father's younger sister. Mother had suggested it, convincing Father that it would be good to build up my independence. It was wonderful to visit with my aunt. She always seemed so fashionable and on-trend and we had had a weekend of shopping and tearooms. We had only just returned from an outing to a local park and Aunt Mildred was expressing how bushed she was from all that tramping about, when the door-bell rang. It was a messenger with a telegram. "My dear, you have to return home immediately," she said. "Why," I asked. She had no sooner read aloud the contents of the telegram than I felt a sort of light-headedness and the ground rushing up to meet me. The next thing I knew I was sitting in a chair by an open fire, a cup of tea in my hands and a heavy blanket about my shoulders.

Some hours later, when I was sufficiently recovered, Aunt Mildred brought me to the station, informing me that someone would be waiting for me at the end of my journey and promising to follow on as soon as possible. So I took the return journey alone, sobbing to myself almost throughout, and arrived in the early afternoon.

As promised, Mrs Douthwaite, a neighbour of ours, had come to collect me from the train. As we were motoring along, Mrs Douthwaite nervously chatted about this and that to occupy the time. I cannot remember anything she might have said, but I do remember that she stopped suddenly mid-sentence when we rounded the mountain and came within sight of the lake. At that moment, she grew silent. Before us a large group of people gathered by the lake. Three men were pulling a small rowing boat to shore. Mrs Douthwaite said something about hurrying home to Rose Cottage, but I remember that I gripped her arm tightly and said, "Stop."

She pulled the car to a stop at the side of the road. I remember that I ran the short distance to the lakeshore and was just in time to see them lying Mother's body on the ground. It is the small things that you notice the most, isn't it? Like how my mother had worn her shoes to drown herself. It made sense of course when I realised later that she probably walked into the lake from the stony shore. I remembered too how her lips were tight together in a sort of half-smile and that her skin was this very strange mixture of blue and purple in colour; like marbled meat. Someone had already positioned a penny over each of her eyes, those same eyes I imagined that had searched desperately for a peace of sorts in the lake's dark depths. My father stood to one side, his hands placed over his face, sobbing. I went to him and we stood there, crying in each other's arms as they lifted her body from the rocky shore and carried it to a waiting ambulance. I would not see her again and have a faint memory only of a simple coffin lowered into the ground under the shade of an old oak tree.

'Yes,' I said, summoning my thoughts to the present and in reply to Mr Burrow's question. 'He was away for a long time. I was born just after the War. Did you go away to the War, Mr Burrows?' I asked.

I heard him clear his throat.

'I did, miss. I don't think *they'll* ever learn, those men who make war, miss. They told us it was the war to end all wars, and yet here we all are, back at the same point as we were before. It's hard to fathom, it is.'

'Was it terrible, Mr Burrows?'

'Yes, miss.'

'I think it must have been. I don't think Father will ever get over it.'

'Yes, miss.'

'It's the bad dreams, you see.'

'Dreams, miss?'

'I've said too much, Mr Burrows.'

'Dreams can be terrible things, miss. Not too far to go now.'

A short time later the car passed over the cattle grate, and I felt Millrace's presence upon me again, like a shroud, taking me into its embrace. 'Millrace,' I muttered under my breath.

'That's right, miss. Millrace.'

The car's wheels rumbled over the cobblestone bridge, where water crashed noisily from a height to continue its journey to the sea.

'There's Tramp come to greet us, miss,' Mr Burrows said.

Tramp barked incessantly and followed us along the rest of our journey, until we eventually reached the house. I remained in my seat, waiting for Mr Burrows to come around, and as I sat there, I heard the sound of hurried muffled voices, and an angry, agitated exchange of words. Eventually the car door opened.

'Are you ready, miss?'

'Yes, thank you,' I said, extending my hand. 'Is everything all right?'

I felt Mr Burrows' firm grip, then I placed one foot on the ground, and then the other, and extended my cane.

'I'll get the door, miss. I'll just get you to stand over to your right a little, please.'

I tapped the ground and the car's wheel and found a space in which to stand and wait. I heard the door bang closed behind me and felt Mr Burrows' hand again upon my arm.

'There's nothing to worry about, miss. It was just a little misunderstanding. This way, miss. Down, Tramp.'

'Can I pat him?'

'I'd be afraid he'd knock you over, miss.'

I supported myself with my cane and bent down to feel for Tramp's head. He nudged my hand, as if he had the knowledge that I could not see him. He had a large head, eager to be stroked. A happy dog, I concluded, and well fed, if his broad back was anything to go by.

'Tramp's young Mr Charles' dog,' Mr Burrows explained.

'I see. You're a good boy, Tramp,' I said, patting the dog's head. I stood upright again and felt the effort of doing so, in a slight light-headedness and a certain ache in my limbs.

'Watch the step now, miss,' Mr Burrows said, guiding me along.

I placed my foot on the first step and had that unusual sensation again. It felt like the house was watching me as we climbed towards the entrance. It is true that houses can smell of damp and age and people often joke that walls have ears, and houses have ghosts, but Millrace had a presence.

'I'll bring you through, miss.'

I followed Mr Burrows' lead, my cane tapping the ground, making that now familiar tick-tick sound, until I was eventually standing in the spot I had been the day before, only this time there was no invitation for tea. Instead, footsteps receded away, then the door closed. I felt for the high-backed chair I knew was there, and took a seat.

'No tea this time?' Pipe-smoker inquired.

It was then I got the smell of that unusual pipe-smoke.

'Still enjoying the view?' I said.

'Actually, I was watching the tide. It's higher today. And this weather has been so strange, don't you think?'

click-click

'It has been a little colder than expected, yes.'

'As I mentioned on your previous visit, I like to come to this very spot and watch the sea and the comings and goings of the tide. It seems like the tide is pushing further and further up the river every day. There's a lagoon forming too. Do you know that the river there is in the wrong place?' he said shortly.

'What do you mean?'

'Great-uncle Thomas, in his eternal wisdom, changed the course of the river to build—'

'A mill,' I added.

'Exactly right. You are the smart one. The river, the original river that is, ran a mile west of here, but it was too slow, and unsuitable for mill wheels. So Thomas in his wisdom—'

'You said that.'

'Yes, I did, didn't I?'

click-click

'Well, he built a new course, the one in existence now, with several drops, to increase the flow, and allow the wheels of industry to mill and spin a little faster. They built seven mills in total, and dye houses, and could process and finish in record time, eventually putting all of their competitors out of business.'

'They were successful then?' I said a little sarcastically.

'All things must come to an end,' he said.

'What do you mean?' I asked, tilting my head to the side to catch his response.

'Success became a curse. The beautiful river, with salmon and trout, and birds, and everything that was natural in the world eventually died. The salmon could no longer find their mating ponds, and even when they did, the river had become so polluted with the dyes used to colour the fabric, that nothing could survive. The salmon died. Then the trout were no more. They say it smelled of death and decay, and all that death ran to the sea. Where the river meets the sea, it turned a sort of yellow colour, and everything died. There were grumblings in the village. My uncle underpaid his workers. He and his siblings were hard taskmasters it seems. They forced their workers to labour long hours. The conditions were unsafe, what with all those dyes and chemicals, but when you are poor you have little choice but to do the bidding of others. Isn't that so?'

'Yes, I suppose it is.'

'They say the workers handling the dyes could never remove the stain. Even after the mills had closed, and the last of the workers had left, their bodies remained a reminder of a cruel past. The fetid pools of long dead fish and spawn and chemicals meant the villagers could no longer use the river for fishing and bathing. It was a terrible legacy. It has been a terrible burden to bear.'

'The river has recovered, I think.'

'Perhaps it's for the best then.'

'What do you mean?'

'It doesn't matter. You'll see.'

'No, please go on. Tell me. What became of your relations, and their wealth?'

'Perhaps another time,' Pipe-smoker said. 'We have company.'

I gave a little jump when I heard the door crack open and the sound of other voices. It was Mrs Butler and someone else. Mr Burrows, I thought at first but then I heard someone give a little shriek; as if they had been suddenly frightened by something.

'You can leave now,' Mrs Butler said.

'Yes, Mrs Butler.'

I heard hurried footsteps retreating and then the door closed. I let my ears become accustomed to the new presences in the room, someone fussing about something. There was a moaning sound then an apology. The earlier conversation had occluded the noise I could now discern. It was the bellows noise, a breath in and out. I remember that I felt a little nervous as the squeaking sound grew louder, until it seemed as if it was almost upon me.

'I'm afraid our session today will need to be a little shorter. The Master did not sleep very well.'

I remained silent, waiting for further instruction.

'Well do make ready,' Mrs Butler said hurriedly.

I took my cane in hand and made my way to the seat.

I checked my reach, the foot pedals, and ran my fingers along the fret to feel for each key separately. My left hand ached a little.

'It's such a fine piano. Isn't it?'

There was a sort of grumbling, mumbling sound in reply.

Then, a few moments later Mrs Butler said sternly,

'Well do carry on.'

There were whispered voices in the background, but I turned my thoughts to the task and remembered that I was in the mood for some Claude Debussy that day. *Claire de lune* was an appropriate number, I thought. So I played Debussy, and then Chopin, then a Shostakovich number, and some Beethoven for good measure, and when I finished I was perspiring a little around the collar of my blouse. I took a breath, allowing myself a moment of silent rapture.

'That's enough for now,' Mrs Butler said. 'Mr Burrows will be here shortly. Please wait here until he comes to fetch you.'

'Yes. Yes, of course,' I said.

I heard the squeaking noise fade away then the door closed firmly. I readied myself, putting on my hat and coat, and a little scarf about my neck for the day that was in it. I was just taking hold of my cane when he startled me.

'That was very fine,' Pipe-smoker said.

'Thank you,' I said under my breath.

'Where did you learn to play like that?'

'I attended the London School of Music.'

'You must have been quite good then,' Pipe-smoker said.

'My parents always tried to give me the best in life. A teacher told them once that I had a talent for music and that she would help if they were able to pay a small amount towards tuition. They found the money somehow. I don't know how, but they did. Then, some years later, when I was ready she put me forward for a scholarship. I am going on ... Sorry!'

'So that brought you to the city, did it?'

'Yes,' I said.

'And that's where all this business happened?'

'What business?'

'The accident.'

'If you call it that.'

'A shame.'

'I suppose you want to know the details?'

'Would you like to tell me? Ah, there you are Burrows,' Pipe-smoker said. 'It seems your story will have to wait until the next time we meet.'

'All ready to go, are we, miss?'

'Yes. I'm ready, thank you, Mr Burrows.' I tapped my path towards Mr Burrows and felt for his arm.

'Here you are, miss.'

I felt Mr Burrows' hand guide me then he wrapped my arm around his.

'Well, goodbye,' I said.

'I look forward to your next visit,' Pipe-smoker said by way of goodbye.

Mr Burrows led me to the door and into the hallway.

'You'll be back again tomorrow. I heard that Mr Charles is very much enjoying your visits,' Mr Burrows said.

'Did you eavesdrop again today?' I asked him.

'Not today, miss. Mrs Butler gave strict orders. I had my duties, I'm afraid, and much the worse for it.'

'Why do you say that, Mr Burrows?' I asked, as he led me down the steps towards the car.

'Mr Broom found one of the mares dead in the field. She'd been in foal, the first pregnancy in many years—'

His voice trailed off then and he changed the subject. He made some comments about the weather and the heat. Sure enough, by the time we reached the bottom of the steps, I was almost ready to discard all three items of clothing. It was even hotter inside the automobile. When I had eventually removed my coat I could feel the heat of the leather against my bare skin and had to move around every so often to prevent myself from sticking to its surface. I rolled down the window as we drove away. There was no Tramp to bid me farewell this time. I daresay he had found some shade against the heat of the day. Even the motion of the car and the breeze blowing through the open window was not enough to cool my skin. We were a short time into our journey when I noticed a terrible smell. It was so terrible that I pinched my nose and tried to prevent myself from retching.

'It's bad today,' Mr Burrows said. 'But you get used to it. It's the heat, you see. You don't notice it as much when the weather is a little colder.'

'What's causing it?' I asked.

'It's the river, miss. It gets that way sometimes. Did you have a nice day, miss?' Mr Burrows said, changing the subject again.

'Yes. I enjoyed it very much,' I replied, remembering Pipe-smoker's story about the mill and dyes and how the river had turned fetid and lifeless.

We drove along in silence for some time. I let myself linger on some thoughts, things I remembered about Millrace, from before, when I was younger. I remembered the long meadow leading to a beautiful lawn area. I remembered too, the crypt built for the family I believe, situated close to the tree line and just to the left of the main house.

A path curved from the gravel courtyard, before descending to the level of the lawn, and leading away to the trees. There was a separate area nearby, ringed by a wrought iron fence; a graveyard for the family's pets, I remember.

I imagined soirees on the lawn, and games of tennis or croquet on long summer days, followed by afternoon tea or lemonade, and scones with jam and cream. I imagined those things still existed in some other world, outside Millrace.

'There we are now, a little shade from the sun.'

True to Mr Burrow's words I felt the coolness offered by the part of the journey around the backside of the mountain, which stood, like it had for millennia, offering the mercy of its presence, and protecting too, our side of the valley, from the violent storms which sometimes rolled in off the sea.

'I was wondering,' I said, 'if you have noticed a change in the air of late.'

'I can't say I have, miss,' Mr Burrows said. 'Why do you ask?'

'It's just a feeling, like a storm is coming. You know the ones, Mr Burrows. First the calm, then the fury.'

'Aye, I've known such storms, miss. Terrible to behold. Like the world itself is going to end.'

'I had forgotten how it can be here … in little old Rashleigh, when the storms are brewing. In the city it's quite different, you see. There is always a tall building, or a tube station in which to shelter in heavy weather. Unfortunately, people tend to have the same idea at about the same time, so you often find yourself shoulder to shoulder in a crowd waiting for the worst of it to pass. It brings out the best and the worst in people too.'

'Can't say I have much knowledge of the city, miss. Only been twice. Once on my way to France, and the second time on my way home from France. I didn't have the urge to linger for too long on either of those occasions. It was the air, miss. Hot and stinky, and filled with a sort of stale energy if you ask me, miss. It can't be good for you. Some of the lads I'd been to France with … you know the ones from the cities, well they had survived just about everything the War could throw at them only to arrive home in time to die from the Spanish flu. Bad air in those cities, I tell *ye'*. Bad air.'

'Poor souls. My brother died from the flu too.'

'I'm sorry to hear that, miss.'

'Yes, he was just a baby. And now this new predicament.'

'It's not the flu now, miss.'

'No. The terror overhead is what we've come to fear most now, Mr Burrows. I've always felt that the air seemed a little more charged than normal just before a bombing raid. Maybe it was the sense of expectation that something terrible was about to happen.'

'It was just like that before a big barrage, miss. Why, it was almost as if you could strike a match and the world itself would explode.'

'Doesn't it feel a little like that now?' I asked, and clasped one hand tight around the other. 'Bad air.'

I heard Mr Burrows take a deep inhalation as he rolled down the window on his side, and I got the hint of cologne wafted in my direction. I tried to picture what he looked like.

Clean-shaven with a tight haircut, I thought. Although I had not known him to smoke cigarettes in my company there was also a distinctive odour of stale tobacco. Perhaps in trying to mask the smell he applied a little more cologne than necessary. He was at least middle aged because he had served in the Great War.

I thought him as broad and thickset in build, given the noises he made when getting in and out of the car. The fact that he had callused hands suggested that he was used to physical labour. I also pictured him as sallow or ruddy in complexion based on the plentiful sea air and the outdoor nature of the tasks he performed.

'The weather's changeable. I'll give you that, miss. I've not heard a forecast ... Speaking of forecasts, well, Mr Pine, the undertaker, now he has a knack for predicting the weather and who might kick the bucket next. He claims he can tell by the cut of a man's jib. He claims to be more accurate than all the weathermen in Britain, does Mr Pine. I can't say he has been wrong too many times on either subject. I'd wager he'd have something to say about your bad air theory, miss.'

'I'm just being silly, I suppose,' I said casually.

'This is you now, miss,' Mr Burrows said, changing gear.

We turned right then the car came to a stop with a squeal of brakes and a belch from the exhaust.

'Are we home already?'

'Aye. A bit of conversation makes the journey fly. Let me get that door for you, miss. You stay right as you are.'

When Mr Burrows had left I stood there by the side of the road and soaked up a little of the sun, and thought about the day's events, and took a deep breath of air, before eventually turning on my heels to go indoors.

*

'I'm so very glad you came.'

The room was hot and stuffy and I was already perspiring. I played for one hour; an assortment of tunes. The assembly, which included past pupils of the school and invited guests were there to hear the music recital in aid of wounded servicemen. In one corner of the room, a former music teacher of mine, Miss Russell, sat behind a table, on which was positioned a large wooden box. Every so often someone would drop a brown envelope, or rolled-up note into it, as they passed by, and Miss Russell would smile and ring a bell.

'Thank you,' she would announce loudly, and people would turn and stare.

'There's a good turn out,' Henry said. 'And you played beautifully.'

I could feel my face redden at the compliment.

'It's for a good cause,' I said.

'Yes,' Henry said. 'I see some of the chaps over there.'

He nodded in the direction of a small group of men who were variously standing and sitting in another corner of the room. Some of the men wore blue hospital uniforms. They looked strangely out of place amongst the other attendees.

'Poor souls,' I said.

'They must have had a bad time of it,' Henry said. 'See that man over there. The man with a bandage around his head.'

'Yes.'

'An explosion damaged his hearing so that he's almost deaf.'

'How terrible. He looks so young.'

'I had tried to engage him in conversation but he just stared at me. Eventually someone explained.'

'Do you think you'll have to go away?' I said, guiding Henry towards a table which was laid with plates of sandwiches.'

'I shouldn't think so,' he said, taking a sandwich in his fist. 'Egg.'

'The least we could do,' I said, and poured tea into a cup. 'Tea?'

'Yes, thank you,' Henry said, and stuffed the sandwich into his mouth. Between chews he said, 'Sorry, but I'm quite famished. I've been too busy to eat.'

'The Ministry.'

Yes. I'm afraid I can't say any more than that.'

'I understand.'

'Listen, I wanted to apologise. You know … for being so forward. I didn't ...'

'I liked it,' I said, furtively.

'It's just that, I …'

'You don't have to explain.'

'No, but I do. There's something that I should have mentioned.'

Before he had a chance to explain I was distracted by someone tapping on my shoulder.

I turned to see who it was.

'There you are,' Miss Russell said. 'How do you do?'

'Henry Morton,' he said, taking Miss Russell's outstretched hand..

'Mr Morton … Well, thank you for coming along this evening.'

'A very good cause,' Henry said.

'Yes indeed,' Miss Russell said. 'Are you in the services, Mr Morton?'

'Yes,' he replied, and left it there.

'I see,' Miss Russell said, wrinkling her nose as if she had just inhaled an irritating scent.

'Would you mind dear … I want to introduce you to one of our benefactors. He's enjoyed the recital so much that he just has to meet you in person.'

'Go ahead. I'll be fine,' Henry said.

'I won't be long. I promise.'

'Take your time. What with egg sandwiches and tea, why would I need to go anywhere else.'

When we had moved to a different corner of the room Miss Russell whispered, 'He's ever-so handsome. Is he a relation of yours? An uncle, perhaps? Ah, there you are Mr Kingston. See, I told you I'd manage to drag her away.'

'Harold Kingston,' the man said.

I smiled and shook his hand and listened distractedly as he explained who he was, and what he did. Every so often I stole a glance across the room to see if Henry was still there.

On one of those occasions, as Harold Kingston was explaining the metallurgical processes involved in the manufacture of gun barrels for twenty-five pounders, a very fine artillery piece according to Mr Kingston's account, I managed to catch Henry's gaze. He was looking in my direction. He smiled, then gave a faux expression of surprise. I laughed to myself. Then an unusual thing happened. My pulse quickened and I found myself feeling a little hot and bothered. I took a deep intake of breath and returned to the conversation.

'Hot,' I heard myself say.

'What was that?' Mr Kingston asked.

'I bet it is very hot.'

'Where, my dear?' Miss Russell said.

'In the foundry …'

'Tremendously hot,' Mr Kingston replied. 'The furnaces can reach well above fifteen-hundred degrees centigrade.'

'British steel. That's how we'll win the war. Isn't that right Mr Kingston?' Miss Russell said, giving me a knowing look.

'If you'll excuse me,' I said. 'I have someone waiting for me.'

'Of course. Of course. It was very nice to meet you.'

'And you, Mr Kingston,' I said.

As I was moving away I overheard Miss Russell say,

'Cold, hard steel, that's what we need to win the war, Mr Kingston. Steel and determination.'

I passed through the crowd to the place where I had last seen Henry standing, but he was gone.

I asked one of the ladies who were serving teas if she had seen where he had gone, and she said,

'I believe I saw that very gentleman collecting his coat from the cloakroom.'

I went through the adjoining room and into the entrance hall, to where the cloakroom was located, but he wasn't there either. I collected my coat and went outside. He was standing with his back to a pillar.

'Thought I'd run off?' he said. 'I needed some air and a cigarette. Didn't think it was correct of me to smoke inside … seeing as no one else seemed to be doing so.'

I buttoned my coat against the chill of the early evening. Almost by reflex I looked up. A clear, blue sky stretched out before my eyes.

'Perfect conditions,' Henry said, seeming to read my thoughts. 'Should think we'll get a hammering tonight.'

'It doesn't bear thinking about,' I said, and felt that tingle of nerves running through me.

'I have business to take care of quite early in the morning. Ministry work, and all that. I have to stay in the city tonight.'

'Where will you stay?'

'My secretary has organised a room at a boarding house close by. It's quite convenient.'

'Gosh! I do hope they stay away. I don't think I can spend another night in the shelter with Mrs Simpson.'

'Your landlady?'

'Yes. She has a nervous disposition.'

'And where's your friend … Doris isn't it?'

'Doris had to go to Brighton to take care of her elderly aunt.'

'I see. You're all alone with Mrs Simpson, and maybe the Luftwaffe dropping by for company,' Henry said, taking another pull on his cigarette before tossing the butt on the ground.

'Yes, I suppose you could say that,' I said.

'I have an idea,' he said.

CHAPTER EIGHT

That night, as I slept, I dreamt again of the burning man, with his face as black as soot. He was sitting on a sort of throne, surrounded by ornaments and skulls of all sizes. He was staring at me, or through me, in my dream. His eyes were dark and menacing. Around him danced little men, half-naked, carrying spears. I heard loud drums and women crying. A man's face came into view. It came closer and closer, as if his image was at the end of a camera lens, and he was one of those unnamed actors, whose cameo was to stare wide-eyed and maniacal into the camera.

He made some terrible sound and it must have caused me a moment's distress because I woke with a start and a shortness of breath. I realised quite quickly that the window shutters were banging and in the distance, I could hear the sound of a thunderstorm approaching. I placed my feet on the floor and walked to the window.

The air was still sticky-warm despite the storm coming to clear it out. I felt the screen to keep the insects out, and ran my fingers over its mesh surface then I fastened the shutters in place before returning to bed. I tossed and turned for some time, the noise of the storm growing louder with every passing hour until sometime later on I fell asleep again, lulled into my dream state not by the sound of jungle drums, but of thunder in its stead.

This time I had no further dreams of a burning man, and dark savage people. Henry came to me instead.

*

The boarding house was a rather shabby affair in Piccadilly. I had agreed to Henry's proposal without giving it much thought. Perhaps I did it because I was afraid; not of nighttime bombing or Mrs Simpson's banshee-like screams, but of letting something rare slip away. The war had brought with it such uncertainty that every opportunity seemed like it might be the last. So when he smiled and took my hand, and led me to our destination, I was all the while thinking, hoping and wishing that the Germans would bomb somewhere else. Somewhere far away from Piccadilly. But that wasn't to be the case. Instead, they came with such fury and intensity that everything I hoped for became impossible.

We had only just arrived at the boarding house, when the air raid sirens began to sound.

'Bloody Luftwaffe,' Henry said.

'Maybe it's a false alarm,' I said, hopefully. 'It's too early for a raid, don't you think?'

The single bed was unmade. A rolled up woollen blanket sat atop a lumpy mattress and a single pillow completed the bundle. It had all the hallmarks of transience—a sort of passing through of one soul after another. There was nothing to indicate any homely comforts. A grimy-looking washbasin was attached to a badly painted wall, above which hung a shaving mirror.

I saw Henry move a little closer in its reflection.

'I wish …' he said.

I placed a finger on his lips and said, 'It doesn't matter.'

'We better get to a shelter,' he said, softly.

He kissed the back of my hand, and then he kissed my forehead and pulled me into an embrace. I wrapped my arms around him, and held on for dear life. I could hear the percussive thud of anti-aircraft batteries opening up, and the distant drone of the enemy bombers. He kissed me again; this time on the lips, then took my hand and we went out into the hallway.

A rather serious looking gentleman passed us in a hurry. 'Bloody Luftwaffe, at it again,' he said, and continued on without looking back.

Out on the street people hurried by, their heads bowed as if they were sheltering from a shower of rain.

'The tube station,' Henry said. 'We'll take shelter there.'

CHAPTER NINE

The next day I dispensed with my coat, choosing instead to wear my summer dress and a wide-brimmed hat to protect my delicate skin from the scorching sun. That morning, after breakfast, I visited with Jess and the new pups, seven in all, little balls of fur and funny noises. I cradled two of them, one in each arm, for quite some time, until they started to pine for their mother. Jess was hardly able to stand after all her labour, poor thing, so I left a bowl of goat's milk on the ground, and heard her lapping at it for a while, before she crashed exhausted back into the wicker basket. I heard the pups then, squealing and guzzling their fill.

I happened to be sitting in the shade of the portico when I heard the rumble of wheels on the road. There was a squeal of brakes and the engine sputtered and died, then the sound of a car door opening and closing. A few moments later, a second door opened and closed.

'How do?' a man's voice said.

'How do,' Father replied.

'*War Ags Committee*,' I heard a man's voice announce.

'I've already submitted my stock levels,' Father said a little defiantly and without a moment's hesitation.

A farm inspection had already taken place. We were not hoarding, or skimming, as some farms had done. Everything we had was there for all to see. The War Agricultural Executive Committee, or War Ags, seemed to have a different opinion on the matter.

'We are here to check whether those numbers are accurate, or not,' I heard the man reply sharply.

I heard the approach of footsteps, Father's familiar gait, and two more pairs. The first was heavy on his feet, a large man, I concluded, but the second pair was more delicate.

'We're sorry to have to disturb you,' a woman said. 'Might I trouble you for a glass of water?'

'Of course,' I replied. 'Won't you follow me?'

I went inside and heard the sound of footsteps behind me. We entered the kitchen and I went to the sink and pumped the handle until water began to flow. It gave a gurgling sound at first, and I put my hand under the tap to feel the stream.

I kept pumping, past the point where it spat and sputtered, until I felt the cold water on the back of my hand. I filled a glass and let the rest drain into the pan we kept beside the sink. I turned to face our visitors and sensed a presence close to me.

'That'll do nicely,' the man said, grabbing the glass from my outstretched hand.

'Oh,' I said, suddenly surprised to find him beside me.

'The name's Campbell and this *fine* young lady is Miss Wilkins.'

'You're new to these parts,' Father said.

'Drafted in from Launceston. The Committee feels that the law is not being sufficiently enforced in this neck of the woods.'

'And you're the man that's going to fix that, are ye'? Father said.

'My detection rate is one of the highest in the land.'

'Is that so? I expect you won't find much to be bothered with in these parts … Mr Campbell.'

'Well, why don't you let me be the judge of that?'

There was silence then, but the air seemed full of tension. Launceston, I thought. It seemed such a distance to travel just to check on little old farms like ours, and even farther for Mr Campbell to travel given that he was from somewhere different altogether. Northern, I presumed. I had heard a similar accent before, in London.

'You know, you're one of the lucky ones, what with your well and all. Most small farms about here would kill for something like a well with clean water. I've been to others. The water is bitter, and smells of something sour. Yours, well it's different. Sweeter, isn't that right, Miss Wilkins?'

'I haven't—'

'We share with our neighbours,' Father said.

I heard Mr Campbell empty the glass of its contents.

'Just what I needed,' he said, grabbing my still outstretched hand. 'Perhaps you would fill another for my colleague here.'

I felt the glass in my hand and turned towards the sink to rinse and fill it once more then I held it out for our second visitor to take it from me. A few moments later I felt my burden lighten.

'Thank you,' she said. 'It's been terribly hot again today.'

'Yes. Yes, it's been very hot,' I said.

I heard her drinking, more slowly than Mr Campbell had done, and less noisily too, and when she was finished, she placed the glass on the countertop. As she did, she came a little closer.

'Well? Was I right? Sweeter, don't you think?'

'Yes,' she replied and leaned a little closer still. 'My colleague is a brute,' she whispered. 'I'm so terribly sorry.'

She had one of those plum accents, one associated with places like Mayfair and Chelsea. I wondered how she wound up in the War Ags of all places.

I was thinking about this when the sound of raised voices distracted me. Father and Mr Campbell were arguing about something.

'Do you have a pig?'

'No,' Father replied.

'You know that the government allows one pig per household?'

'Yes.'

'Then why don't ye' have one?'

'I've been waiting to go to the market,' Father said.

'I love the taste of pig. Don't you?'

But there was no reply.

'Bacon, sausage, pig's trotters. I say to my Mabel … Mabel you can eat all of a pig, from the tail to snout. My Mabel is a very fine cook. *Ooh!* All this talk of food has brought on an appetite. I don't suppose you folks have any juicy morsels to hand.'

I was about to say something when Father snapped,

'Will this take long? I have work to do.'

'Aye! Your work. I see here that you're a writer then too?'

'That's right,' Father replied.

'Written anything I might have read?'

'I wouldn't think so,' Father said. 'Trade journals and such things.'

'Trade journals. Not my cup of tea. Don't think I'm uneducated though. I am a learned man myself. Isn't that so, Miss Wilkins?'

'I wouldn't know,' she replied.

'Yes, well, my Mabel says I should be a politician. Westminster, she says. An MP, you know. Perhaps you could be my secretary, Miss Wilkins.'

'Not likely,' she said.

He took a deep inhale of breath and said, 'Well, let's get on with this inspection then. I don't have all day.'

'We've already been inspected several times. I can't see what reason demands another,' Father replied.

'Leave that up to those who make decisions at a higher level,' Mr Campbell said. 'Shall we?'

Their voices faded away then, as if they had stepped outside to continue their discussion.

'We don't hoard you know. Everything we have is there for all to see.'

'My colleague thinks he can put the squeeze on small holdings such as yours. He does it to get something for himself. I'm afraid there's nothing I can do about it. He has the ear of the Divisional Head. It's Mr Campbell this, and Mr Campbell that. He received a medal for his work. He goes on and on about it. For services rendered, he says. By the way he goes on you would think that he had taken on the might of the German Army itself.'

'Is there no one you can speak to?' I asked, and suddenly realised how naive my question must have sounded.

'My dear girl, women are seen and not heard from. Haven't you realised that yet? Mr Campbell is the type who doesn't need a justification or authorisation for anything. He's a law all unto himself.'

I heard her fiddling with something.

'Mind if I smoke?'

I shook my head. Why did I always have to be so amenable? I thought.

'He was a conscientious objector in the last war,' she said, striking a match. 'Not that there's anything wrong with that, in and of itself, but people like Campbell give one pause for thought on the matter.'

There was a smell of sulphur, followed soon after by thick, choking cigarette smoke.

'It's the small things in life that make it bearable, don't you think?' she said, between puffs and drags, and a brief fit of coughing.

I heard her inhaling through her mouth and I imagined there was this small gap between two of her teeth because she made a sort of whistling noise as she did. It was the sort of sound a bomb made as it hurtled towards the earth, spinning ruthlessly through the air, whistling out its malevolent tune. I shuddered at the memory and grasped the countertop with both hands.

'Is anything the matter?' she said. 'Why don't you sit down? You look a little peaked.'

'Yes. Perhaps I should sit for a moment.'

'Shall I make a pot of tea?'

'That would be nice.'

She moved towards the sink and I heard her fill the kettle.

'Gosh! You keep the range good and hot. Almost burnt my fingers there,' she said.

'There's a forest beyond that top field,' I said. 'Father cuts enough to see us through even the harshest of winters.'

She moved closer and pulled out a chair to join me. I heard that whistling sound again as she puffed and dragged on her cigarette.

She began to chat about this and that, but I was already distracted, a sudden remembrance of things past, the smells of the city, the crush of people crowding into the shelter and the sound of the anti-aircraft guns as they lit up the night sky.

'Here's your tea,' I heard her say, then her voice faded, and was replaced instead by the sounds of a blaring klaxon-horn.

*

We spent the night on the station platform among the hundreds of others seeking shelter from the German bombs. During lulls in our hushed conversations, I found myself dozing off, waking only if the noise became too much, or the vibration from an explosion on the surface reverberated through the station. Each time I woke, sometimes startled to find myself still there in the dim light, I found Henry staring at me.

'Try to get some rest,' he repeated, and kissed me.

'You were right when you said it was perfect conditions.'

He smiled but said nothing.

'Kiss me.'

He kissed me again, but then someone lying close by groaned and said,

'Give it up, luv. Bad enough with Jerry overhead.'

I realised he wasn't talking to me but to someone else, when a woman's voice replied, 'We might all be killed, Cyril.'

'No point in thinking about it, luv. Get some shut eye. There's a good girl.'

'You were going to tell me something. Before. In the room. Was it important?'

'Yes,' Henry said, 'but it can wait for another time.'

I was going to say something in reply when the all-clear sounded and people began to move about.

'I wonder how much damage has been done,' someone said.

'Sounded like it got a right going over, up there,' a woman said.

As we made our way out of the station Henry said,

'I'm away for a few weeks. Can I see you again when I return?'

'Yes,' I said. 'I'd like that.'

The raid had continued for most of the night and it was

already morning by the time we emerged onto the street again. Crowds of people milled about at the entrance, and for a few moments I lost sight of Henry, before he reappeared, moving against the stream of people, and making his way in my direction.

'I thought I'd lost you there,' he said, his voice raised above the din of the all-clear, and noisy chatter as people moved about.

The area around Piccadilly Circus appeared to be, from first impressions, relatively unscathed. It was impossible to tell for certain where the damage might be, but thick black smoke seemed to be coming from the direction of Spitalfields. I said a silent prayer that Mrs Simpson had found shelter in time.

'Can I see you home?' Henry said, following my gaze over the buildings.

'No. I'll be fine. Don't you have work to do?'

'I think they'll understand.'

'No, it's perfectly fine. I need to check in with the headmistress at St George. She'll be concerned about us all … staff that is. It's not far to walk. I do hope it has escaped unscathed.'

'If you're sure.'

'Yes. Please don't worry,' I said, nervously brushing the front of my coat and checking for my mask and tin helmet.

'I'll walk you as far as the Circus.'

We made our way in the direction of Piccadilly Circus, walking mostly in silence, with exception of a cursory 'mind your step' or 'let's go to the other side of the street'.

The Circus was empty of vehicles except for when an ambulance sped by, followed closely by a fire engine, its bell ringing loudly for all to hear. People hurried along the footpaths trying to avoid each other, making their way to work or to complete their journeys to their intended destinations. As we reached the Burlington Arcade Henry stopped and said,

'I should cross here.' He pointed in the direction he would need to travel to Whitehall. 'I've grown terribly fond of you,' he said, glancing about before leaning forward to kiss me.

'Will you tell me what's so important?' I asked.

'The next time,' he said. 'Must dash now. Work you know. I'll call you in a few days.'

He kissed me again then looked up and down the empty street before hurrying across. Once he had reached the opposite side he turned, raised his arm, and waved. I waved back but he had already disappeared out of view.

*

'Mark my words.'

'What was that?'

'Nothing. It was nothing,' I said, slowly remembering where I was, staring moronically into the blackness, hoping that Henry's face would reappear, but it never did. Instead, as time went on it was becoming harder and harder to remember what he looked like at all.

There were certain things of course, the way he held a cigarette between his lips, the turned up collar of his macintosh, a broad brush of his face.

I still had a sense of him through other details, yet there remained a space, occupied only by features I conjured up, until in the end I couldn't tell if it was Henry at all, and not some figment of my imagination.

'I was just remembering something,' I said.

'Your tea will get cold,' the woman from the Committee said.

'I wonder what's taking them.'

'That'll be Mr Campbell weaving one of his schemes.'

'Father is wise to such things.'

'I hope he is. Others have not been so lucky, or wise. Do you mind if I make another pot of tea?'

'No, please. I just wish we had something else to offer you. I've used our ration already, I'm afraid.'

'What, no cake or biscuits?' she said jokingly.

'No,' I said and gave a little laugh.

In that moment of humour, she reminded me of Doris. Perhaps that's what had led my thoughts astray in the first place.

'You're dressed as if you are ready to go out,' she said.

'I'm on my way to Millrace.'

'*Millrace*. I was there once … a garden party before the war. All very *la-di-da*. It seems like such an eternity ago now though,' she said in an exasperated tone.

'What was it like?' I asked eagerly.

'The party?'

'Millrace. What was Millrace like back then?'

'A ramshackle old pile. It had that whiff of splendour long spent. And that old fuddy-duddy who owns the place, well he was—'

'He's had a stroke. He's in a wheelchair.'

'Is that so? Well I am not surprised in the slightest. He struck me as a man in a constant state of torment and pain, as if he had what I like to call *man trouble*. You know, as if the weight of the world is upon his shoulders, and his shoulders alone. Well it isn't, is it? They might have caused this silly war, but we are all in it now, and us girls will have to stick together, you know. It just won't do to think otherwise. Man trouble, that's what we have.'

The description seemed to sum up the world's problems.

'I volunteered, you know. Before you ask the question.'

116

'I wasn't …'

'You were. How did a posh girl like me get stuck with a fat slob like Mr *Whatshisname* out there?'

'Campbell,' I said.

'The very fellow. Good old pork chop himself.'

'You are funny,' I said.

She struck me as terribly gay and liberated all at once. Society girls, like Miss Wilkins, moved in different circles. They always seemed to be flitting from one party to the next, one soiree after another, without a care, as if money simply grew on trees and the world's problems were for someone else to sort out.

'I remember that he walked about with a cane.'

'Who?'

'Well Mr Millrace himself. Charles senior, of course. Perhaps he had an injury of some sort. He had a son, quite a dish and very popular with the ladies. I remember that he possessed this deep mahogany tan, which he acquired in the Far East or Africa, or some such place. I say possessed because it suited him so much. I cannot stand people who go about looking as if they have just come out of a tannery. It just will not do. The sun is to be appreciated, and nothing more. We got rid of sun worshippers a long time ago, don't you think? Expelled them to places like the Côte d'Azur and Cap d'Antibes, and the like.'

'Isn't that where …?'

'Poor Eddie,' she said, 'I'm not quite sure what he sees in that ghastly woman. They love the sun. Her nibs, especially. Perhaps that was it in the end. Worth giving up a kingdom for, do you think?'

'I don't' know, I …'

'Oh don't be so serious,' she said, 'I'm just having a little fun. I didn't mean any of it, of course.'

'What did he look like?' I said.

'Who? Eddie …?'

'The younger Charles.'

'Oh, got a little crush have we?'

'No, I …'

'My dear girl, you are quite the serious one. Young Charles, as you call him … I believe his name was Charlie to his friends. I can't be certain about that, so don't quote me.'

'No,' I said. 'Of course not.'

'He looked a little like that Errol Flynn chap, with dark eyes and slicked-back hair and a rather fashionable pencil-thin moustache. I remember remarking at the time that he seemed a little underweight for the clothes he was wearing … if memory serves me it was a navy jacket and pressed grey trousers. The clothes just hung off him. Did him no favours despite the good looks. He was a pilot in some far off place.All that heat can run you down. I expect he joined the fly-boys when the war started.'

'Yes, he did for a time. He lives at Millrace now.'

'I see. Well I don't expect he'll stay there for too long. What a dreary old place. Views of the sea were rather splendid though. I do remember that. Yes, it had one of those long lawns that swept down to the sea. There was a river too. It ran through one section of the grounds. Terrible stench in the heat of the day. I don't suppose they realise that the old world is gone, poor dears,' she said, her words clipping along at a tremendous pace.

'The Master of Millrace …'

'Old Humpty Dumpty himself.'

'Humpty Dumpty, as you call him, has employed me to play piano for one hour every day. It seems such a luxury in these trying times, don't you think?'

'How very aristocratic of them indeed. I used to play a little myself, you know. Gosh, it reminds me of that time *mama* hired a music teacher. He was quite a handsome type. I fell head over heels in love with the boy, that I shouldn't think I learned anything at all, musically speaking, if you follow me ...'

'Not really but, I...'

'Yes, very handsome boy,' she said and made that whistling sound. 'I couldn't play a jot if you sat me down, right now, and commanded me to. Gosh, good old Jimmy.'

'Jimmy...?'

'James. I called him Jimmy. He liked that. He studied music at Oxford. Can you believe it? He gave piano lessons to anyone who could afford the price. I wonder where he is now?' she said, and seemed to leave the question hanging there as if she were expecting me to answer.

I said, 'Practice makes perfect.'

'Oh, it did,' she replied and gave a little laugh. 'What about you? Do you not find it stifling ... you know, washed up here in Rashleigh, and the world outside throbbing with excitement. I cannot wait to get back to London. Thinking of joining the WAAF, you know. All the girls are doing that.'

'The Women's Auxiliary Air Force! Wouldn't that be quite dangerous?'

'What's life without a little danger?' she said, and gave my arm a nudge. 'Oh, how very silly of me. That came out all wrong.'

'It's all right. I am rather used to it by now.'

'How did it happen? You don't mind if I pry.'

'A bomb.'

'Damn them all to hell.'

'Yes. No. Oh, I don't really know what I meant to say. I ...'

'You don't have to say anything, my dear girl.'

'You are correct, though.'

'How do you mean?'

'Rashleigh can be frightfully dull, sometimes, then something exciting happens and it seems like everyone and everything comes alive, together and all at once. It is like we're all sunflowers waiting for the sun before spontaneously bursting open, then just as quickly closing down again. That's little old Rashleigh for you.'

'How very strange.'

'Parochial, you mean.'

'Yes, *rather* ... I do expect the sea throws up a thing or two though. I thought this is the place where smugglers bring their booty ashore to hide it in caves, and the like.'

I thought about the body that had washed up at Craggy Cliff. "A terrible sight," Constable Barnaby had said. "All bloody and mangled by the rocks. Crabs in his pockets."

'A German sailor washed up recently by Craggy Cliff. They say he was very badly mutilated. The rocks ...'

'Sounds ghastly.'

'He's buried in the local cemetery, along with the rest of them. They have a separate section for the Germans.'

'You mean there has been more?'

'Every few weeks a dead body washes up, somewhere along the coast. Sometimes it is one of ours. Sometimes it is one of theirs. More often than not, full identification is impossible. The sea can take its toll, you know. Nonetheless, they all get a Christian burial.'

'I thought you said Rashleigh was rather dull. I'm seeing the place in a completely new light,' she said and leaned her shoulder against mine, as if she was having an intimate chat with a lifelong friend. 'What about smugglers?'

'What about them?'

'Have you heard anything?'

'I don't know what you mean.'

'Do you mind …?' she said, and lit another cigarette.

'No!'

'Oh, would you rather I didn't smoke?'

'No, I mean … it is perfectly fine.'

'Splendid. Well …!'

'Well, what …?'

'Have you heard about any smuggling going on? Let me explain. There is a rumour that contraband is being landed here which then makes its way on to the black market.'

'Are you a spy?'

'God, no, my dear. I am just doing my job. Actually, if I was able to get to the bottom of this inquiry then I might just be able to wangle my way out of War Ags and into the WAAF.'

I could feel a pang of jealousy growing inside. I was no longer able to contemplate such things and felt in that moment, adrift, with no hope of finding land.

'I'm sorry. I can't help you,' I said, and rose from my seat.

'But, surely, you have heard something.'

'I am afraid not.'

'Look, it doesn't really matter if it is me or Campbell that solves this problem for the Committee, but they are determined to stamp it out. I expect whomever it is will face a lengthy time in prison. Black market offences are not looked upon very kindly.'

'I really don't know anything about the matter,' I said.

'Campbell's walking this way,' she said hurriedly.

I felt the table shift a little with her weight as she pushed her chair back.

'Are you quite finished with your tea? I'll give that a quick rinse before they come in.'

She made that whistling noise again then there was a fizzling sound and I realised that she had extinguished her cigarette. She pumped water and I heard the motions of washing and drying and the back door open with a creaking noise.

'Our business here is almost done. Isn't that so?' Mr Campbell said.

'I expect it is,' Father replied gruffly.

'Well, let's get along then, Miss Wilkins. We have more work to do before the day is out. We need to count and verify the herd on the farm.'

'Yes, Mr Campbell.'

'The figures don't add up,' Mr Campbell added.

'I'm afraid Mr Campbell here doesn't seem to trust our numbers,' Father said.

'It's simple arithmetic. I have my numbers and you have yours, and my numbers are gospel.'

'Thank you for your hospitality,' Miss Wilkins interjected. 'I hope we haven't been too much of an intrusion.'

I shook my head side to side in reply, 'Not at all.'

'Well, I'll see you out then,' Father said.

Before she left Miss Wilkins came closer and said in a low voice, 'If you, or your father, think of anything, you will find my number on the back of this …' She took my hand and placed something into the open palm. I closed my fingers around the piece of paper to make a fist. 'Don't forget. Anything at all.'

'Yes, of course.'

'Miss Wilkins, if you please' Mr Campbell said, his voice raised as if he was eager to get going. 'We have work to do.'

'Coming,' she said.

'I will be back shortly, my dear. Campbell is keen to survey the top field. I don't for the life of me know why, but …'

'Smugglers,' I said.

'What's that, dear?'

'The Committee believes that there are smugglers operating in the local area.'

'Do they now?'

'Black market goods.'

'I shouldn't know anything about that, dear.'

'I told Miss Wilkins the same thing.'

'Well, let me go and see to their concerns.'

Father had no sooner closed the door behind him than there was another noise, and as if on cue, I heard the now familiar squeak of brakes. Mr Burrows had arrived.

CHAPTER TEN

It was as we were journeying I told Mr Burrows all about the visitors from the Committee. He listened without saying a word, a cursory *hem* and *haw* now and then perhaps, but I sensed his mind was somewhere else, and for the most part, he simply remained in his thoughts.

I must have rattled on and on, in that excited way I used to do, when some topic stirred my enthusiasm for chit and chat. It was in one of those moments of silence between *hem* and *haw*, as we were passing the lake, that I said,

'Do you believe in God, Mr Burrows?'

'Which one?' he replied.

I had never heard it put like that.

'Well, the only one,' I said. 'The one true God.'

'The way I see it, miss, there can't be only one, if there's any at all,' he said, and gave a little chuckle. 'No, there can't be only one, miss. Not with the terrible mess, we have ourselves in. We'll need more than one god to get us out of it.'

'Whatever do you mean?' I said in reply.

'The war and all this deprivation, miss. I thought we had left all of that behind us. We had rationing in the last war of course. Not as bad as now. It's the submarines, you see. You can't get a thing these days without a ration card. It's not that I'm complaining, mind you. We all muck in, miss. I've heard the grumbles at Millrace though. Mrs Butler is always complaining about the lack of this or that. The young Master Charles doesn't seem to mind. I expect he has bigger things with which to concern himself. '

'Perhaps Mrs Butler should remember that it's more than the big houses that have suffered. Why, only the other day I was telling Father how we were running short on tea, and if there was any possibility, we could get extra on our ration card. I thought because we were herd owners that might at least count for something, but Father told me that we would not get any special privileges, and we would have to do without, until the next distribution. We must continue to sacrifice for victory like everyone else, he said.'

'Sacrifice for victory indeed,' Mr Burrows said. 'I'm afraid that might not be enough. Well, never mind. I'll tell you what, when we get to Millrace I'll try to rustle up some tea for you, and a few of those nice oat biscuits. Did you like them?'

'I did, Mr Burrows, thank you. That would be very nice.'

Oh, how could I lie like that? Those terrible little hard tack biscuits tasted of nothing more than sawdust. I would have spat them out, there and then, if it wasn't for company, but I couldn't tell him that. I lied instead.

'What's that?' I said, as the smell of smoke pinched my nostrils.

'We're almost there now, miss.'

'What's that smell?'

'Oh, they're just burning some carcases. It's to prevent the spread of disease.'

'It's terrible.'

'Yes, miss. Nearly there now. Close your window if you need

to. Though I daresay the heat might become a little too much for you.'

I left the window open and the smell filled the small compartment in which I sat. I retched a little at the stench, a sort of sickly sweet odour and tried to distract myself then with thoughts of Mrs Butler. The poor woman always seemed to be in a constant state of constipation. I wondered if it was the strain of running a house such as Millrace, or the added burden of taking care of the invalided Master of Millrace. I put these wanderings of the mind aside when Mr Burrows announced our arrival, and we went about the daily ritual of the excited greeting from Tramp and climbing the steps to the entrance. Except, this time, I was left standing in the hallway, waiting, while Mr Burrows went to see about the day's proceedings. It seemed there had been an accident and I heard panicked voices, as servants ran about, rushing down corridors and out of earshot, or climbing stairs, and whispering. It was something to do with Master Charles. That much I caught. Mr Burrows was required immediately. I stood there for what seemed like an age until someone familiar came to rescue me.

'Won't you come with me?' he said.

'Oh, it's you,' I said.

'Follow me. Come on. Turn right and walk straight ahead.'

I followed the sound of his voice, not in the usual direction towards the drawing room, but in the opposite. I thought this quite queer at the time, but since everyone else seemed so preoccupied with whatever emergency had befallen the house, I followed his instructions.

'Tiger's head to your right, about four paces,' he said.

I gave a little jump. 'Oh dear.'

'Don't worry, he's long dead. It's just his head.'

'Poor thing,' I said in reply.

'Uncle Thomas shot him on safari.'

The mention of safaris conjured up images of jungles and wild snarling beasts, and Kipling-like characters in safari hats atop elephants, and the like.

'Where are we going?' I asked.

'No need to be afraid. It's just a short distance.'

'Three steep steps down, about four paces in front of you.'

I tapped with my cane and found the steps.

'I thought I'd show you a different part of the house. Secret passages and all that,' he said. 'It's in here.'

I heard a click and the slide of a door or panel, and a waft of cool air brushed across my face.

'Take my hand,' Pipe-smoker said.

I did, and felt the smooth, hairless skin of his hand. I remembered what Miss Wilkins had said about tanned leather and it caused me to loosen my grip a little, while his hand remained firm and reassuring.

'Don't be afraid,' he said.

'I'm not.'

'This way. It's quite dark. Wait a moment. It's for my benefit of course,' and he struck a match.

There was a smell of sulphur then candle wax and that faint whiff of gasoline again.

'All set.'

I nodded and let him guide me onward, tapping every so often to ascertain the dimensions of the passage.

'This one takes us past the kitchen and pantry.'

A smell of baking pinched my nostrils then a different smell, something gamey.

'Mr Burrows caught some rabbits. You can see them hanging

through a little spyhole.'

'Why would you need a spyhole for a pantry?'

'It served some function in the Civil War. My ancestors supported Cromwell, God help us.'

'So they spied on servants?'

'To learn where loyalties lay, I suppose. Come along.'

He led me further along the passage and I had the sense that we were descending on an ever-so gradual gradient. The air was damp and cold.

All about me I could hear the sound of water trickling and that *plink-plink* noise it makes when dropping into little pools.

Underfoot the surface changed from the surety of rock and stone to a wooden surface that creaked and groaned.

We continued, until eventually he said, 'Nearly there.'

I felt warmer air on my face then and tasted salt air on my tongue. 'The boat house,' I said.

'Bravo,' Pipe-smoker replied.

'So this is where you steal away to.'

'They don't even notice I am gone.'

I heard the dull sound of wood knocking on wood, and water lapping about, and grew a little anxious that I might trip and fall, and be washed out to sea.

'Do you trust me?' Pipe-smoker said.

'I've come this far, haven't I?'

'You've grown tense. You're perfectly safe.'

'It's just the water. I know we're close, so—'

'We're still at a distance. There is a series of steps leading down to the jetty to where a boat is tied up. I can fetch the oars from the rack if you like. The tide is about to turn. Would you like me to take you out?'

'I think I've had enough excitement for today,' I said.

The lapping of the water and the sea air caused me to suddenly become quite nauseous and I felt myself getting a little dizzy. I leant on my cane to steady myself, and gripped Pipe-smoker's hand tightly.

'Is anything the matter?' he said.

I was about to reply when I felt myself falling and then nothing, nothing at all.

*

'You've gone and done it, haven't you?' she said, hanging her gas mask and tin hat on the hook on the back of the door. 'I leave London for two days and what do I return to …?'

'Keep your voice down. Mrs Simpson will hear you.'

'Reckon she's listening through the wall, do you?'

I nodded to confirm a suspicion I had long held that Mrs Simpson occasionally listened to our conversations through the paper-thin wall that existed between two rooms; our bedroom and the vacant room next door.

'Well, if she is listening, then *she has nothing to be concerned about here,*' Doris said, raising her voice. 'I'll be down for a cup of tea though, if you want to stick the kettle on, Mrs Simpson.'

A few moments later we heard the familiar top step creak and groan.

'See, I told you. Didn't I?'

'It doesn't mean she was listening in.'

I shook my head and said,

'Doris, she doesn't have any other excitement in her life, except idle gossip and reading the death notices in the paper.'

Doris laughed. 'I'll give her gossip to redden her ears, I will.'

'Oh, Doris!'

'Now, back to my original question. Dish it all. C'mon.'

I bit my bottom lip and tried to stifle a nervous giggle.

'You didn't?'

'Don't tell a soul.'

'You little harlot you. And you, a country girl and all. Whatever will they think back in what do you call it?'

'Little old Rashleigh.'

'That's it. Rashleigh. Even the name sounds proper.'

'They won't think anything, because no one is going to tell them. *Are they?*'

'Of course not,' Doris said, and made a long, exaggerated winking action.

'They better not.'

'Well, go on then. Tell me about this affair of yours,' she said, making herself comfortable on the bed.

*

'You've been out for some time,' Pipe-smoker said.

'Where am I?'

'Rest,' he said. 'You're perfectly safe.'

His voice boomed and echoed. As I began to come to, I felt a soft, velvet surface under my fingertips.

'It's mostly books and ledgers and a bit of bric and brac in here,' he said then. 'We're in a storage room. Thankfully it has this old and tattered chaise-longue too.'

'How did I …?'

'I carried you back through the tunnel. You can rest here until you feel better. We are just below the drawing room … so, we don't have far to go. I couldn't risk going any further … not in the condition you were in. We'll have to wait until you feel better.'

'My head hurts,' I said.

'That will be the knock you took. Luckily, you fell on a wooden surface. A few inches more and you might have tumbled down the stairs and who knows what might have happened. You have a small bruise. Nothing much to worry about I should think,' he said and touched his fingers to my forehead.

I flinched at the sudden contact.

'Didn't mean to frighten you,' he said.

'You didn't,' I lied, and put my hand to my head to feel the large bump, which had resulted from my fall. 'Oh!' I gripped the arm of the couch with my free hand and pulled myself upright.

'Steady on. Slowly.'

'Help me sit up,' I said.

'Here,' he said, gripping my arm.

'Let's get you comfortable.' I felt hard cushions behind my back, then, 'Drink this.'

'What is it?' I asked, and he pressed a metal cup into my hand.

He had filled the cup to the brim and it felt heavy in my hands.

'Just water. I am afraid I don't have anything stronger, though I'm sure if I searched long enough I might be able to rustle up something. Perhaps a jot of rum, or brandy.'

I felt the bump on my head again and sipped the water from the cup. It had a metallic taste, which made my tongue tingle a little.

'That's one of those old cups. They called them Loving Cups. They passed them around at weddings. Don't worry I washed out the dust and cobwebs first.'

'My tongue ...'

'That's the lead, I should think. They used it to make such things back then.'

'Oh!' I said, and handed him the cup.

'I'm actually quite surprised by what I've found lying around. It appears that Mrs Butler and Mr Burrows have outdone themselves.'

'Yes,' I said rubbing, my forehead again, half-listening to Pipe-smoker's words, and fighting the urge to sleep.

'Tins and tins of ham … American, you know?'

'Yes, I know …'

'Canned peaches from Florida, USA. Hard cheese from Melton-Mowbray. Flour from Hungerford, Berkshire and several jerry cans of petrol. Rabbit sandwiches indeed. If I had known that we had this stored away, well …'

'You said it yourself, it's a storage room. One might expect to have certain provisions stored away.'

'Mrs Butler has outdone herself. Clever old thing.'

'Mrs Butler …? Ooh, my head hurts.'

click-click

'Here … try a little of this for the pain.'

That alluring smell wafted towards me. I felt the weight of the pipe in my hand.

'It's quite strong. One or two puffs should do the trick.'

I placed the tip of the pipe between my lips and inhaled.

'Give it a few moments.'

I felt a strange sensation at the back of my throat, warm and tingly, then a little light headed. 'Oh!'

'I don't know what I would do without my little puff-puff. Life wouldn't be worth living.'

'Don't say that,' I said, and felt the light-headedness replaced by sleepiness instead.

'On more tootle should be sufficient to take the pain away.'

I dragged on the pipe again.

'There's so much pain in the world.'

'Rest,' he said.

'I do feel a little sleepy. Would you mind? Just a few moments to recharge.'

'Rest now. Everything will be right in the world again.'

I could feel my heartbeat slowing to an almost indiscernible beat and my mouth becoming very dry. All the while I had this feeling of being outside of my body, floating above it, and imagining myself lying there, care-free as the world spun.

'I think I'll play a little music.'

Then a scratching noise, like a needle running across a record, before something familiar: *'While we have moonlight and love, let's face the music and dance.'*

How lovely, I remember thinking. He hummed along with the music. I imagined him swaying around the room as if no one else existed. Then a sleepiness descended and the music became just a background noise, replaced instead by the sound of waves crashing against the rocks. The next voice I heard was Pipe-smoker's.

'Do you feel well enough to stand?' he said.

I felt dizzy and out of sorts but said, 'Yes. I think so.'

'Let's give it a go then.'

I gripped his arm and he helped me to stand. After a moment or two of unsteadiness, He handed me my cane and I tapped a path but quickly found my way blocked.

'You have managed to find the canned peaches. Care for some?'

In truth, canned peaches sounded quite delectable, but I had other things on my mind. I was beginning to wonder if our absence had been noticed.

'Thank you, but no.'

'Let's get you back then, shall we? Before Mrs Butler raises a search party.'

'Would she do that?'

'Mrs Butler takes the orderly running of Millrace very seriously,' he said. 'I daresay she would have me hung, drawn and quartered if she knew I had spirited you away.'

'Very Cromwellian.'

'*Touché!*'

'Do the servants know about the secret passages?' I asked, trying to slow the spinning world just a little more with every step.

'Yes, of course, how do you think … Never mind. Did you like the music?'

'Yes,' I said, 'Fred Astaire…'

'And Ginger Rogers. Don't forget Miss Rogers.'

'No, of course.'

'Here, take my hand again.'

We proceeded from the storeroom into a tight passage. I know this because my shoulders rubbed the walls as we passed through it. From the other side of the wall I heard footsteps scraping along the floor and the noisy sound of pots banging about. Someone was tuning in a wireless. A man's gravelly voice eventually came through.

'If you haven't guessed already, that is the kitchen on the other side of the wall,' Pipe-smoker said.

'Listen,' I said. 'Can you hear that?'

'*This is the BBC Home Service. The German flagship, Bismarck, has been sunk in the North Atlantic …*'

The announcer then proceeded to detail the order of battle and a reminder of the brave sacrifice of the crew of HMS Hood .

'Well, that's a turn up for the books. The Royal Navy has sunk her at last,' Pipe-smoker said.

Just then, I heard, 'Master Charles will have tea in his room today.'

'No recital then, Mrs Butler,' a voice replied.

'Recital, *pfff!* Well, what are you waiting for Daisy? Be quick about it.'

'Yes, Mrs Butler.'

'Poor girl,' Pipe-smoker whispered. 'Old Maggie can be hard at times. Let's get along, shall we?'

We left the sounds and smells of the kitchen behind us and continued through the passage until I heard a door creak on its hinges then Pipe-smoker said,

'Back where we started.'

I tapped the cane against the edge of an opening and followed the sound of Pipe-smoker's voice until I felt warm air on my face.

'Fire's still going. That's one blessing,' he said.

'Yes,' I said, and placed one tentative foot in front of me, then another.

I heard the sound of the panel sliding close again and a *clicking* noise as some mechanism fixed itself in place.

'Mind if I light up again?' he said. 'How's that bump?'

'No, please,' I replied. 'It's quite alright.'

click-click

The now familiar pipe-smoke wafted towards me and made my head spin a little.

'Well then, shan't say a word!'

'Do you mean that I shouldn't mention canned peaches?'

'You are the funny one.'

'Oh! You mean secret passages.'

'Yes that and that little knock on the head. Come up with a good excuse yet?'

'I'm not a very good liar.'

'I doubt that.'

I was about to answer when the door opened and someone entered.

'You can take our guest home, *now*,' Mrs Butler said.

'Sir, do you think it's a good idea to …?'

'Hush now Mrs Butler. All will be well. We were just getting comfortable. Isn't that so?'

I smiled but said nothing, for fear I might trip myself up in some silly web of lies. In truth, it was taking whatever energy I still possessed to compose myself. The heat of the fire, and pipe-smoke, and the throbbing headache were just about to overtake me when,

'Come along, miss. Let's get your things,' a second voice said.

It was Mr Burrows.

'Here's your coat and hat, miss,' he said, handing me my things. 'That's a nasty knock you've taken, miss.'

'It's nothing really. A silly accident.'

'Show here, girl,' Mrs Butler said, and I felt a grip on my arm. 'Well, how in heaven did you come by that?'

'It was my fault,' Pipe-smoker interjected. 'You see I was showing our guest into the drawing room when, of all things, I led her past that piece of rug … you know, that part over there, the piece with the tear, and …'

'I tripped and fell and knocked my head.'

'Oh, dear,' Mr Burrows said.

'Well that won't do,' Mrs Butler said. 'It's quite a sizable bump you have there. Wouldn't you say, sir?'

'Like a Florida peach.'

'Begging your pardon, sir?'

'A turn of phrase, Mrs Butler. A turn of phrase.'

'I'm sure I don't know what a Florida peach might look like, sir, but perhaps we should have the doctor look at it.'

'I'm fine,' I said.

'Is the heat getting to you, Mr Burrows? It's just that you appear to have become quite flushed about the face.'

'Just the heat of the fire, sir.'

'Yes, that must be it. Now what shall we do?'

'With—?'

'With our guest, of course, Mrs Butler.'

'Yes, sir, well …'

'I'm perfectly fine, really. Perhaps Mr Burrows could drive me home.'

'That might be for the best,' Pipe-smoker said. 'You will come back though, won't you? Don't let this little trifle put you off.'

'No … I mean to say, yes. Yes, of course.'

'Well that's settled then. Mr Burrows, if you would please.'

*

Later, as Mr Burrows was driving me home, I chanced to ask him.

'Young Mr Charles,' I began, 'was he badly injured in the war?'

Mr Burrows was silent for a few moments, gathering his thoughts I should think, before giving me an answer.

'I'm afraid so, miss.'

'What happened to him?'

'It was towards the beginning of the war. He was flying, a reconnaissance mission I think they call it, over enemy territory, he was. The plane caught fire. The poor boy got himself trapped in the cockpit, didn't he?'. When he managed to free himself well, the damage was mostly done. Burned, he was. It hurts me to say

137

it, miss, for he was such a handsome boy.'

'Yes, I've heard it said.'

'Like one of those matinee idols, miss. He cut quite a dashing figure, he did. As for the young women ... Well, there was a queue for his attention. I knew young Mr Charles as a headstrong boy too, and he has lost none of that, but … those injuries, miss. No man, or woman, should have to suffer such a terrible thing. I believe it has affected his mind.'

'How do you mean?'

'It's not my place, miss, but seeing as you are keeping regular company at Millrace perhaps you should know.'

'Know what …?'

'Young Mr Charles returned from the war, changed physically, yes… and mentally too. I believed he experienced some terrible things, miss. I've witnessed something similar in my time. I've known men to go a little doolally. You've heard that term before, haven't you?'

'Yes,' I said, 'a little mad. Is that what you are implying?'

'Yes, miss. He can have flights of fancy, and the like.'

'Tall tales, you mean?'

'Tall tale indeed, miss. Young Mr Charles believes some terrible things about his father. I don't know where he got the notion at all.'

'Such as …' I pressed.

'Why, he believes his father to be a cruel and uncaring man.'

'And is he?'

'Quite the opposite, miss. It's the curse,' Mr Burrows said.

'It's a curse on the house.'

'What do you mean?'

'You've heard of it,' he said. 'It's since that time when all the workers got sick from the mills, and the water turned fetid, and

138

villagers could no longer wash or feed themselves.'

'But that's more than one hundred years ago. I thought it was just some old wife's tale, to scare children.'

'It's not, miss. I could tell you some things. Things about that house that would make the hair stand up on your pretty, little head. Aye, there is some strangeness about it. I have been there nigh on twenty years now. Since just after the—'

'Just after what, Mr Burrows?'

'Never mind, miss. This is you now. Safely home. Let me get that door for you.'

The car came to a stop and the handbrake squeaked as it was being applied, then the door on the driver's side opened.

'I can't say if I'll be here tomorrow, miss. It's the Master, you see, he isn't well … It would be a shame, miss. A terrible shame. You see. I believe that you have brought some life back into that old house. You have lifted young Mr Charles's spirits into the bargain, you have. What's more, miss, I think you play most beautifully. Yes I do. And the others, well, they say just the same thing they do.'

'That is kind of you to say, Mr Burrows. I—'

'They say something cold will work wonders to bring down that swelling,' he said.

Instinctively I touched my forehead and felt the bump, like a hillock, still in place. 'Yes, something cold …'

'Here's a little something to get you through the rest of the day,' he said, and pressed a tin box into my free hand.

'What's this?' I said but Mr Burrows had already started the engine again.

It sputtered and spat as he drove away. I wondered if I would hear the sputtering, spitting sound again, or if the whole affair had just been a strange dream, one from which I would awaken

139

to find myself on the bedroom floor having knocked my head on something. It was as I was standing there that my attention was drawn to a noise getting louder with every passing second. It was the sound of hobnail boots marching determinedly in my direction. There was just the one pair from what I could tell, and I could hear someone whistling as they walked along. It always seemed to me that a person who whistled knew something more about the world. It was as if they held a secret inside which was bursting to get out. I cocked my head to the side and listened; listened as the whistler got nearer, and nearer, until he was almost upon me. Then he stopped.

'Good afternoon,' he said. 'I think this must be the place.'

'Good afternoon,' I replied, and gripped the tin box tighter in my hands.

He moved about a bit, his boots scuffing along the ground, as if he was kicking pebbles, or moving obstacles out of his way; like shyness. I found myself blushing and an involuntary frisson of both excitement and fear coursed through my entire body. I could only imagine how that looked to the stranger. Then, of all the silly things, I found myself lost for words. I was distracted from the silliness by a cawing noise, a crow or magpie passing by, and the sound of wings flapping noisily.

'I'm sorry,' he said. 'Did he frighten you?'

'Who?' I asked.

'It's my companion, Raven. He travels everywhere with me.'

'No, of course not. He didn't frighten me,' I replied. 'I was just a little distracted.'

'Yes, I saw that car leaving.'

'We must have passed you on the road. I'm surprised Mr Burrows didn't stop to offer you a lift.'

I tried to conjure up an image in my mind of the stranger

accepting the lift, cradling his bird in his arms, and Mr Burrows and little old me in the back. What a sight that would have been.

'Is he actually a raven?' I said.

'Yes,' the stranger replied.

'Describe him to me.'

'He is tall and beautiful, and his feathers are the colour of coal. He is ever watchful. He is very smart. We've travelled quite a distance together,' he said. 'Would you like to touch him?'

I heard Father's voice. He was calling out, not to me, but to our visitor.

'You're Fallada,' I assume, Father said.

'I am Wilhelm Fallada,' the stranger replied.

'The Committee wasn't long about sending you out. I will give them that. Well, if it was petrol I required, or extra tea on my ration card, I would probably still be waiting. You are here now nonetheless and you are carrying neither Tetley's or turpentine. Did you walk all the way?'

'Ten kilometres,' the stranger replied.

'We don't use those fancy measurements around here. We use miles. You're in England now.'

'Of course,' he said.

'It's a good seven miles, give or take a yard, from here to the train station. Well, I expect you are a man who has done his fair share of walking in his time. I see you have a good pair of boots. You will need them. I won't be supplying you with a new pair if you wear them out. So take good care of them. Moreover, you will mend and darn your own clothes while you are here. My daughter will not be doing it for you. God knows she has enough to do. You speak English well enough.'

'Yes,' the stranger replied. 'I studied English at university in Germany before I came to England. I have been working the farms here since the beginning of the war, so I have perfected it a little.'

'Well, you'll have no hardship from us. We are ordinary people. We don't have room for you in the house, so you will be sleeping in the barn. It is warm at least, though I daresay you won't need much in the way of blankets. It has been so very warm. I expect you've experienced worse conditions?'

'Yes,' he said softly, without giving any further explanation.

'You'll eat with us, breakfast, lunch and tea. I will not have any man say he was unfairly treated under my roof. We will see how you work out and if we get along, then you'll be welcome to join me for a smoke on occasion. I daresay every man deserves food and shelter, and the odd puff on a pipe, despite the times we live in.'

'That would be good,' he said in reply. 'And you won't mind if I keep, Raven?'

'He doesn't bother me. You can feed him with scraps, same as the other animals.'

'Thank you,' he replied.

I was too busy composing myself to notice that their voices had begun to drift away.

'Father, I said. I—'

'I'll be back shortly. I'm going to show Mr Fallada where he'll be staying. Why don't you go inside, dear?'

'Yes, I'll do that,' I said, drawing a breath.

I stood there for a few moments longer listening as the men's voices faded further away then suddenly remembered the box in my hands. I gave it a shake. It made a rattling noise, like sugar or sand, but to my surprise when I opened the lid a wonderful smell greeted me. Tea. What a wonderful gift.

'Tea …' I said aloud. 'Not turpentine.'

Raven cawed loudly and flapped his wings to take flight. I imagined him circling above me, looking down and watching me, as I stood there, savouring the sweet aroma. I closed the lid and turned to walk inside. A thought occurred to me. It was something the woman from the Committee said.

CHAPTER ELEVEN

On the fourth day, I rose with the hope that the day would be different; light where darkness reigned. Instead, there was the constant greyness filled with a perception of shadows, like the ghostly spectres of the dreams and storms I had left behind.

In my dream, I had found myself cast upon the pebble beach, the one just beyond the point, where jagged rocks discouraged most, and to which only the most determined of souls would travel. A terrible storm was blowing and waves crashed upon the shore with such ferocity that the whole world in which this dream took place seemed to shake and shudder. I remember, after some effort, getting to my feet, and feeling the pebbles between my toes, cold, and oily slick from the pounding of the surf. I felt suddenly frightened by the forces that surrounded me. A gusting wind danced with white horses and driving rain, with such ferocity as to make my efforts seem inconsequential, and my progress a futile exercise against the raw power of nature itself.

Voices called out. The faint echoes of souls lost to the sea over millennia. My anxiety at these circumstances suddenly possessed me of the power that only exists in dreams. It was the ability to be in more than one place at once so that I was suddenly transported to the cliff-top, from where I looked down upon my other self; the dark-self still struggling in the surf, dragged back by the weight of a heavy and water-soaked cloak. I looked out to the boiling sea where the same white horses pranced across the grey horizon, and saw a massive wave, building, building, and building still, as if every ounce of the sea's energy had been summoned, to hurl at the crumbling shore.

Run, I shouted, and saw the fear in my own eyes reflected back at me. Run. It was no use. My legs were heavy and my words extinguished, on one powerful gust of wind, after another. Still the wave built. The sea is coming, I called, and the fear built like the waves themselves until at the very last moment, the moment before all is finally resolved I woke, my hands clenched tight around the bed blankets, my breath still held with fear, and watched the faint grey spectre leave the caverns of my mind.

After some moments of a dawning realisation that I was no longer dreaming, my breath returned, in heaving, necessary gulps of air. I released my grip on the bed sheet and lay there for some time, remembering, feeling the sweat-soaked nightdress against my back, and adjusted my position to make myself more comfortable. After a few more moments, I grew restless and had a sudden desire to use the chamber pot.

As I sat there, squatting in place, I thought about the nature of my dreams. The doctors said it was my mind's means of compensating for blindness. Every night a different dream. Every dream held my deepest fears and greatest regrets, all bundled into a matinee of vivid sights and sounds. You should take some sleeping pills, the doctor had suggested. Vivid dreams are not uncommon in cases such as yours, he continued. Medication will help you get a good night's rest.

It wasn't lack of sleep because plentiful fresh air made up for that. It was my nightly journey to dark places. I couldn't tell the doctors or they would surely have locked me up. I shook my head a few times side to side, stifled a nervous yawn, then pushed the chamber pot under the bed and stood in place. I splayed my toes apart to ascertain the reality of my grip on the world, and then I dressed slowly, carefully; conscious, in a slowly dawning sort of way that a stranger had come to live with us, and I had better look my best.

When I had made myself presentable I made my way down the stairs, pausing in the hallway, just as I always did, to wind the clock, then proceeded to the kitchen. Father was already busy. I could hear him mumbling to himself. There were the usual smells, breakfast porridge a little overcooked, and the wood-smoke from the range. I heard the pups yapping in their cosy bed and went to pick one up.

The sound of music was coming from the wireless set. It was a Vaughan Williams composition, *In the Fen Country*. How beautiful it sounded.

'Good morning,' I said, as I took a pup from the litter and cradled it in my hands.

'I didn't hear you come down,' Father said, as he switched the wireless off.

'Oh, please leave it on.'

'Have to save the batteries,' he said, then said nothing more about it.

I wondered if it was Father's way of sheltering me from any further harm, perhaps thinking that by keeping out the sounds of the outside world might somehow nullify its woes. Nevertheless, the echo of the music rang in my ear a little longer, then the yelp of the pups distracted me, and when I tried to bring it back, I was unable to. I stroked the pup's head instead.

'You're blind like me,' I whispered. 'The world is still

146

unknown but you are safe here with your mother.'

I ran my fingers along the length of the pup's body and felt the thick layer of fat around its ribcage. Jess was fattening them up with her milk and it would not be long until they would be ready to go out into the world for themselves.

I brought the pup closer to my face and rubbed its soft fur against my cheek, and smelled its new dog smell. I felt a sudden sadness. It was as if a pin-sized hole opened in my heart, and emotions had flooded in. My eyes grew moist at the thought of what was lost to me, forever.

I stooped and placed the pup back with its squirming mass of siblings, and heard the squealing of excitement as they fed.

'Come and get your porridge before it gets cold,' Father said.

The moment was gone. My eyes filled with darkness again. I made my way to my chair, and moved it a little closer to the table before taking my seat.

'Good morning,' a voice said, startling me.

It was Mr Fallada.

'I'm sorry, again. I didn't mean to frighten you,' he said.

I had hoped for some time for a distraction to my day and longed perhaps, in a strange sort of way, for sounds of busyness, like the sounds of the city, and people's voices, an interaction with someone other than the familiars of Rashleigh. I drummed my fingertips along the table top and cleared my throat,

'Good morning, Mr Fallada.'

It had been such a long time since we had had anyone for breakfast, and a strange, exotic man into the bargain, that I was all at sixes and sevens, and managed to take the first mouthful of porridge with my fork, and not my spoon as I had intended. How silly I must have looked. He didn't say anything. Instead, Father pointed out my error.

'That's your fork,' Father said, and I felt my cheeks flush with the heat that comes with embarrassment. My mistake was almost catastrophic since the fork was almost to my mouth, and the porridge was falling through its prongs. I slowly, purposefully, returned it to the bowl, and scraped its edges then I found the spoon, which I had intended to use. What has come over me? I thought. I was never one to be so fidgety.

'Will your Mr Burrows be coming to collect you today?' Father said.

I was still reeling a little and did not feel like eating anything then. I felt the spoon heavy in my hand. There was nowhere to escape. All I could do was sit there, unable to answer Father's question. I could feel him staring. He was probably wondering what had come over me, and then he changed the subject rather quickly and turned his attention to the day ahead.

'We'll tackle the top field first.'

'Yes.'

'This weather is confusing everything. Never have I known it to be so warm, and damp, then freezing cold. When it rains, it seems like it will never stop,' Father said.

How disappointing, I thought.

I expected Mr Fallada to add to Father's observations, but he remained silent. I could hear him chewing, and drinking his tea, but not another word. 'We'll plough the top field in any case, and hope for the best. The draught mare is powerful. You've handled a work horse before?'

'Yes.'

'Good then,' said Father. 'It will be a good day's work.'

I almost felt like screaming. Say something, I thought. Say anything. Only moments later did I realise that I was still holding the spoon aloft and quickly put it down.

'You need your strength,' Father said, observing my frozen posture.

'I'm not hungry this morning,' I replied.

'What's come over you?'

When I didn't answer he said, 'Well, it'll be in the pot if you need it.'

'Thank you, Father,' I said, and pushed my chair away from the table.

I was about to excuse myself when I heard a car's horn.

'That'll be your Mr Burrows,' Father said.

I heard him rounding the table and the sound of his steps fading towards the front door.

'He's not *my* Mr Burrows, Father. He's just, Mr Burrows,' I said after him.

'Your father told me that he is also a writer.'

'Yes. He has written for trade journals and the like.'

'Interesting.'

'Do you think so?'

'Yes,' Mr Fallada said. 'It is an occupational hazard of mine. Journals and scientific articles.'

'Occupational hazard?'

'I'm a physicist. Actually, I was studying for my doctorate before the war.'

'Oh! Where?'

'Oxford.'

'Then why are you working on farms?'

'I am one of those doubtful cases. The authorities don't really know if they should trust me or not.'

'Should they?'

He made a slurping sound as he drank his tea then said, 'I shouldn't see why they wouldn't.'

'Perhaps they suspect you of being a spy. Are you a spy, Mr Fallada?'

'A spy …? An English attempt at humour, *ya!*' he said, slipping unconsciously into his mother tongue.

I heard the door opening and Father exchanged words with someone before returning.

'A young man says he's from up the Big House, come to collect the young lady.'

'If you will excuse me, Mr Fallada.'

'Of course,' he replied.

I rose and made my way to the door, 'Mr Burrows. Is that you?'

I heard the garden gate swinging open.

'If you'll excuse me, miss, but I've been sent from the Big House. It has taken me an age to find this place. I couldn't bother you for some water?'

'Of course, I said. Where's Mr Burrows?'

'I'm Christian,' he replied. 'I'm Mr Burrow's son. I work at Millrace too. I'm afraid my father is poorly. I've been sent to pick you up instead.'

'Oh!' I said. 'I do hope your father is not too unwell.'

'Food poisoning, miss. That's what the doctor says.'

'Food poisoning. Well that is terrible news. Won't you follow me, Mr Burrows …?'

'Christian, miss, please. Everyone calls my father Mr Burrows.'

'Christian. Of course.' I turned then to go to the kitchen to fetch the young Mr Burrows a glass of water and practically ran into Mr Fallada on his way out. He grunted an apology of sorts and stood there waiting for me to say something. I had stumbled forward and he had grabbed my arm just in time. As he helped me up, I placed my hand on his chest, and could feel, for just a

150

moment, the warm beat of his heart. It was slow and strong, and echoed through the palm of my hand. I felt suddenly embarrassed and quickly made my excuses.

'I've been so clumsy,' I replied, and felt again that strange rush of heat. 'It's this weather, I should think.'

Once I had regained my footing, I moved past him, and in the direction of the kitchen. My heart was pounding in my chest. I pumped the handle and placed the glass underneath, and when it was full, I drank it down, then filled it again, and drank the second glass. I stood for a few moments with my hands resting on the sink bowl, then pumped the handle again and filled a third glass. This one I meant for the young Mr Burrows.

'Are you all right, miss?' I heard him ask.

It was young Mr Burrows. He must have been standing there all the time.

'Yes. Perfectly fine,' I said.

'Thank you, miss,' he said.

I heard him drink it in one go.

'Another?' I said.

'No, thank you, miss. That will do just nicely. I'll go and start the motor again. It was overheating, so no harm in letting it cool a little. I'll leave the empty glass on the table, will I?'

I nodded my head in reply and heard him going to the door, then the crunch of gravel under his feet as he made his way to the end of the path. There were no sounds in the house then, just the sound of my own heartbeat, and the shallowness of my breath, and the *plink-plop-plink* of the precious water falling from the tap into the bowl underneath. That was the way it had been up to the point; silence in the early morning and the darkness of my thoughts, as I went about my day. Now, all had changed and so many new sounds had entered my daily life; Jess with her yelping pups, and Mr Fallada to add to my list of strangers, the daily jaunts to Millrace in a noisy automobile with Mr Burrows, and now young Mr Burrows. I went to ready myself for the journey ahead, thinking to myself about a suitable musical accompaniment to my changing world. Rachmaninoff, I decided, a little Rachmaninoff for the blind rabbit.

We reached the house in the late afternoon with a short delay caused by a puncture of all things. I sat in the stifling heat, while young Mr Burrows went about the change of wheel, feeling useless as he struggled under the weight of the machine. I heard him swear several times in the effort. No one should have to do such laborious work during the heat of the day, I thought. As I sat waiting for young Mr Burrows to complete the task of changing the wheel I thought of Mr Fallada in the top field, guiding the plough in the unforgiving earth. I tried to visualise what this strange man might look like. I ran my thumb over the palm of my hand, building a picture of him in my mind, imagining the raven resting on his shoulder, as he went about his business, like a pirate on dry land, shipwrecked in a place far from home.

'That's us done, miss. Are you ready?' Young Mr Burrows said.

I climbed aboard once more. We journeyed onwards and arrived at Millrace a short time later. Tramp arrived barking and running alongside. As I stood in the courtyard, I could feel Tramp's tail beating against my leg. I put my hand out to him and let him smell my scent, and that of the pups.

'I'm to bring you straight through,' young Mr Burrows said. 'They'll be waiting for you in the drawing room. I'm sure Mrs Butler will be none too happy with our tardiness.'

'There was nothing that could be done,' I said. 'I'm sure it won't be all that bad.'

'You don't know Mrs Butler,' he said, as we climbed the steps to the entrance. 'She's a terror, is what she is. She has the whole house shaking in their boots. Ever since young Mr Charles returned, well—'

'There you are,' a voice said, and I knew at once who it was. 'You took your time getting here.'

'I'm sorry Mrs Butler, but—'

'We had a puncture,' I interjected. 'There was nothing that could have prevented it. I wasn't much use. I'm afraid Mr Burrows had to change the wheel by himself.'

I heard her sigh noisily, then she said, 'Well do come along then. We shouldn't leave the Master waiting any longer.'

Young Mr Burrows took my arm and steered me towards the drawing room, whispering every so often to let me know of obstacles and the like.

'Well, it's about time,' Pipe-smoker said and made a wheezing, whistling sound on his breath. 'You've caused quite a stir, you know. Poor Mrs Butler is at her wits end. Isn't that so, Mrs Butler? First Mr Burrows falls ill then you arrive late for your appointed time. This just will not do at all.'

I was about to make my excuses when I heard Mrs Butler say, 'I think you're having fun on my account, sir.'

Now, Mrs Butler, have you ever known me to do such a thing?'

'The Master is feeling unwell too. This will have to wait until he feels better.'

I breathed a sigh of relief. I would be going home again.

'You will stay of course,' Mrs Butler said, and I felt my heart sink in my chest.

'Stay?'

'Yes. You will have to stay awhile. I'll arrange for tea.'

153

'But, I can't—'

'Don't be silly, girl. You'll stay and that will be the end of it.'

With that, Mrs Butler barked some instructions and I heard voices fading away until the door closed heavily behind them.

'How is that bump on the head?' he began.

'It's fine, thank you.'

'Good. I'm sure that little puff-puff helped the healing. I don't know what I would do without it. Good old, Maggie.'

'I'm afraid I don't know …'

'Mrs Butler. I call her Maggie,' he said.

'Oh, I see …'

'Without Maggie I would be lost. Cast adrift.'

'She seems to be quite efficient.'

'Efficient. That's one word for it. As long as Maggie keeps me in puff-puff, I don't care. She could knock off everybody in this house and I wouldn't care one iota.'

'That's not very nice,' I said, suddenly remembering Mr Burrows' words.

'Does that make you uncomfortable?'

'Yes.'

'I'm sorry. It's just a turn of phrase. I didn't mean anything by it.'

'That's quite all right.'

'No, it's not, damn it. You see, if I didn't have my tobacco well, the pain would be unbearable. It's become a habit now. I just can't live without it. I don't know what I would do. Perhaps my demons would escape their confines and …'

'I'm sure you won't run out,' I said. 'Mrs Butler appears to have everything in order.'

'I expect you've heard about Burrows then?'

'He's unwell.'

'Silly old fool. Rancid peaches of all things. If you are going to take the odd thing from the bounty then choose wisely. That's what I've always said. What was he thinking? We had to have the doctor here. There were awkward questions. Where did the canned peaches come from? Things like that. Maggie assures me that everything will be fine.'

'Where did they come from?' I dared to ask.

I heard a deep intake of breath and then he said, 'Feels like snow today.'

'Snow. How silly,' I said in reply.

'I've been watching the change in the clouds. They're sitting much lower in the sky today. They're heavy with moisture.'

'It'll probably rain then,' I said smartly.

'No. No, it won't rain today.'

I let him talk, trying to fix his position in my head. 'It's much too warm for snow, don't you think?' As I spoke the words, I rose from my seat and tapped the floor with my cane.

'I'm over here,' he said, and I heard the sound of furniture moving. 'Just by the window.'

I felt the sun on my face and made my way towards it.

'The storm is blowing in from the sea.'

click-click

'I know these things,' he said. 'I've observed them. The tide carries everything before it. Soon it will carry this house and all its demons away, and good riddance.'

'You can't mean that,' I said.

'I do. This house and all its terrible sadness will be carried away upon a tide.'

'The sea is at least one quarter of a mile away,' I said, recreating the image from my youth.

The room grew colder and I felt the goose bumps rising on

my skin. The gloomy grey at the back of my eyelids turned darker still.

'The winter is upon us again,' he said. 'It will snow, and snow. I expect you will be spending some time here.'

I felt a shiver run along my spine and heard for the first time the sound of a storm come to turn the world upside down. Rain or hail, I couldn't tell, pelted the window glass. I turned my head in the direction, in which I thought Pipe-smoker might be standing, and said,

'Rain.'

'Hail,' Pipe-smoker replied.

click-click

'What strange weather it is.'

'The snow is not far behind it.'

'I can't stay here if it snows. Father will be worried.'

'Why don't you take a seat? Take this chair and I will describe the world from where I sit.'

I moved to my right and tapped the ground until I felt an object in my path. It was a wooden chair with cloth-covered armrests. It presented an image of a chair one might use at a dining table, stiff and functional. I sat down and waited.

'From here you can see the world,' Pipe-smoker said.

I didn't see anything of course.

'I'd like to tell you a story,' he said, and I heard a clicking noise. It sounded somehow familiar, metallic. Just like a cigarette lighter might sound.

'If you like,' I replied.

'Where shall I begin? At the beginning, I suppose. At the end of all beginnings.'

'This one is reliable.' I studied the small, silver-coloured lighter the saleswoman was holding in her hand. 'Would you like to try it?'

'Yes, why not,' I said, and picked the lighter up with both hands, as if it was something rare and delicate.

'It's silver-plated. You might consider the cigarette case as well,' she said, and procured a rectangular-shaped object from under the counter.

I studied the lighter for a few moments then handed it back, and took the case in my hands instead.

'Is it possible to have it engraved?'

'I should think so. Both items madam, or just the one?' The reason I ask is that it might make sense to have both inscribed, in case one should ever be mislaid.'

'Yes, yes, of course. I suppose that makes sense.'

'Well, what do you think?'

'They're very nice. May I?' I said, and took the lighter in my hands again. I ran my thumb over the polished-metal surface, thinking all the time how it would make such a perfect gift.

Henry was always complaining about running out of matches, and the old lighter he occasionally produced was almost on its last legs.

'Is it for someone special?'

'Yes,' I replied, and ran my thumb over the little metal barrel.

'You light it like this,' she said, taking the lighter from my outstretched hand.

It made a clicking noise then a long bright flame erupted from the top.

'You can adjust the height of the flame here,' she said, pointing towards a small serrated dial. 'Do you want to try again?'

'Yes,' I replied, and took the lighter in my hand.

I thumbed the roller bar mechanism several times, and on the fourth or fifth attempt I heard that clicking noise again and saw the bright flame.

'See. Quite easy, isn't it?'

I nodded a few times and handed the lighter back.

'For your husband, is it?'

I smiled and said, 'How much is it?'

'I'll have to speak with Mr Jones, the manager. He'll have a better idea how long it might take to make the engraving.'

'Of course.'

'... and the engraving will be extra.'

'Yes.'

'Now, if I could just have your name, I'll add it to our sales ledger.'

I gave the saleswoman my name and address, and after she had finished writing them in her book she said,

'And what engraving would you like?'

'Oh! I hadn't given it much thought.'

'That's alright, madam. Take your time. I'll speak with Mr Jones while you're making up your mind.'

She turned and walked along the length of the counter towards a door at the end.

'There's no need,' I said. 'I know what I'd like the inscription to be.'

She stopped and turned to face in my direction. 'Yes, madam.'

'H.M.'

'Just the two letters on each then, madam?'

'Yes. H.M. will do just nicely,' I said.

*

Pipe-smoker began his story. He told me of his family and how they had ravaged nature for profit, and how the village people bore terrible scars and illnesses, and how those illnesses persisted, even up to that very day. He told me again of the vast riches amassed by the family whilst all about them suffered. And from this wealth, the family built another two houses, just like Millrace.

'Millrace was one of three?' I asked.

'Yes,' he replied, and went on to tell me of their lavish lives. All was well until each of them had children of their own, and when each child came of age, they staked their claim on the wealth of the family. One child, in particular, Charles, was unscrupulous and mean. He was the eldest of his brood, and on reaching the age of eighteen, he became heir to his father's dynasty.

On his father's death, he evicted his siblings from the house, and sent them away to boarding schools abroad. Well, this caused consternation in the family, Pipe-smoker explained, and when his surviving relations confronted him, Charles had a great wall built, like that of the gable-end of a grand house, so that he could no longer see the estates of his relations. Since the mill was on the land on which he laid claim, he controlled the comings and goings of people and materials too. There was a sort of standoff between all of them and things came to a head when Charles announced he would marry. He was to marry a daughter of a merchant of Venice, a woman who was engaged to his cousin, Alexander. At this time, a woman came from the village, and begged Charles to pay the villagers compensation. He refused. It was said, Pipe-smoker continued, that the woman was an elder of the village, and known to have possessed certain magical powers.

'I know what you're going to say,' I said, noticing that in the thrall of his story I had been holding my breath. 'You're going to tell me that she put a spell on Charles.'

'Worse,' Pipe-smoker said. 'The woman cast a spell on the house, the woman to whom he was to be wed, and on all the progeny of Charles' line. And Charles would live to see this terrible legacy bear fruit before his eyes.'

'There's no such thing as spells,' I said.

'Would you like me to go on?' He said.

'Yes,' I replied, eager for more.

'Charles did indeed marry Francesca. That was her name. Francesca Roveri. She was very beautiful. Even though Charles had been ostracised by the rest of his family it was said by maids, and servants alike, that they were a very happy couple. The business continued to grow and grow, and Charles became even wealthier than he had previously been. His lawyers ensured that he wrested control of the entire company from the rest of his siblings, and his extended family, several of whom died in mysterious circumstances.'

I noticed that I was holding my breath again and shifted in my seat to stretch. I heard the storm grow stronger as the wind shook the window glass.

I pulled my coat about my shoulders and waited.

'Charles and Francesca had two children, a boy and girl, twins, the girl older than the boy by no more than a few minutes, yet poor Francesca died giving birth to the boy. Charles inconsolable. The girl was sickly you see, and the boy, well, the boy was the cause of his mother's death in his father's eyes.'

'And the girl?' I asked, even more intrigued now.

'I'll get to that,' he said. 'But before I do, I'll explain what happened to Charles. You see, Charles was increasingly convinced that the old woman's curse had come to pass. His wife had died.

160

His daughter was sick, and his son eventually ran away to sea. His relatives ostracised him. He turned increasingly to alcohol and rarely left the house.'

'Poor man,' I said aloud.

'The man who comes here to hear you play is my father. My father's name is Charles. Now you see the irony of course.'

'The irony of what?'

'We two are trapped, Father and I. Trapped here in this house. Perhaps it's the curse.'

'I don't believe in such things,' I said, and suddenly remembered the fate which had befallen me. 'It's a silly old wive's tale.'

'Yet, here we all are.'

Just then the drawing-room door opened.

'There you are,' Mrs Butler announced. 'Whatever are you doing?'

I waited for a moment before replying. 'I was just listening to the story of this house.'

'As you are probably aware,' she said quickly changing the subject, 'the weather has changed. Where this snowstorm came from I shall never know, but the Lord works in mysterious ways. There is no other option, I'm afraid, but you will have to remain here, at the house, until it passes. The automobile, for what it's worth, cannot travel in such conditions. I have arranged a room.'

'But my father will want to know where I have gotten to,' I said. 'He will be worried if I don't return.'

'I'm sorry, but there's nothing for it. There is already quite a blanket of snow on the ground. You are here now. You are safe. You will be fed and have a warm bed for the night. You should give thanks for the kindness shown.'

'Yes, of course,' I replied, my voice faltering a little. 'I am very

161

glad of the kindness. Will you please let Master Charles know I am very thankful?'

Mrs Butler harrumphed loudly, as if to dismiss me.

'I will send someone to fetch you once the dinner is ready. Meanwhile, you will remain here. I will send in tea.'

'I thought I might stretch my legs,' I said.

'That is out of the question,' Mrs Butler replied sternly. 'What will you see that you cannot already see?' Mrs Butler said.

I'm not sure if she meant her words to be so cold. There was truth in what she said of course, but I was beginning to feel a little like a bird in a box. A little jaunt about the house would give me more of a sense of things as they were, and I could conjure up an image in my mind of everything.

'Of course,' I replied, 'you're perfectly correct. I don't want to be a further nuisance.'

I heard the door close before I had a chance to say anything more.

'I think she likes you,' Pipe-smoker said. 'I can show you about,. We can take one of the secret passages again.'

'We better not. Anyway, you were telling me your story.'

'Yes, yes, I was, wasn't I?'

click-click

Smoke wafted towards me.

'I went away, you know. Far away. I wanted to be far away from Father, and this house. My travels brought me to Indo-China. That was before the war. I was in Singapore when hostilities began. You've heard of the Naga, of course?'

I shook my head, 'No, I replied.'

'Nagaland,' he said. 'Like England. Nagaland.'

'Nagaland,' I repeated like a child learning the word for the first time.

162

The sound of the snow pelting the window had diminished, replaced instead by a sort of eerie calm.

'Has it stopped snowing,' I asked.

'No,' he said. 'It's heavier now. The wind has died and the snow is falling straight down.'

'Would you describe it to me? I want to imagine it in my mind.'

'It's pure and white. Everything is covered. I once heard such a scene described as God's quilt covering the land. For just a moment it gives the impression of absolute perfection in the world.'

'I'm sorry,' I said. 'I've distracted you from your story. You were telling me about Nagaland.'

He puffed on his pipe and inhaled the smoke, and made this sort of smacking sound.

'I wished I had seen them as I wanted to see them, under different circumstances, but it didn't happen like that. Vast areas of the jungle had been devastated, their lands taken from them by one side, then the other. The enemy had enslaved the men to work on their railroad. The women they had used as concubines. The children became orphans and had to fend for themselves. I saw first-hand from the air, what I did not understand before, the devastation of a world on fire.'

Circumstances were difficult on the home front. There was rationing of course, and those interminable visits from the Committee, and the melancholy sound of hobnail boots on a gravel road. There were snide remarks too from the women who worked at the greengrocer's, Miss Worth and Miss Penney. I didn't know people could be so cruel. To think that they might once have treated me as their equal. Worthless and Penniless I called them. I could survive the Miss Worth's and Miss Penney's of the world. I was made of sterner stuff than that. It sounded like it was much worse in places such as Nagaland.

'I should explain how I got to fly missions over the jungle. As I was saying, I was in Singapore when the war began …'

Pipe-smoker's words faded into the background and I was lost in thoughts of snow. I thought of the eerie peacefulness. It was just like the day Henry revealed the truth to me. It was snowing that day too.

CHAPTER TWELVE

How silly I was. A silly young woman with notions and music, then Henry told me the truth of it all. I had wanted to run away, but the snow, the snow and the truth had stopped me from leaving. I remembered that it was heavy, the streets packed with a thick blanket, and not a soul about. I was standing by the window, with a narrow view of the park across the street through the blackout blinds. We were in a shabby old place, a room rented for just such a rendezvous.

Perhaps that should have been my first clue; always a shabby old room in some out of the way place. Dinner in a quiet café, then fumbling in a darkened doorway trying to put the key in the latch.

I had known Henry for six months by that time and not a day went by when I didn't ask myself the question that he would someday have to answer. Then we would arrive at another shabby little place, never his or mine, and I would ask myself the question again. Is there someone else?

I remembered he came to stand next to me. I was shivering a little from the draft blowing in from a crack in the windowpane. He placed his jacket around my bare shoulders and rested his chin at the nape of my neck, then he held me as we stood there and watched as searchlights went up across the London night sky, illuminating the snow as it fell.

'There won't be any bombing tonight,' he whispered. 'The weather's too bad.'

I didn't say anything in reply. I was waiting and perhaps he sensed it.

'There's something I need to tell you,' he said matter-of-factly.
click-click

That sound had somehow come to irritate me, ever-so slightly. I don't know why.

'Yes.'

'It's a rather delicate situation.,' he said, and blew a cloud of smoke over his shoulder.

'Don't you think you should move over there,' I said. 'In case the air raid warden sees the ember.'

'You're right. of course,' Henry said, releasing his hold, and retreating to the opposite side of the room.

I returned to gazing through the crack in the curtain, and watched the snowflakes landing on the window pane, and dissolving before my eyes. I could hear Doris' fateful words echoing around in my head. All the good ones are already spoken for, she'd said.

'Who is she?' I eventually said, without looking around.

'Darling, you know that I'm so very fond of you.'

'Fond of me?'

'You know what I mean,' he said.

I heard his footsteps moving towards me again.

'Don't Henry. Leave me be.'

'You don't understand,' he said, turning me about so that his face was close to mine.

'No. No I don't,' I said, meeting his gaze.

'The truth of it, darling, is that, well, there's no easy way to say this, but I'm married you see. You must understand that it's an unhappy marriage. Sarah ...'

I heard the name drop like such a heavy thing and land with a dull thud in my brain.

'Why don't you leave her then ... this Sarah of yours?' I snapped.

I felt worse then. Sarah, a name to go with his infidelity, and I, the *other* woman. I freed myself from his grip and went to the armchair where I had hung my clothes and hurriedly began to dress.

'All these months, Henry. Allowing me to love you. Knowing that there was always something—though never knowing exactly what. Let's call it intuition.'

'Didn't you hear what I said? It's an unhappy marriage. It has been since the very start.'

'Then why did you marry *her* in the first place?'

I didn't want to say her name again. To say it was to give this guilty feeling, which was suddenly creeping over me, more power.

'It's complicated. Perhaps another time. Look ...'

I saw him come towards me again and hurried to fix the buttons on my blouse.

'Don't ...'

'I wanted to tell you because you deserve to know,' he said, and held my arms tight by my sides.

'Let go. You're hurting me.'

'I'm sorry darling, I didn't mean to ...' he said, and loosened his grip.

I felt this sudden urge to pinch his cheek. Why, I shall never know. It just came over me. So, I did. I pinched his cheek for just a moment, and felt the tiny, rough stubble between my fingertips, and then I released it and watched the spot where I had pinched the thin folds of skin together, return to its normal pinkish colour.

'I'm sorry …'

He grabbed my arm and brought the palm of my hand to his lips, and kissed it. He kissed each finger one at a time, then the back of my hand, and as he did, I felt the minor storm, which had been building inside me subside into a nothing, a wisp of wind on a summer's day, and I let him. I let him kiss me, drawing me close, one arm around my waist, then his breath upon my neck, his fingers unbuttoning my blouse again. My heart was beating, *ta-thump, ta-thump, ta-thump*. His lips met mine again.

'Henry …'

He didn't reply, except by placing another kiss on my lips, and nose and cheeks, and forehead and I weakened in his arms, and let it happen. I wrapped my arms around him and felt the soft mattress rise up to meet our twisting, contorting bodies once more.

When it was over, that last groan subsided into a deep sigh of contentment, he rolled to his side of the bed and lay there, staring at the ceiling, breathing deeply, closing his eyes shut, one hand resting on his chest, his fingers intertwined in mine with the other. I worked my fingers through his thick chest hair, and placed my head against his shoulder and watched him. Watched him, because I knew he was somewhere else in a world slowly spinning out of his control.

'What is it?'

'I love you,' he said, and turned towards me.

He had never uttered those words to me before. Love.

'There's something more, something you haven't told me. And it's not about *her*.'

'Sarah.'

'Don't say her name.'

He looked away as if he had been scolded.

'I remember Doris' words. All the good ones are already spoken for, she said.'

'And yet you stayed. Why?'

I felt hot tears welling in my eyes and pushed myself away to sit, my legs pulled up so I could fold my arms across my knees and rest my chin on top.

'Don't you know by now?'

He reached his hand across, stroked my back, and rolled in my direction.

'Darling, there's no need to cry.'

'There's every reason. Don't you see?'

I pulled away from him then and swung my legs over the side of bed until my feet reached the cold floorboards. I stood, and for just a fleeting moment a terrible feeling washed over me, like a premonition, or a sense of deja-vu, and I had to steady myself against the bedside table, with its little oil lamp perched on top.

'I've been given an assignment,' Henry said, in a very matter of fact way. 'I'm being sent overseas.'

I felt nauseous and light-headed again.

'Overseas?'

'Yes, I'm not supposed to tell anyone, but, well it's the Far East. I wanted you to know the truth so that there would be no more lies between us. I intend to divorce Sarah when I return. Then we can be married.'

'Married. Did you really think …?'

'You will marry me, won't you?'

'No. I can't,' and a thought flashed through my head and disappeared just as quickly without my having a chance to interrogate it. Then another thought came to mind. That tune, *Here Comes the Bride*, and, 'Yes.'

'That's my girl.'

'Your girl?'

'I didn't mean it like that. You know what I meant.'

'I couldn't possibly dress in …' I said, and then tears came again.

'Oh darling. What is it?' he said and gripped my hand in his.

'There's no such thing as fairy tales and happy endings, is there? I mean, for a moment I saw an image of myself, all in white, and you at my side. A nondescript little room and the pair of us standing there, with a rather solemn-looking man wearing a fabricated sense of the occasion on his face, eager to usher us over the threshold.'

'It wouldn't be like that, darling. It would be …'

'What?'

'When do you leave for this Far East place of yours?'

'That's the damned thing,' he said breathily. 'I leave the day after tomorrow. Can't you just see your way past all of this? I can arrange everything when I return … the divorce, then whatever you wish. We can do anything you want.'

I pulled my blouse about my shoulders and buttoned it closed with trembling fingers and fussily tightened my skirt about my waist again, all the time avoiding Henry's gaze. I had this sudden need for air to clear my head, and time to think about what it all meant.

'I leave on Monday from Victoria Station,' he said.

'This is worse than any bombing raid,' I said and put on my coat and scarf, and stood there wondering what to do next. I slung my gas mask over my shoulder.

'Stay.'

'I have to get back. I'm already late.'

'There's a clock, just past the turnstiles, and a kiosk selling newspapers. I'll be there, under the clock, at nine, waiting for you. You'll be there. Won't you? 'Make me a promise.'

'This is all so sudden. I need to think.'

I gathered the rest of my belongings and made my way to the door, turning just once to see him standing there, the braces of his trousers hanging loosely by his sides, one hand thumbing the lighter I had bought him, the other holding a cigarette to his lips.

He had that expectant look, as if I was going to give some indication, an answer there and then.

'Oh Henry,' I said meekly and placed a trembling hand on the doorknob.

'Why couldn't it be someone else? Why does it have to be you? This damned war.'

' I'll call you tomorrow. Maybe you'll have considered my proposal by then,' he said as I twisted the handle and pulled the door towards me.

'Yes,' I said, without turning around.

I made my way into the narrow hallway and down the stairs, trying all the time to hold back the tears, which filled my eyes. The landlady sat at a tiny reception desk, unwinding rollers from her hair and checking herself in a handheld mirror.

'Are you leaving us already luv'?' she said, without looking up.

'Yes,' I said and continued to the door.

'You'll freeze your knackers off out there,' she said. 'Haven't you been watching the weather? Don't expect you've *'ad* time,' she said and gave a little cackle of laughter to go with her underhand remark.

I pulled the door towards me without answering and stepped outside. The snow was already ankle deep as I trudged my way in the direction of the nearest tube station. I turned to look back just once and saw the building was in darkness. The blackout blinds were still in place. As I reached the station, an air raid warden stepped forward.

'That's a cold one, luv',' he said, shining his blackout torch to light the way towards the steep stairwell down to the tube. 'Be careful as you go.'

'Thank you.'

Someone brushed past me, a dark silhouette against the dimmed light of the stairwell. Then another. And another. Hurrying for their trains. I descended into the station and a hot updraft greeted my arrival. There was a smell of compressed bodies and sweat. There was the stench of urine, and worse. I continued on, going even deeper into the bowels of the station.

There was the high-pitched squealing noise of metal on metal as a train entered the station, and the sound of a train accelerating as it left. Mechanically I pushed through the turnstile and continued to the platform. As I waited for my train, I stared blankly at the people opposite waiting for theirs. I looked from the platform to the tracks, leading from the dim light to the dark tunnels at each end and decided upon a game of chance.

If the train arrived first at the platform opposite, I determined then I would not marry Henry. If my train arrived first, then it was decided, I would marry Henry and damn the consequences. I waited, nervously twiddling my thumbs, until the sound of an approaching train drew my attention. Then there was that grating noise of brakes applied, and a feeling of pressure as air was forced through the tunnel ahead of the train. Just then, the strangest thing happened. The two trains arrived at the station at the exact same time. That was the damned thing of it, in the end.

CHAPTER THIRTEEN

'That was in nineteen-forty. We were running out of fuel, you see, so our commanding officer made the decision that we should fly north until we reached the relative safety of Burma. When the invasion of Burma came, it forced us further north again. We eventually reached Nagaland.'

'I'm sorry, but you were flying where?'

'Weren't you listening at all? My squadron had been ordered to fly to Burma. The Japanese were driving north at a ferocious pace, burning, and killing everything in their path. I could see from the air what I was missing from the ground. Whole tracts of forest destroyed and laid bare, a road snaking its way through the jungle. There were rumours that prisoners of war were being used, as a sort of slave labour. It was harder to discern that from where I sat, in the relative safety of the cockpit of an aircraft. It was true though, that there must have been an army of thousands at work below, like ants, burning and clearing. I could only imagine the suffering of those poor buggers, whoever they were.'

I shuddered at the thought.

'On one of those missions, I had just crossed over the border when my plane was hit by ground fire, damaging one of the engines. I thought if I killed the fuel supply and went into a dive then the fire might extinguish itself. So, I put the craft into a deep dive and watched the flames go out. With thick black smoke billowing from the engine, I pulled the nose up. Just as I did, I heard a *ping-ping* sound as rounds from the ground punctured the fuselage. The fuel tank exploded in flames. I didn't have time to try any of the usual manoeuvres before the whole damned thing was burning. Burning, you see. Burning, burning, burning ...' he said and I could feel hot tears welling in my eyes as he spoke.

click-click

'It must be really hard ... to remember these things in such detail.'

'I need to tell my story. I need to ...'

'All right then. If you insist.'

'I tried the canopy but it wouldn't budge. Something had jammed it in place. Then the fire reached the cockpit floor. How terrible that is in such a confined space. Entombed. It's like being fed into a crematorium as the little gas burners flicker into life, one after the other, and you are stuck inside your coffin trying desperately to get out, before the door slams shut forever. I remember asking myself if that was it. If that's what my brief life was all about. To arrive at that moment between one world and the next. I decided that *I* should take my fate in my hands. I took my pistol to shoot myself, rather than be burned alive. I was stopped only because the plane suddenly pitched and rolled and I found myself upside down with flames lapping at my legs. I aimed at my head but put two rounds into the plexiglas instead. Air rushed in. I reached my arm outside, found the clasp, which was jammed in place, and pulled it towards me. The canopy fell away from the rest of the machine. So too my pistol. I grabbed at my safety harness and pressed the release and as I did the whole aircraft exploded into flame.'

I found myself taking a deep intake of breath and holding it in as Pipe-smoker continued with his story. What a terrible vision, I thought, to be like a human torch, the sky above, and the ground below, and no one to hold your hand.

'I fell then, screaming and crying out, with nobody to hear me. I fell, and fell, until my parachute opened, and wrenched me skywards again. When I looked up, from behind my goggles, I saw that the parachute was also on fire; shredding and peeling apart like my skin. When I looked down, I saw the jungle canopy racing up to meet me. You see, the parachute was not much use then; merely strings held together as the silk burned bright, and so I fell, faster and faster with every passing moment, accelerating towards the ground. I could see it happening before my eyes, flashes of bright orange and yellow, and black. For a few brief and desperate moments I watched my own immolation thinking that I wouldn't reach the ground fast enough for the misery to end.'

click-click-click

I turned my head quickly to my right. There was a barely perceptible whiff of gasoline. He was beside me. I could reach out and touch him.

'I still reek of it,' he said. 'I still reek of gasoline.'

click-click-click

'I'm sorry,' I said.

'I fell through the top layer,' he continued, 'then the parachute wires became entangled with branches and trees, and the thought flashed through my mind that I would linger there in the canopy like a candle on a Christmas tree, burning bright, forever forgotten. But I didn't. I continued to fall. I fell until the trees gave way to nothing. Then splash, I was in water. It was a fast-flowing river. Over and over I tumbled, dragged along by the current. It was so fast that I did not get a chance to take a breath

175

before I disgorged onto a flat, muddy riverbank. I rolled onto my back and stared skyward, and saw nothing but blackness. I don't know how long I lay there. The pain had become so bad I must have lost consciousness at some point. When I came around I heard the sound of voices. "Shoot me," I said. "Shoot me." The voices continued a jibber-jabber until I sensed movement. I waved my arm to tell them to go away, but instead of going away, I felt someone grab my hand. I screamed. That must have frightened them. Then a few moments later, someone grabbed at my other hand, then my feet. I caught glimpses, a face, eyes wide like saucers, a bandolier, bare feet. They tied me to a long bamboo pole, like a pig on a spit. I vomited then and the smell of gasoline pinched my nostrils, and oh the misery, the terrible, painful misery of it all. Christ himself would not have endured it.'

'You were saved.'

'As I hung there, upside down, enduring every movement through gritted teeth, I saw their world as they would see me, through cracks in the jungle canopy, brief flashes of blue, then the darkness would return. After a time I could not bear it anymore, and started to make quite a fuss, only for one of them to hit me over the head several times, until I suppose I blacked out completely.'

'How cruel,' I said, 'after all you had already suffered. Oh, how terribly cruel.'

'Perhaps it was a blessing. I suffered terrible burns you see. I knew things were bad, so bad I would gladly have died, there and then. If I had my pistol I would have ended it.'

click-click-click

'You mustn't say that. It is a sin to think such things.'

'Have you never thought of it?'

'Never,' I shot back. 'Never.'

176

I lied of course. The thought had entered my mind many times. I wondered how God could be so cruel as to condemn me to the darkness, when I once had the benefit of sight. Where was the justice in that?

'I awoke in the night and thought for just a moment that I had already died. It wasn't to be. I was alone, in one of their huts you see, surrounded by the darkness. It was too painful to move. When I allowed my eyes to become accustomed to the gloom, I could make out the dimensions of the hut, mere six or seven feet in diameter. When I moved my head a little side to side, I felt a gentle swaying action as I did and could determine only that I was suspended, in a sort of hammock. I did not know it then but a jungle rat had made its way from the roof of the hut to the hammock and was seeking out exposed pieces of my burnt flesh on which it was determined to gorge itself. If it wasn't for the arrival of one of my minders then I would have surely lost even more fingers and toes.'

'A rat, oh my god,' I said. I imagined the creature and the horror of it all. I have known some rats to be the size of a kitten, larger even. What terrible little creatures.

'Yes, such a creature exists there too. My saviour came in the shape of a young boy of the tribe. Rama was his name. He chased the rat that night, the next, and the next after that. During the day, women of the tribe came to the hut, bathed my wounds, and covered me in oil, from head to toe. At first, the slightest of touches would send pain coursing through my body and I would lose consciousness. Then days, maybe by the end of the first week, it became more bearable, and each day I remained there I got better and better, until perhaps a month had passed and I could sit upright. The men of the tribe would come to inspect my progress; fierce-looking warriors who carried spears and hung the shrivelled heads of monkeys from the end of them. They would discuss my progress amongst themselves. Often there was angry debate, and I thought that was it, they were going to kill me. Instead the women continued to treat me, and Rama came to chase the rat away.'

'You had no conversation with them?'

'I tried to speak, but no words came out.'

'Could you eat?'

'Just soups and broths, and even that was terribly painful.'

It was just then that I heard three hard knocks at the door and the sound of it opening.

'Hello, miss,' a voice said. 'I've come to bring you some sandwiches and tea.'

I heard her approach. She was carrying a tray in her hands. I knew this because of the rattle of china.

'Thank you,' I replied.

'Will I set your tea down here?'

'Is there a table?'

'Oh, I forgot, miss. Yes, there's a table to your right.'

'Thank you,' I said after her, then the door closed and we were alone again.

I reached out and felt the metal tray and on it a plate with several thin sandwiches. I took one in my fist and nibbled at the edges like a little dormouse.

'I wonder if I might ask why you hide away when Daisy comes into this room,' I said, between mouthfuls of bread and Marmite.

'The girl faints at the sight of me,' he said bitterly. 'It's the burns you see. She's not had to deal with such horror before. That's why she knocked to give me warning that she was coming in.'

'I'm sorry. I didn't mean to pry again.'

I was slowly realising that I was there, not for the Master's entertainment, but as a companion to a lonely young man who could no longer venture into the world without gawks and stares. I too had found myself in such circumstances; a whisper here and there, poor thing they'd say, look at her now, terribly sad, and on it went. In the city, the pain of such sleights didn't have the same effect. Perhaps it was because of the cacophony of voices, the anonymity of the city, the busyness of the war effort, or the number of similarly damaged souls floating about the ravaged landscape, that people didn't bother to notice, or even care.

It was just such insensitivity, which caused me to return home permanently, to the countryside I knew best, out of further danger, only to find myself the subject of idle gossip, whispered loudly to my ear. One cruelty, simply replaced by another.

I saw Pipe-smoker in that light too, a damaged person, caught between an almost death, and an almost life, unable to transcend into either one. I stirred the tea, poured myself a cup, and thought for just a moment about the snow again.

I thought too about Father, and Mr Fallada, and the top field left unploughed.

Is it still snowing?' I asked, taking another sandwich in my fist.

'Yes. It's heavier now.'

'Heavier?'

'The snow has begun to drift too, now that the wind has picked up again.'

Almost on cue, I heard the window glass, as one gust after another assailed it. I heard a door or window shutter perhaps banging against something, as if it too wanted to get inside out of the storm. I wished there was a fire at which I could have warmed my bones, but they had neglected to light one, or it was so insufficient as to be useless against the freezing cold.

'Are we quite safe here?' I asked.

'Perfectly,' he replied, and lit his pipe again.

click-click

'Can I tell you something?' I said.

'What's that?'

'I think I know how you feel.'

'You do?'

'Yes. I believe I do. You see, I can feel the eyes upon me, the vacant stares and sideways glances.'

'The gawkers.'

'They think I don't know they're watching me, but I do know. I daresay I would probably do the same thing in different circumstances. The world is cruel like that.'

'I was still very weak when I came home and took to my bed for several weeks. My system you see was still fighting off one damned infection, or another. When I eventually felt well enough I asked Burrows to bring me into the garden. The roses were in full bloom. It seems such a trivial thing but for the first time I found myself unable to find any beauty in the sight of them.'

'I've always found that roses always look best when cut at the stem and stuffed in a vase.'

'It wasn't just the roses. It was everything really. Maybe I was just feeling sorry for myself, but I couldn't make myself content with anything, the roses, the long meadow, the fresh air, so I ordered Burrows to take me back inside, and I haven't been out there since.'

I let my fingers play distractedly with the edge of the plate; searching for something to do, tempted for the briefest of moments to finish the nibbled sandwich, but then a memory came to me instead. Images flashed before my eyes of the burned and injured. Another night of bombing over London. Balham station packed to the rafters and a woman giving birth amongst the throng. Overhead the dull *thump-thump* of explosions echoed through the tunnel and shook the ground where we stood. Dust and fragments of the tiled ceiling landed on our tin hats and made a pinging noise. The helmet's strap digging deep into the flesh beneath my chin causing me to swear under my breath. I remembered a boy, no more than six or seven, lost in the crowd, crying out for his mother, and Doris gripping my hand with fear, her fingers tight between mine as we made our way to an unoccupied patch of ground at the far end of the platform where it sloped away towards the darkness of the tunnel entrance. From the dim depths, wide and frightened, saucer-like eyes glared back at us, describing by their number how overcrowded the tunnel had become.

'Doris …'

'You were you saying something?'

Pipe-smoker's words jolted me back to the present.

'I was remembering something,' I said in a low and breathless voice. 'I'm sorry; please continue with your story.'

He made a tamping sound, then *click-click* and moments later the smell of pipe-smoke wafted towards me again.

'There isn't much else to tell, I'm afraid. I spend my days in splendid isolation, free of the societal demands, which would normally be required of someone such as myself. Who would like to visit someone like me now? A beast. That's what I've become. It's almost as if I have some terrible disease. I'll have you know, there was a time when I had to beat the ladies back with a cricket bat, and now, now … well, you would have to be blind, to …'

The words had already spilled from his lips before he realised his error, and by then it was too late.

'I didn't mean for it to sound so cruel. It's a figure of speech.

That's all. A figure of speech. Won't you forgive me?'

I made an effort to get to my feet then thought the better of it.

'We have similar circumstances, I suppose. It seems such a tragic thing, don't you think, you were once handsome and debonair and I was once attractive …?'

'You still are,' he said.

'No man would come near me now.'

'I don't think …'

'It's true. It doesn't matter anyway. I'm waiting for someone. He's away to the war.'

I thought about the horrible scar that ran across my face, where the surgeon had made an incision in an effort to save the sight in the eye. It was no use in the end and I lost the sight in both eyes, and had an ugly scar to match the shrapnel-mottled skin on my forehead to add to my woes.

'This fire doesn't seem to be up to much. Does it?' he said, changing the subject rather suddenly. 'The room is so draughty, don't you think?'

I heard the sound of a poker on a grate then the crackle and hiss as a log took light.

'Come sit by the fire,' he said. 'I want to tell you the rest of my story.'

CHAPTER FOURTEEN

I made my way to a space close to the fireplace and sat in one of the high-backed armchairs. I was too close to it at first and found myself moving a few feet back such was the heat.

'You must understand that it is so very important that I tell you my story. It will help to know the rest too,' he said. 'You see the Naga, you remember the Naga ... Yes. Of course you do. They were most kind to me. Kinder than one might expect under such trying conditions. I was very close to death those first few days and weeks. If there had been a priest there, I suppose he would have anointed me. Priests can be useful at those times one is close to one's creator, a sort of reassurance, a spirit guide. Most cultures have something similar I think. They did bring someone to me. I can't remember much about it as I was quite delirious most of the time, but I have a memory of someone, with wide eyes staring down at me from above, shaking his head side to side and waving a stick in the air. It's funny now that I remember it, that this man, a medicine man, I assume, was shaking his head and his stick to summon his gods, when I thought he was telling the assembly that there was no hope. His *no* was actually a *yes*. I was going to pull through. The gods would see to it. And pull through I did, despite my terrible injuries. I suppose you think I am making all of it up, but I'm not. What would be the point?'

I imagined what it must be like in those terrible moments, the flames consuming the body, and then the aftermath, screaming in unbearable pain, wishing for death, then …

'Well, I'm not. I'm living proof that a man can walk through the flames of hell and return to tell the tale. I was with the Naga for about two months, it could have been longer because I lost all track of time and space, occupied as I was in my own world of torment and daily ritual, when they brought another man to the hut. He was English too, but I didn't know that at first. You see, he was in a delirium. He'd been shot. Tribesmen had carried him through the jungle for days and nights until they reached the village, but at that stage, it was too late. Gangrene had set in by then. He was tall. I could tell this at the time only from his position in the hut. I suspect that whatever time he had spent in the jungle hadn't allowed for pleasantries, such as shaving, as he had quite a long, scraggly beard. He was very thin, almost skeletal. I noticed his uniform was ragged, frayed at the edges, but I could see he was Naval Service, officer rank, a commander, I believe. A holster hung limply from his hip. I could see it still held a service revolver. I remember envying him for that one thing. I thought to take it from him while he slept, but I was too weak. Yes, I would have used it to end my miserable life, once and for all, but it didn't happen like that.'

'It's just too terrible to think about.'

I could feel hot tears welling in my eyes again and a sort of uncontrollable quivering of my bottom lip. I stood, unsteadily at first, unsure of where to go, the heat of the fire was building and the room was becoming increasingly warm and claustrophobic, like the jungle Pipe-smoker had transported me to, with his tale of burned men and headhunters.

'I should go.'

'But you must know,' he said, and I felt his hand grip my forearm. 'It's important that you know.'

'No,' I replied. 'No, I do not want to know any more of your story. I'm feeling unwell.'

I felt his grip loosen and used the moment to tap my cane, searching for a path to manoeuvre through. I almost fell over a footstool in my haste but a few moments later I found my way to the door. In a panic, I felt for the handle and pulled the door towards me. It opened with ease, but only because Mrs Butler was on the way in at the same time.

'Where are you going in such a hurry?' Mrs Butler said.

'I must leave, I said. I must leave now.'

'What are you talking about girl? Have you gone a little mad, as well as blind?'

I could feel a little anger rising in me then and pushed by her as I attempted my escape.

'I can't stay here,' I said. 'I will walk, even if it takes me all night and day. I will walk home.'

'You silly girl,' Mrs Butler said. 'Mr Burrows.'

'Yes Mrs Butler.'

'I'm afraid our guest is not feeling terribly well,' Mrs Butler said. 'I'll fetch a sedative. Please, show her to the guest room.'

'I don't want a potion. I want to go home. This house …'

'Now, now, miss. Mrs Butler will take care of you. Let me show you to the guest room.'

'Oh. Mr Burrows. You must hear me out. You said it before. You told me that this house has a history to it.'

'Indeed it does, miss. Indeed it does.'

I felt his grip upon my arm. 'Daisy, come and help me here,' he said.

'Yes, Mr Burrows.'

I felt more hands grip my free arm.

'It's just this way, miss,' Daisy said. 'Perhaps if you take some rest then we can see about getting you home in the morning.'

I felt my resolve slip away then. 'Yes, perhaps if I lie down I will feel a little better. It's such a shocking story. You all know it of course,' I said.

'The first step is here,' Mr Burrows said.

I felt the step with the toe of my shoe and as we climbed the stairs I could sense disquiet between my two companions.

'We're almost there,' Mr Burrows added.

We had reached the top step when I felt suddenly unsteady, like someone finding their sea legs for the first time. The unsteadiness worsened and I felt myself swaying back and forth until I could no longer resist the pull of gravity and plunged headlong into the dark abyss.

I heard Mr Burrow's anxious voice calling after me. 'Miss. Miss …' he said.

Then there was nothing. Nothing at all.

*

When I came around, I was lying down with a firm mattress and pillow beneath me, and a soft-textured blanket at my fingertips. I wiggled my toes. Someone had removed my shoes. It must have been a dream, I thought, but then I heard whispered voices growing steadily louder as my senses returned.

'I've given her a little sedative to help.'

'Do you think that's wise?'

'I don't think it will do her any harm.'

'It's you that knows best about these things, Mrs Butler.'

'Yes, well. I've spoken to the Master.'

'If you don't mind me saying, but the Master can't exactly speak his mind, one way or the other.'

'I would appreciate it if you kept your counsel on such matters.'

'Yes, Mrs Butler. Of course.'

'Now, I'm sure you have other duties to perform.'

'Yes, Mrs Butler.'

'There is much to be attended to. See that the rest of the staff has taken care of their tasks. You must be my eyes and ears, Mr Burrows. I'm afraid I will be kept quite busy. She'll need a guide. I'll need to reassure her.'

'Yes, Mrs Butler.'

'What is wrong with me?'

I found it so hard to form the words. A sort of numb, tingly feeling coursed through my body.

I made to get up, only to feel a pair of hands pressing my shoulders down again.

'Allow the potion to take effect.'

I gave in to the sleepy feeling, though a persistent, nagging voice in my head continued its hum. The voice was telling me that it was not a good idea. Not a good idea to sleep at all.

*

The essential aspect of a dream is whether you ever possessed the sense of it in the first place. The dream is in a vacuum. I saw, in my dream, with the perfect clarity of a soul sure of purpose, who I really was, and then who I never was, the woman with sight, the world once revealed to me. Then back into the darkness, I plunged. It is the dream of dreams, a voice said, before I felt myself blasted into space and the sudden, sharp shock of dissolution and the fragmentation of my soul, scattered like thousands of particles of space dust.

Am I dying?

That's not the question, the voice replied. We are all dying.

A wall of mirrors presents itself. In each one, I see myself differently.

Which one am I? I said.

Whichever one you want to be, came the reply.

Then I sit in the kitchen. Father is by the stove. He has his back to me. He is stirring something in a pot. He looks different than I had known him. Taller, perhaps. Thinner. Darker. He is smoking his pipe and humming a tune.

I know it. It is *Gymnopédie*.

Is it my porridge you're stirring? I ask.

Stew, he replied.

But you're not Father, I say, confused.

He turns then, slowly, and I see who he is. Before he has a chance to speak, I am transported through a tunnel, twisting and turning, across the boiling ocean to a green pasture. I float like a feather eventually coming to a gentle rest on a bed of flowers of many hues. I close my eyes and let the dream sleep take me.

CHAPTER FIFTEEN

'Good morning,' a voice said, and I sat bolt upright.

'You frightened me.'

'I didn't mean to, miss. It's just that Mrs Butler ordered me to come and wake you. It's almost nine.'

'Nine o'clock?'

'Yes, miss. You've been asleep for almost twelve hours. You must have been terribly tired.'

'Daisy, isn't it?'

'That's right, miss. Daisy Broom. My father's Mr Broom, the horses' groom.'

'And your mother?' I said, stretching my arms and legs.

'She's quite dead, miss. Died when I was a young 'un. It was just after that war. The last one, that is.'

'I'm sorry,' I said, fixing the pillows behind my head.

'At least it's stopped snowing,' Daisy said. 'There was an awful storm last night. I couldn't sleep a wink myself. Shutters were clattering and windows were groaning with the ferocity of it. I thought the house itself might fall down on our heads. Wouldn't be no harm either.'

I heard her pull the curtains and felt the sunlight on my face.

'You don't like it here, then?' I asked, stifling a yawn.

'It's not that, miss. The work is fine. I like my job. If you'd be so kind as to not mention any of this to Mrs Butler?'

'I won't,' I said.

'It's the house, miss. Ever since young Mr Charles returned, the Master hasn't been himself. I've heard him screaming, miss. In the middle of the night, this terrible roar. I'd hear Mr Burrows and Mrs Butler scurrying along the passageway, heading for the upstairs rooms.'

'The Master has bad dreams then?'

'Young Mr Charles, miss. Oh, I can't bear to think of it. I've seen him just once of course. Oh my, how terrible it must be, to be scarred like that. It gives me the heebie-jeebies, it does. And my father, Mr Broom, that is, well, he made sure we were all brought up right and sensible, taught to stomach most things, as you do. Well, I wouldn't last long in this job if I didn't know how to empty a chamber pot, and the like. It's the way of these old houses. They don't have the conveniences that newer houses have. Lavatories and the like. I think it was that first time, when young Mr Charles returned from the war and they were bringing him to his room. I caught sight of him, miss, and I must be truthful … Never did I think I'd see the like of it. It was a terrible shock. The poor young man. I told Mrs Butler. I told her that I couldn't be taking care of young Mr Charles. Oh, that was a day in Hell itself. But she relented in the end. Could see the sense of it, I suppose. Perhaps young Mr Charles got wind of it and understood, in his way. He is a kind soul I'm sure of it, but terribly troubled into the bargain. I suppose you've noticed his little habit.'

'The pipe.'

She leaned closer and said, 'Who would have thought it?' she sniggered.

'What do you mean?'

'He smokes that funny stuff, opium or something like that. Developed quite a habit, he has. I don't know where he gets it from. No, that's not entirely true. I know Mrs Butler organises it.'

'How do you know that?'

'I shouldn't really say.'

'It will be our secret, Daisy. I promise. After all, who could I tell?'

'All I know for sure is that every week a delivery arrives. I only know that because the place is all a flurry. They don't think I know.'

'Know …?'

'About the tunnel, of course.'

I played dumb and said, 'Tunnel?'

'I suppose it's only keeping with tradition … smuggling, miss. There's a tunnel running under the house. It leads to a boat dock. A boat arrives there laden with all sorts of goods. If only the authorities knew I'm sure they would lock us all up. Oh! I shouldn't have said that. You won't tell. Promise you won't tell. My father would have my guts, he would.'

I shook my head, 'Of course not, Daisy.'

It seemed the illicit trade that built the house continued through to the present times.

'Did you know young Mr Charles before?' I said.

'A little, miss. I was not in service then but I would see him from afar. We live in a cottage down by the river there. He was a handsome one. I'll tell you. I don't suppose I've ever spoken a word to him, but I've heard by reputation only that he was once a prize catch hereabouts. Don't suppose he's that now,' she said.

I heard her moving about, as if she was dusting or cleaning. There was a little creak and groan of floorboards then the sound of a match being struck and the scent of burning candle wax and sulphur.

'Just a little candle to take away the stale air. Can I tell you another secret, miss? It is a strange thing, but you see, one of my chores is to light the candles around the house, upstairs and downstairs, penny candles everywhere. The electric hasn't come this far you know. You would think, a big important house such as Millrace, and no electricity, but there you go. Anyway, where was I? I'd no sooner have a candle lit and wax a drippin' than I return a short time later to find the corridor dark and the candle snuffed. It's as if a ghostly breeze had come along and blown it out. But I have my own theories on it.'

'What would they be?' I asked.

'I think young Mr Charles snuffs them out. It's a reminder, I suppose.'

'Reminder?'

'A flickering flame.'

I remembered the drawing room and the open fire, the heat, and Pipe-smoker rattling the poker in the grate.

'I don't think it's young Mr Charles,' I said. 'When I was cold he stoked the fire in the drawing room.'

'That doesn't prove it's not him. Who else could it be?'

'I don't know,' I said. 'It does seem strange though. These old houses do have drafts everywhere. I suppose it's enough to keep the place from falling down on itself.'

'A draft? I doubt that, miss, unless there's drafts everywhere, down below, and up above.'

'I think someone has been teasing you,' I said.

'But who. Who would do such a thing? It's right creepy, is what it is. Ever since young Mr Charles returned it's been happening.'

'Well, if it is him as you say, then I'd say it's a game he plays, to keep himself from going mad.'

'A game?'

'Yes. It's not the fear of the fire but simply something to occupy his mind. He doesn't go outside. I'd expect I'd do the same.'

'I never thought of it like that, miss. It makes sense, I suppose.'

I felt a little breeze on my arms and remembered that I needed to dress. 'Can you fetch my clothes for me?'

'Yes, miss. They're just over here. I'll get them for you.'

I stretched out my arm and ran my fingers over my tweed skirt, and the silk blouse I had worn the previous day. I grew a little concerned that someone had taken the time to undress me, or perhaps I did it myself and didn't have a memory of it. I let my naked legs hang over the edge of the bed and for the first time felt the chill of the day.

'Have they cleared the snow from the drive?'

'I should think the men will set to work on it after all their other work has been seen to. Mrs Butler sent young Mr Burrows into the village to hire some of the locals to help with the clearing.'

I pulled my skirt about my waist and fixed the little metal clasp to keep it in place, and pulled my blouse about my shoulders.

'Have you seen my stockings?'

'They're right beside you, miss. I've laid them out on the bed.'

'Thank you,' I said.

I ran my hands over the bed sheet and once I found what I was looking for I set about putting them on, then placed my feet on the floor again. To my right I located my shoes and slipped them on then I marched in place. The room had a musty smell, as if it hadn't been occupied in some time.

Perhaps, I thought at the time, it was the reason that Daisy had set about dusting and moving things about.

'Whose room is this?' I asked.

'It was the young mistress' room, miss. I never met her but I've heard she was quite beautiful, just like her mother.'

'Where is she now?'

'She went away, miss.'

'Where?'

'I think she was sent away to a special school, miss.'

'A special school?'

'Yes, miss. Somewhere in the country, I heard.'

I suddenly felt a little queasy and had to sit down again.

'Is everything all right, miss?'

'Yes, yes, just a little light headed.'

'Shall I open the window, miss.'

'Yes, that would be good. Thank you, Daisy.'

I heard her huff and puff with the effort then I felt the sudden rush of cold air.

'It's quite cold, miss. Are you feeling better?'

'Yes, Daisy,' I replied, though in truth I was still feeling a little at odds with everything.

'Where was this school you spoke about, Daisy?'

'Why, I don't know, miss. I've heard Mr Burrows speak of it, but it was always in whispers. Mrs Butler was very stern whenever the subject arose. She reprimanded Mr Burrows several times. I've heard her do it, with my own two ears and all.'

'Have you seen my cane?'

'Right beside you, miss. Here I'll get it for you. Now, there you are,' she said.

I felt her cold fingers on the back of my hand. She held my hand for a moment, slowly opening the fingers, which were clenched tight, and eased the cane into my grip.

'Will that be all, miss? I'm afraid I have other duties to attend to this morning. I'll be back in a little while.'

'Yes, Daisy. Thank you. I can figure the rest out myself.'

I heard the sound of footsteps then the door opened and closed. I stood there for several minutes, dwelling on the situation, and wondering what to do.

Would Daisy remember to come for me?

Surely, she would, I thought.

What if she didn't?

I could make my way down that long staircase, and leave, just like that. There was the small matter of the snowfall, of course, but what of it?

I could tramp along by myself. Perhaps the roads were clear of snow. I navigated my way to the window, running my hand around its frame and sill, and drummed the window glass with my fingertips. I felt the cold breeze on my legs and arms, and little goose bumps forming at the chill.

I tried to imagine the scene, the white blanket of snow, the trees standing in awe, and the sea beyond pounding the rocks, and the big wall described to me, of which I had only the vaguest memory. Perhaps it had been covered over by ivy and time, blended back into the landscape, so that it was not as imposing as it had been. I imagined the village beyond the gates, the generations who had passed through the Big House, and mill; the mill wheel still turning, nothing more to mill, now just a mill stone marking time. And beyond the Big House and village, and along the road which wound its way to the crossroads, one way for Rashleigh, the other for the cliffs at Towey, and a reminder of the Salt Path to connect it all to Millrace and the sea. Somewhere out there was the small farm on the side of the hill and Father waiting, wondering what had become of me, like the day he waited for Mother to return but she never did. I wondered if he thought the same of me. That I would never return. I thought then that Father would come for me, or at least if he didn't come himself, that he would send Mr Fallada in his stead.

I had a vision of Mr Fallada then tramping determinedly through the snow, Raven circling overhead to guide his path, warning him of dangers and the like, until he arrived at the door, and called out my name and I standing by the window like a modern-day Juliet, waiting for my knight to rescue me.

'Silly girl,' I murmured to myself.

I tapped a course around the room, pausing every now and then, to get a feel of its dimensions, and the objects in it. I found a doll on a small chair close to the window. I ran my fingers over its porcelain face, and through its curly hair, and smelled its musty smell. I imagined it as like one of those old Victorian dolls, with its little sailor cap and long petticoats. It is the strangest of things, but as I stood there, holding the toy in my hand, I had a memory, like a flash, one moment there, the next gone.

I tried to repeat the image in my mind, stretch it out a little, so that it made more sense. Still, it came back to me in fragments, fractals of time, jumbled up, real or imagined sights with sounds now to accompany the memory.

In the background, there was a man. He was mouthing something. You must go away, he said, then disappeared into the shadows. I shook my head and placed the doll where I had found it. 'Silly girl,' I said aloud.

'Yes,' a voice said, startling me.

'I didn't hear you enter, Mrs Butler,' I said in reply.

'The men are clearing the roads. I expect you'll be able to return home today. Perhaps by this evening, if it doesn't snow again. We might as well make you useful while you're here. The Master would like you to play for him.'

'Of course,' I said.

'Daisy, show our guest to the drawing room.'

'Yes, Mrs Butler.'

I felt Daisy's arm link mine. 'This way, miss,' she said softly.

There was a smell of sour milk, as if Daisy had been churning buttermilk or some such thing. We walked down a long passageway, pausing every few moments so Daisy could point out an obstacle in my path, or to draw my attention to something I might be interested in. There seemed to be a lot of trophies, heads of various animals and the like, a bust of some member of parliament or other.

'And this one you might be interested in, miss. It's a painting and a very big painting at that.'

'What's the painting of Daisy?'

'Well, there are four people dancing in a circle. Birds and animals surround them. To the right in the picture there's a man looking on and a sort of imp playing a harp.'

'*A Dance to the Music of Time,*' I said.

'What's that miss?'

'It's the title of the painting. *A Dance to the Music of Time.* It's by a French painter. Nicolas Poussin. It's very famous,' I said, rattling off facts that were buried in the furthest recesses of my mind.

'How do you know that, miss?'

'Someone described it to me once. The old man on the right represents Time. The dancers represent Poverty, Labour, Riches and Pleasure. Some say the dancers represent the seasons. Aurora precedes Apollo's chariot in the morning sky, and both are followed by the Hours.'

'You must be ever so clever, miss,' Daisy said. 'Playing piano and knowing about art and the like. I wish I were clever. I wouldn't be working here, I can tell you. I'm sorry, miss. I didn't mean it like that. I must sound ever so ungrateful.'

'Don't fret. I know what you meant, Daisy,' I said, letting my fingertips rest on the canvas a moment longer.

I felt the oily grooves, the places where the paint had cracked and worn away.

'Oh, I don't know, miss. Mrs Butler encourages me to do needlework. She says it's useful to have such skills. What with rationing. We mustn't waste anything, she says. We must economise. We must do this. We must do that. What I'd really like …'

I heard her clicking her fingers, as if she was searching for words, or inspiration. 'Yes, Daisy, go on.'

'Well, miss, what I'd really like to be is a secretary, or something like that, miss,' she said. 'I'd have a career of my own. I can see it now. I'd wear bright red lipstick and I could afford makeup powder. You know. Just like those women in the magazines. I'd be glamorous.'

'Aren't you glamorous now?'

'Oh, miss. This is the last place I'd ever wish to be glamorous. London, miss, that's a place I could be glamorous in. It has all gone to hell in a handbasket now though. The Prime Minister says we should ready ourselves for more war. Can you imagine, miss? War in little old Rashleigh. I don't know how it could get any worse. Mrs Butler says there was talk they might convert Millrace into a convalescent home, for the wounded soldiers. What a terrible fate awaits the poor souls.'

'What do you mean, Daisy?'

'It's nothing, miss. I must learn to keep my lips sealed. That's what Mrs Butler is always telling me. Keep those lips tight like a duck's arse under water. That's what she says, miss. Not a word of a lie. Cross my heart and hope to die, I do.'

'Well, let's hope that doesn't happen.'

'No, miss.'

I ran my fingertips a little further up the canvas. In my mind's eye, I pictured the little imp playing the harp. I could almost discern its outline from the contours of the brush strokes.

'We all dance to the music of time, in the end,' I said under my breath.

'What's that, miss?'

'It's nothing, Daisy. I'm just thinking aloud.'

'First sign of madness, miss, talking to yourself like that. You'll fit in just nicely around here,' she said, and give a little laugh to herself. 'Well, if you're ready, miss … I'll take you down the stairs.'

'Yes, of course,' I said, hooking her arm.

'Here's the stairs now. Be careful now. It's quite steep.'

'I will,' I said, and held onto the banister. I could feel its smooth and polished surface and imagined an adventurous child sliding all the way down it. We reached the bottom of the stairs and I tapped my cane on the stone. Terra firma once more, I thought, orienting myself.

'The drawing room is to my right.'

'Yes, miss.'

'So tell me a little more about young Mr Charles.'

'He had that dark hair and sallow skin. You have that beautiful raven hair too. And he was taller than me. Taller than Mr Burrows even.'

'Is Mr Burrows tall?'

'Ever so tall, miss. I don't know how he fits into that car, I don't. He has to nearly bend himself in two to get behind the wheel.'

'I see.'

The drawing room was warm, the fire already lit, and not a whiff of pipe-smoke. I took my seat at the piano and stretched my fingers along the keys.

'I'd love to be able to play piano, miss,' Daisy said. 'But my father says that I should know my station in life and I should feel very lucky to have secured a position in the Big House. There's many girls who would die to get a job like yours. That's what my father says. Well, he would say that, wouldn't he?'

'Why do you say that?'

'He doesn't want me going anywhere else, miss. He says that the world out there is a very troubled place.'

'Maybe your father is correct.'

'If it wasn't for this war, miss, I think I'd go somewhere else. London or Paris, or somewhere there are lights and people and music. Somewhere I can feel alive.'

I thought about Daisy's words. That a world existed outside of places like Millrace, and little old Rashleigh, and the farm. Even Pipe-smoker had seen the sense in escaping the confines of privilege and place.

'Can you play something, miss?'

'What would you like to hear?'

'I had heard a tune on the wireless. It was music that someone had requested. *Roll out the barrel.*'

'Perhaps we should wait for Mrs Butler to get here.'

'Go on, miss. It's just you and me here. You can say you were warming up.'

I thought then of the day before and the strange events, which led to my late arrival, the sudden snowstorm, and Pipe-smoker's story of—oh—I couldn't bear to think of it. It was too ghastly.

'Some Liszt instead?'

'What's that miss?'

'The composer. Liszt.'

'Sounds foreign, miss.'

'Yes,' I replied, and laid my fingers on the keys.

Transcendental Etude No. 5 was always a favourite of mine. It's technically quite challenging. Oh if my right hand could tell a story it would be of the hours and hours of practise required to perfect the piece while my left hand waited idly by. It is music to suit hands like mine, small and precise. It suited too that, having lost the dexterity of my left hand somewhat, that I could play it without a feeling of inadequacy. I was mid-way through the piece when I heard,

'Daisy, you may return to your duties.'

'Yes, Mrs Butler,' Daisy said obediently.

I felt her hand rest for a moment on my shoulder then I heard her leave.

'The Master will be down shortly,' Mrs Butler said. 'I expected to convince his doctor that this experiment is a waste of time, but they inform me that the Master has improved, and since nothing else has changed in his regimen they assume that the small happiness he enjoys listening to you play must be having some positive effect. I'm not yet entirely convinced but—'

'Music is always of benefit,' I said, closing the piano cover and turning to face towards the sound of Mrs Butler's voice.

'Young Mr Charles learned to play piano in this very room.'

'You were employed here then?'

'No, Mrs Butler replied. I worked at a different house. I remember though, it was quite a scandal at the time.'

She paused then, as if gathering her thoughts, or reluctant to say more, so I pressed the subject.

'Scandal?'

'The day young Mr Charles left,' she said. 'It was all around the county.'

I thought I heard a sort of sobbing noise. 'Are you quite all right?' I said.

'Perfectly,' Mrs Butler snapped. 'Yes, I'm perfectly fine.'

'Where did he go?'

'It was not long after his sister was taken into care. She was troubled from birth, and as she got older the affliction worsened. She was nearing her sixteenth birthday when the Master decided that she should be sent away to an asylum.'

'An asylum?'

'It was for her own good, you see. She could get treatment there and the very best care. The doctors assured the Master that everything would be done to treat her affliction.'

'What was wrong with her?'

'She would have these fits. Well, there was no one here that could take care of her. She would speak in tongues, like a devil she was. It is said that she would cry out in the night, claiming she had lost the ability to see, but she wasn't blind, it was her madness, you see. The locals said it was the curse on the house. The Master dismissed the idle gossip, but the girl's problems were always on his mind.'

'What happened to her?'

'It was a new treatment. A sort of shock therapy. The treatment proved unsuccessful. The poor girl's condition worsened until she no longer recognised her father. The situation is beyond hope, I heard the Master complain to Mr Burrows once. That was a long time ago.'

I shifted uncomfortably in my seat. I couldn't imagine such a terrible thing as electricity coursing through my body.

'Them that knows said that young Mr Charles was inconsolable. He stole away on one of the merchant ships. He was no more than a boy then. I can't understand it to this day. What sort of man, and a ship's captain into the bargain, would take a boy on board like that? The truth was revealed much later, one year perhaps, when a letter arrived telling of his journey to the far side of the world. He wasn't heard from again until that time he returned home. He had grown into a young man, tall and handsome. He inquired after his sister but his father refused to give him any information about her. Oh, if only someone had spoken up, but it wasn't my place. Perhaps it's this house that feeds upon all our fears.'

'But what about the others, Mr Burrows and Mr Broom? Were they not in the Master's employ then?' I said.

'Mr Burrows and Mr Broom came back from the war. They had a terrible time of it, you see. Mr Burrows had nearly died. He was discovered in an asylum many months after the war had ended. He had no memory of what had happened, you see, buried under all that earth. Can you imagine how dark and suffocating that must have been? Poor Mr Burrows. Mr Burrows had been a batman so he knew his way around the servant's quarters. As for Mr Broom, he returned uninjured. Well, the Master had heard of his expertise with horses. He had been in the cavalry, you see. Now we have another war to deal with, and all of its terrible consequences.'

'Do you have anyone …?'

'You lived in London?' she said.

'Yes, for several years until my injury. I was a music teacher at a school for girls.'

'I remember last year,' Mrs Butler continued, 'I had cause to visit London. Not that I'd do it now though. My sister, you see, she was living there. She had three children, my three little nephews. Just lambs really. I remember pleading with her to leave the city, or at a minimum to send the children away to somewhere safe. I even offered for her to send the children to me. God knows how I might have coped, but I was willing. I could see that she was terribly stressed. The planes were coming over almost nightly, and dropping their bombs indiscriminately. The last night of my visit, the docks were bombed. It was only a few miles from where Gertrude lived. She was almost convinced that leaving was the right course of action, but at the last moment, she changed her mind. She said that the good Lord had spoken to her and that she should not send her children away. Well, it pained me to see the anguish the decision had caused her, but you see, I don't think Gertrude was in her right mind. She had gone a little mad.'

'And how is Gertrude now?' I asked.

'A bomb had landed close to the school but it didn't detonate, you see. It just sat there, undiscovered, like it was waiting for the school to reopen, for the children to return to play, then—'

'That is too terrible,' I said. 'All of them?'

'Yes, all three died that day. Gertrude was inconsolable. She went mad, you see. They found her body washed up in the Thames estuary. She couldn't take the guilt. She said so, in the note she left behind. She said, God had told her she must do that too, to repent for her sins.'

'I don't understand. You say, God had told her to stay in London despite the danger, and when her children were killed, God also told her to take her own life?'

'Madness, don't you think?'

I heard Mrs Butler blow her nose.

'I'm terribly sorry,' I said.

'No tears or prayers are worth the effort now. It will do them no good. I will see them again someday. That will be enough reward for my misery.'

'Yes. Of course you will,' I said.

I reached out and felt Mrs Butler's cold hand under mine. She was thinner than I'd assumed; given the spindly, bony fingers which met my own. My gesture was the fulfilment of that most natural of things, and yet just as soon as I had laid my hands on hers she pulled them quickly away again. How lonely she must be, I thought. Like a candle flame in a draughty room, flickering with every little wisp of air, always on the verge of extinction. What a burden it must be.

She stood and walked to the fireplace. I heard her rattling the grate and placing logs on the fire. The logs crackled and hissed, a burning ember brushed my leg, and I gave a little jump. I heard Mrs Butler scramble to extinguish it. Just then, Mr Burrows came in.

'I've checked the roads, Mrs Butler, and it appears from all reports that we will get a clear run to the far side of the valley.'

'Good,' Mrs Butler replied. 'We shall see you tomorrow, unless the weather turns against us again.'

'You're feeling better, Mr Burrows?' I said.

'Yes, thank you. Just a little food poisoning. I'm over it now.'

'That is good to hear,' then I turned the conversation back to Mrs Butler's question. 'Yes,' I said, 'Until tomorrow.'

When I had put on my coat and hat I stood there and waited for instruction.

'Well, this way, miss,' Mr Burrows said, and took my arm to guide me towards the door.

'Tomorrow then,' Mrs Butler said. 'I will inform the Master.'

It seemed to me then, that I really did not have any choice in the matter at all; that this daily jaunt to the Big House and this strange request to play was preordained.

CHAPTER SIXTEEN

'I'm afraid this is as far as we can go, miss.'

'Where are we?'

I shivered a little at the cold and pulled the blanket tighter around my shoulders.

'I should have asked Mrs Butler for extra blankets, miss. I'm very sorry about that,' Mr Burrows said.

'I'm fine,' I said in reply, straining to make my voice heard over the sound of the engine. I was, in truth, feeling colder than I had expected. 'I could walk from here.'

'But it must be more than a mile, miss. There's at least a foot of snow on the road ahead, miss, and it doesn't look like there has been anyone this way in some time. Perhaps the valley is cut off, miss. Perhaps I should take you back to Millrace.'

'No,' I snapped. 'I must get home.'

'Truth be told, miss, it seems to be warming up a little too, and we'll have plenty of daylight.'

I heard the creak of leather as he turned in his seat. He was looking directly at me, I thought.

'Best to get you where you need to go then, miss.'

I gripped the door handle, gave it a twist, and felt the cold wash of air greet me as I leaned my head out and felt the tepid rays of the sun upon my face. I pushed the door fully open, placed my feet on the ground, and heard the crunch of snow underfoot, and that mix of emotions at the thought of my clumsy step destroying something so pristine then for it to vanish again with the simple act of a human footprint.

I heard Mr Burrows walk around the car to where I stood waiting. He closed the car door behind me and clapped his hands together a few times against the biting wind.

'I'll walk ahead and you will be holding on to the other end of this rope.'

Mr Burrows took my hand, prised the fingers open, and placed the rope into my hand.

'Are you sure you're up for this?'

'I'm sure.'

I had taken just a few steps, before I stumbled and fell face first into the snow.

'Miss—'

I raised my hand. 'I'm perfectly fine, Mr Burrows.'

I used my cane to find some purchase and brushed the snow from my coat. I felt the wind at my back and took a few tentative steps. My footstep sank into the snow but I found firmer ground and plunged my cane forward. There was a tug on the rope and Mr Burrows moved forward again. It continued like this, ploughing through knee-high snow at times, falling occasionally and rising to brush myself off until tired from our efforts, we stopped to gather our breaths.

'I'm not getting any younger I'm afraid,' Mr Burrows said.

'I'm not getting my sight back either,' I replied.

Mr Burrows walked on and the rope became taut in my hand.

'Well, on we go then,' he said.

I lumbered after him, dependent on the feel of the rope to

indicate which direction I should go. I imagined what the scene must look like, a sea of white, the occasional rocky outcrop, where a mountain stream flowed. The crunch of snow underfoot, and our laboured breathing as we trundled on, broke the silence.

I managed a rhythm of sorts, step, pull, plunge my cane into the snow to find a platform for my next step, and all the while thinking, remembering Balham Station.

*

'Have you made up your mind?' Doris asked.

'Why does it have to be so hard?' I replied.

'Because he's bloody well married I suppose. I would have told him where to go and all,' Doris said.

'No you wouldn't.'

'Just you watch me,' she said. 'I warned you. All the good ones are already dead or gone off to war.'

'You didn't say that. You told me that all the good ones were already spoken for.'

'Well … you know what I meant. And him with his wife, and a bit on the side.'

'I shouldn't have said a word.'

'I'm marking it down in my little black book.'

'You don't have a little black book,' I reminded her.

Doris laughed and said,

'If you're going to give him your answer today then I'm coming with you.'

'I don't want you to,' I said.

'I insist. I have the evening off. What else am I going to do? Anyway, I want to get a look at this man you are determined to give up your life for.'

'I—'

'There's no discussion. I want to give this fancy fellow of yours, the once over, before he takes you away forever.'

'He's not taking me away forever. He's being shipped overseas. I'm the one being left behind.'

'Well, I want to have a look at him anyway.'

*

The train to Victoria Station stopped abruptly at Balham Station and all passengers disembarked. A sea of people assembled on the platform and our train's arrival made an already crowded situation even worse.

'What's the hold up?' Doris asked a man wearing a warden's armband and struggling to keep a too-big tin hat, with a *W* writ large across the front, on his head.

'Air raid warning, miss. All trains stopped,' he said hurriedly, his eyes darting around, obviously overwhelmed by the whole situation.

I glanced at the station clock. It was almost eight o'clock and it was another twenty minutes to Victoria, if the trains were still running. However, everything had stopped and I drew some small consolation from the fact that the trains from Victoria would also not be running as normal because of the air-raid.

'Well, there's nothing for it then,' Doris exclaimed, 'let's find a tea lady. Nothing like a cuppa when the chips are down.'

Doris took my hand and pushed her way through the crowd. I looked over the heads of the people assembled along the platform. It was choc-a-block all the way to the stairway leading up to ground level. At the entrance to the stairwell a policeman was ordering people through a loudhailer to keep moving, even though the platform was already crowded, and people already settled seemed unwilling, or unable to move. It was all becoming a bit chaotic when the first dull thuds sounded overhead. There was a collective moan from the assembly and the section of the crowd through which we were attempting to pass seemed to move as one, in one direction, and moments later in the opposite direction.

'Like Wembley on a big match day,' the man to my right said to no one in particular.

'All right, keep moving there,' the policeman repeated, wiping his forehead with the sleeve of his uniform. 'Keep moving along the platform. There's more room further down.'

'I think we should get into the tunnel,' I said. 'Maybe we can help organise people.'

'Good idea,' Doris said and fixed her tin hat on her head. 'Want some help?'

I struggled to adjust the strap around my chin. 'I'm all fingers and thumbs.'

Anti-aircraft batteries started pounding away, firing rhythmically at the enemy overhead. A miss. A hit. Who knew? The noise of the guns was a mix of smaller artillery batteries firing rapid fire, and then the bigger guns firing with long pauses between reloading, and the next round. I knew those only because Henry had told me so. There were more dull thuds, a little closer this time, six or seven of them in close order, then a gap, and another six or seven. A stick, Henry called them, the number of bombs each plane dropped. I imagined each plane directly overhead, its bomb bay doors swinging open and its deadly load dropping out. I imagined the aircraft banking then and gaining altitude to escape the anti-aircraft flak exploding all around them. I remembered what Henry had told me about the randomness of it all. The bombs could fall anywhere, in no particular order, but with the same deadly intent.

'Bloody Jerries,' someone said.

'Here, just tighten it a notch,' Doris said, and pulled the helmet's chin strap tight. She made an effort to push a thin strand of hair from my face and caught my gaze.

'It'll be alright. Remember your training,' she said.

I nodded robotically and placed my warden's armband on the sleeve of my coat, then followed Doris into the throng.

Dust and masonry fell from the ceiling as the sound of explosions overhead grew louder and louder.

'Adolf's at it tonight, *'ain't* he Daphne?' a man said, turning to the woman sitting beside him, at the entrance to the tunnel.

'Aye,' the woman said. 'Fancy a butty?'

'Just what the doctor ordered,' the man replied.

I caught the man's gaze as we passed by and he gave a wry smile. 'We're all in it together, isn't that right luv?'

'Yes,' I said, and made my way around them and onto the train tracks.

We're all in this together, I thought.

I hurried to catch up with Doris, narrowly avoiding an outstretched leg.

'*Oi*, mind *me'* leg, luv. It's the only one I *'ave.'*

One of the man's trouser legs was pinned high to his hip. He cradled a pair of crutches across his lap.

'I'm sorry,' I said, and moved on.

I followed Doris as we made our way further into the tunnel, with only the dim light of the platform, and the odd lantern placed here and there, to guide our path.

'Looks like I won't get to meet your Henry, after all,' Doris said, without looking around.

Every so often, a pair of saucer-like eyes broke the darkness, eyes filled alternately with fear or curiosity.

'Doris, I think we should turn around. It's no use going any further,' I said.

'This tunnel goes on for miles.' I stopped, peering into the darkness and waited for Doris' reply.

'Doris.'

The sound of my voice echoed against the tunnel's walls but still there was no reply. A squealing rat ran over my foot, then another, and I jumped with fright.

'Doris, I'm turning around. I'm going back.'

'Sounds like she's gone on without you, luv,' a voice said from the darkness. 'Bloody vermin.'

'Doris!'

I waited a few moments more, and when Doris didn't return, I turned around and walked in the direction of the platform. I had gone no more than a few short steps when there was a horrendous bang, and it seemed as if the world itself was turned upside down. I felt a warm stream run down one side of my face, a searing pain then a dull aching sensation in my head. An alarm bell was ringing out and in the background; there was a buzzing noise, like a bumblebee hovering close to my ears.

There was a smell of gasoline, then bang, another explosion, and I felt myself thrown against something hard, and unmoving. There was a shout for help. Someone screamed. The lights went out. It was pitch black everywhere.

'*Doris!*'

I noticed something moving beside me. 'Help me,' a voice said. 'Help!'

'Where are you? I can't see you,' I said, and felt my way in the blackness.

213

'Help!'

I ignored the throbbing feeling in my head and the warm, sticky fluid oozing from the side of my face, and continued crawling towards the sound of the voice.

'Help!'

'I'm here. I'm right beside you.'

'Help!'

'Can't you hear me? I'm right here.'

I noticed then that the pleas for help were not a single voice, but many feeble voices, moaning and groaning in the darkness. I noticed too that I was no longer wearing my tin hat and a mixture of grit and dirt covered my head.

'Can someone bring a lamp? There are injured here,' I said.

'Are you all right, luv?'

'Who's there?'

'Help me out here,' a man's voice said.

I felt hands around one arm then more hands around the other as they dragged me to standing.

'Can you walk, luv?' another man's voice asked.

'I can try,' I said and attempted to put one foot in front of the other. It seemed as if the ground itself was made of quicksand and before I could take another step, I felt my legs disappear from under me.

'Steady on, luv.'

'I'm afraid, I can't …'

'Here, put your arms around us. We'll help you, luv.'

Someone screamed. There was a cacophony of noise.

'Doris!'

'Who's Doris, luv?'

'She's my friend. Have you seen Doris?'

'I'm sorry, luv, but the tunnel is blocked beyond this point. No one is getting through.'

'Has no one thought to bring some lamps? How can anyone see anything at all?'

'Come with us, miss. We'll get you out.'

'But, how do you know we're going in the right direction? How can you see where we're going?'

'You've got a nasty knock on your head, miss. Don't worry, it'll all be taken care of,' the man said.

'We've got to get a move on, Joe,' the other man said.

'I know, I know.'

'I can't see.'

'It'll be alright, miss. We'll get you taken care of.'

I was conscious then of a sloshing sound and suddenly my feet were wet, and then the cold water rose around my ankles, then my shins.

'Where's the water coming from?'

'Nearly there, miss.'

I heard the sound of many voices, some moaning and screaming, others calling out for help. Someone was barking orders. I noticed a smell of rotten eggs, and boiled cabbage of all things.

'It's coming in,' a frightened voice announced.

'Let's get a move on then, son.'

'The water's coming in.'

'Keep going. Keep going, luv.'

'Yes. We have to keep going.'

CHAPTER SEVENTEEN

Later, while convalescing in hospital, I pressed one of the nursing sisters to fill me in on what had happened. It was a horrendous tale. A bomb had made a direct hit on Balham Station, causing the roof to collapse, bursting water and sewage mains, and causing much destruction. I had been one of the lucky ones, I was told, rescued before the water had risen too high.

Poor Doris. Poor, poor Doris. She didn't have to come along. It was out of friendship and mischief that she had decided to make the journey with me. Would Henry still be waiting under the clock? Would he know? Would he have gone searching for me? All these questions floated around in my head as I spent those first few days, half sleeping, jumping then at every noise, clawing at the bandages which had been so carefully wrapped around my head. Two patches, stuffed with cotton wool, and daubed in a stinky petroleum jelly placed over my eyes. A temporary measure, I consoled myself. Until the wounds healed. The pinkie finger of my left hand was broken but I hadn't even noticed, at first, too concerned as I was with the searing pain in my head.

A doctor came by. I know this because someone kept referring to Dr *This* or a Dr *That*. He hemmed and hawed his way through one of my morphine-induced slumbers. I heard someone refer to significant injuries, a poor girl, and a bad infection. It was unfortunate but I'm afraid we could not save the child, he said. A child. I assumed he was referring to the person in the bed next to mine, a middle-aged woman I heard from whispered conversation, who had been on the way to Crystal Palace when the bomb struck.

Poor dear, I thought, and drifted away.

I woke again to the sound of the nursing sister's gravelly voice. She was encouraging me, first with her voice, then with her hands, to sit up. I tried to push myself to sit but the muscles in my arms felt weak and useless. After several attempts, the nursing sister asked someone to come to her aid.

'I've brought some tea,' she said, once I was upright.

'Tea …?'

'Yes, dear. Tea, with a little milk and a lump of sugar.'

I fought back an urge to vomit and shook my head side to side.

'You don't want any tea then?' she said.

I shook my head again.

'All right, dear. No tea then. How are you feeling?'

'How long have I been here?' I asked in an almost whisper due to a strange tight and dry sensation in my throat.

'Don't be bothering yourself with such things, dear,' she said. 'You concentrate on getting yourself better.'

'How long?'

'Why, it's almost a month now, dear. You've been here for one month.'

'It's November 11th,' another voice said.

'November 11th?'

'Armistice Day, dear. If only we had an Armistice to celebrate.'

'Where am I?'

'London Hospital, dear,' she said, and pushed a pillow behind my back.

'Where's the woman who was next to me? You know, the woman who lost the child.'

'Oh my poor dear. No need for you to worry about such things now.'

'It's just that ... it's so sad,' I said, my lips quivering at the thought.

'I know, dear. These things happen, and ... well, there's nothing more for you to burden yourself with.'

'What is it?'

'You need to concentrate on getting yourself well.'

'There's something you're not telling me.'

'You probably didn't even know, dear.'

'Know what?'

'You were expecting.'

'*Pregnant*, no. That can't be right. I was ... we were always careful not to ...'

She held my hand and said, 'You didn't know, then?'

'I'm telling you, it's just not true,' I said, growing more confused with every passing moment.

I tried to remember all the times, thinking of every permutation, every opportunity. Henry had always been so careful. A situation would have caused a scandal. No. It wasn't possible. There was too much to lose. Too much at stake.

'The doctor says you were about six weeks gone. You wouldn't have even noticed dear what with this war going on and food rationing, well, it's easy to miss the signs. You rest dear. You'll feel better in a little while,' she said, lowering her voice to a whisper. 'Now, is there someone we can inform about your whereabouts? Your husband, perhaps?'

'Husband … no,' then I quickly recovered and said, 'No, he's … He's away to the war.'

I placed my right hand over my left to conceal the space where an imaginary band might go.

'Where's he stationed then? We can get word to him.'

'It's very hush-hush. Somewhere in the Far East.'

'There must be someone. A relative or friend.'

'A friend, yes. Could you make inquiries to whether Doris Fleming has been brought in from Balham Station?'

'Doris Fleming. The name doesn't ring a bell, dear. I know most of the patients. You see the injured from Balham were taken here, to Ward C.'

'There was one or two taken over to Chelsea.'

'Doris Fleming, you say?'

I nodded my head in reply.

'I'll ask the other nursing sisters if they've heard anything.'

'Thank you,' I squeaked.

'Now you rest. Are you sure about the tea?'

'Yes.'

I heard the sound of the nursing sister's voice fading into the distance, replaced instead by the din of a busy hospital ward, the rattle of instrument carts and the squeaky wheel of the tea trolley. There were other voices too, such as the man who repeated commentary from the Epsom Derby.

"All the runners and riders are gathered at the starting line. The Epsom Derby, Ladies and Gentleman, the pinnacle of the flat racing season. And they're off."

Over and over he went, the same commentary until he reached a crescendo with, "And by a nose, it's …"

And then nothing.

Someone shouted, "Well who won the bloody thing then?"

But the man would start all over again.

"All the runners and riders gathered at the starting line. The Epsom Derby …"

At least tell us who won, I thought.

"We've heard all this before. 'Ain't you going to tell us who won this time?"

Another voice said.

"And by a nose, it's …"

I let my mind be distracted from the repeated racing commentary by thoughts of Henry. He would have assumed the worst; that I had decided not to marry him, but I was going to meet him to tell him the opposite. Hot tears welled in my eyes. I wiped them away only to discover the thick gauze covering them was still in place, so I made a fist of my right hand until eventually, succumbing to tiredness, I fell asleep, and dreamt of a stranger, walking through a snowstorm.

*

What does an angel look like? My angel came in the guise of a dark silhouette, far away in a snowy landscape, marching determinedly towards me, accompanied by a bird on the wing. A bird dark as coal. Darker even. It is strange what I conjured in my mind, when almost delirious from constant tramping I eventually succumbed to such exhaustion that I fell headfirst into the snow. I lay there, rolling over onto my back to let the sun's rays shine upon my face, felt the sensations of my beating heart and listened to the sound of my laboured breath, all the while ignoring the perilous nature of it all.

I was thirsty so I took a handful of snow in my hand and melted it on my tongue. It had this strange mould-like taste. I threw the remainder away and lay there, gazing up to an unseen sky, wondering if Mr Burrows was staring back at me.

'Are you quite all right, miss?'

'Yes, Mr Burrows.'

'We'll have to get going again soon.'

'Are we nearly there?'

'Yes. It's not far, miss.'

I came to my senses when a dog barked in the distance.

'There's someone coming in this direction, miss.' Mr Burrows said.

The sound of snow crunching underfoot grew louder until the stranger was nearly upon us.

'He's got an armband over his coat sleeve. He's one of those foreign labourers. Category B. A *Doubtful Case* and all.'

'Mr Fallada. Is that you?'

'Are you hurt?' Mr Fallada said when he came closer.

'Do you know this man?' Mr Burrows said.

'It's Mr Fallada. He works on our farm.'

'Are you German then?'

'Yes,' Mr Fallada replied.

'I see. German, he is,' Mr Burrows said. 'Caught on the wrong side of the Channel then?'

'I was a student at Oxford.'

'That's what they all say. Isn't that right, miss? Student! Old Adolf has infiltrators everywhere.'

'Are you hurt?' Mr Fallada said, ignoring Mr Burrow's remarks.

'I'm fine, Mr Fallada. We had to walk because of the snow.'

'Your father has been worried,' he said.

'Help me up then,' I said, and stretched out both arms.

'It's not far,' Mr Burrows said.

'No need for you to go any further, Mr Burrows. Mr Fallada can help me from here.'

'I won't hear of it, miss … Him being one of those Germans, and all.'

'I insist, Mr Burrows. Mr Fallada is a victim, as much as you and I.'

'Just put a rifle in his hand, and …'

'You have to walk back to the car and then you have to drive to Millrace. It'll be late by the time you get back and the roads might worsen.'

'Well …'

'Please, Mr Burrows! Here … you can guide me from here, Mr Fallada,' I said, handing him the other end of the rope. 'How far are we from the farm?'

'Not far,' Mr Fallada said.

'Good. Well, let's be on our way then.'

I turned my head in the direction in which I thought Mr Burrows was standing.

'I'll see you tomorrow, Mr Burrows.'

Mr Burrows cleared his throat. 'Until tomorrow then,' Mr Burrows said, and I heard the sound of footsteps marching away.

'Well, Mr Fallada. I'm in your hands now.'

He said nothing, perhaps somewhat chastened by Mr Burrows' suspicions.

'Are you …?'

'Yes?'

'Are you one of those fascists, Mr Fallada?'

He sighed and said,

'I'm half-Jewish. Even if I could return to Germany, I would prefer not to. There is no future for someone like me there.'

Raven cawed and cawed. I imagined him circling high

overhead, watching the pair of us standing, like specks of dirt on the snowy landscape. Then I felt Mr Fallada's hands grip my arm.

'Time to go,' he said and I heard him walking ahead.

I thought about Mr Burrows tramping back to the car, harbouring thoughts of suspicion and hate like so many people did. Fear of the *other* had crept into the everyday. It was easy I suppose to draw such conclusions about someone from the clothes they wore, or the way they talked, or the colour of their skin, just as you might draw a conclusion about a book by its cover. I have known books to be highly entertaining despite the ordinariness of their look and some of the most ornately bound to be rather disappointing. I think it was one of the benefits of my affliction, that to my eye, it didn't matter in the end.

CHAPTER EIGHTEEN

I slept badly that night, and woke later than usual. The efforts of the previous day caused me to stay in bed a little longer into the morning. The sun was already high enough in the sky for its rays to bathe my face in its warm glow. The melting of the ice and snow continued and I could hear the water cascading into the barrels down below. I stretched and went to the window, and stood there for a few moments, listening for sounds and feeling the heat of the day in the warm breeze. I lacked the usual energy with which I would approach a new day and had to force myself not to go back to bed. I did it with the thought that perhaps Mr Burrows would come for me that morning. I went to the nightstand and poured some water into the basin. I splashed my face and ran a damp cloth over my body, pausing every few moments to adjust my undergarments then I dressed and put on my shoes. I ran my little finger across my teeth for good measure.

When I was done, I went downstairs. I wound the clock and went into the kitchen. There were no sounds or smells of cooking. Instead, there was only silence, accompanied by the ticking of the clock in the hall.

I wondered what to do next. It never occurred to me that someday there would be no one there to greet me. Someday

Father too would be gone, and I would be alone with only my thoughts and the sound of a ticking clock for company. In that moment it dawned on me that it would happen just like it did that morning, and I would rise, dress, and enter the kitchen to stand at the same spot, and I would be alone, in the darkness. I felt suddenly alone and vulnerable; even more vulnerable than I had in the earlier days of my recovery, when I had to relearn the simplest of things. There were days when I would refuse to budge, exclaiming that there was no point to it all. Then one of the nursing sisters would offer words of encouragement, gradually chipping away at the minor resistance I offered, until eventually the bedclothes were thrown back and I put one foot in front of the other. There was a reason to keep on going. There were many. I couldn't see them at first but then they slowly revealed themselves and I took pleasure in the smallest of things.

I learned to recognise different objects by touch and discovered their geometric patterns, how the shape of a cup moulds into the palm of the hand or the sensitivity of the fingertips to different fabrics. I learned to dress myself by the coarseness of wool compared to the softness of linen and everything in between. I learned to imagine my mirror image and lift my heart to address my posture. There were reasons to be alive. There were reasons to be cheerful too.

Music and melody transported me, just as it had always done, but in different ways. Images presented themselves in my mind's eye and I voyaged there unafraid of the obstacles the world threw in my path.

A noise disturbed me from my thoughts. It was the sound of voices coming from outside. I went to the kitchen door, opened it, and went outside. Father was instructing Mr Fallada to go to the top field.

'Father … is anything the matter?' I said.

'Nell has pulled up lame,' Father said. 'We'll need to rest her today.'

'Will she recover?'

'Too early to tell. I'll have to fetch the vet while Mr Fallada continues with the work. Anyway, you go back inside and we'll take care of things from here.'

I closed the kitchen door behind me and tried to distract myself by cooking some porridge. When it was ready I sat at the table and ate a full bowl of it, all the while thinking about Nell, and the vet's expenses and then on the events of the previous day.

In a strange way, I hoped that Mr Burrows would return for me, and I could be distracted for the day.

I thought of a suitable piece, Beethoven's *Moonlight Sonata*, and inspired I went to the drawing room and played for several hours until I heard a knock at the door and went to answer it.

'Yes,' I said.

'It's Mr Burrows, miss, come to take you to Millrace.'

I gave a little smile and said, 'Thank you for coming, Mr Burrows. The roads are clear of snow then?'

'Almost, miss. There's been a big melt. I don't understand this weather at all. It's so changeable, don't you think?'

'It's very strange indeed.'

'I'm afraid Mrs Butler wants you at the Big House as soon as possible.'

'Is anything the matter, Mr Burrows?'

'It's the Master, miss. He's taken poorly.'

'Well then, we shouldn't waste a moment, Mr Burrows. Will I need my coat, do you think?'

'You never can tell, miss. Yesterday it was snowing. Today it is warm. Who knows what the weather will be from one moment to the next? I think the world has gone a little off kilter.'

'I quite agree,' I said in reply. 'I won't be but a moment. I have to tell Father that I am going out.'

'I'll get the engine going, miss.'

I went to the kitchen and went through to the pantry, opened the back door and went outside.

'Father, I called out. Father, are you here?'

When I didn't get a reply I went back inside. I found the pen and paper which was kept in a drawer on the sideboard. I scribbled a short note and hurried through the hallway, grabbing my coat and hat.

'Is something the matter?' I said.

'I was troubled. Troubled all night.'

'Troubled about what?'

'About your good self, miss. Having that fellow about the place. Well, you never know what they get up to.'

I knew to whom Mr Burrows was referring but I didn't feel like making it easy for him.

'Who might that be, Mr Burrows?'

'Why that German fellow.'

'Do you think he might be a foreign agent, Mr Burrows?' I said in a conspiratorial voice.

'He could very well be, miss. You just don't know.'

'Did his presence frighten you, Mr Burrows?'

'Not at all, miss. I'm not one for being afraid in that way, miss. I was thinking about you, miss. And Fritz living under your roof.'

'Didn't you hear the man? He's a student caught up in this silly war, interned because he has a foreign accent.'

'There's more to it than that, miss. He's one of those *Doubtful Cases*.'

'*Doubtful Cases?*

227

'Classification B, miss. It's right there on his arm band.'

'So that makes him doubtful does it?'

'Well the government seems to think so.'

The previous evening Mr Fallada had explained how he had been categorised by nature of his chosen field of study, which was Theoretical Physics, and that the government had placed him amongst individuals with possible fascist sympathies.

'I suppose he's come to spy on little old Rashleigh then. Make observations on crop yields and other farming practices,' I said jokingly.

'It could be, miss.'

'Mr Burrows, I should think that Mr Fallada is merely a person in the wrong place at the wrong time. In fact, it was only last evening that he revealed to Father and I how he was less than one year away from completing his dissertation in theoretical physics.'

'Theoretical what?'

'Science, Mr Burrows.'

'Well there you go, miss. Those fellows are the very people we should be keeping a very careful eye on.'

'I'm certain Mr Fallada obtained his B-classification simply because of his field of study. Perhaps the government is wise to keep fellows such as Mr Fallada here, in reserve, to help with the war effort if it should come to that.'

'What do you mean, miss?'

'Well, the likes of Mr Fallada will be the very experts we'll need if the enemy decides to invade us, don't you think?'

'Well, I …'

'Yes, I'm certain Mr Fallada's skills will be put to use at some future point.'

'An educated man like that would go to waste in Rashleigh.'

'Well, there you go then. We agree.'

'I see what you mean, miss. Yes. Well if it was me I would have sent him packing but there you go. It does show what a little education can do for you. Thinking ahead like that and all.'

I was going to tell him that I thought it was common sense but it seemed like a trite remark to make. I simply said,

'You don't have to be a music teacher to come upon ideas like that, Mr Burrows.'

Then the car swerved and I had the sense that he had turned around in his seat to address me.

'Sorry about that, miss. I took my eyes off the road.'

'That's all right, Mr Burrows.'

'It's just that you reminded me of something. I was in the last dust up, you know.'

'Yes, you've mentioned.'

'When I was away to the war … well, the one thing that kept me sane, was a little bit of music, miss.'

'Is that so?'

'Some of the lads, they played the harmonica or the whistle, or wooden spoons, miss. Now don't get me wrong, some of it was terrible, miss, and we'd let them know it.' He gave a little laugh before continuing with his story. 'A few of the officers would organise for evening entertainment, you see … when there was a lull in the fighting, or when we went back to the rear to rest. Well, miss, I'll tell you, but there was this one time when this lady came to play for us, the whole battalion at once. Well, she played the piano, miss, and you could have heard a pin drop. It was so beautiful. It transported me to somewhere else entirely, far away from the flash and bang and other terrible things. I dare say it transported all of us, to a man, away from that terrible place. I remember the lady was so very beautiful.'

'Do you remember her name?'

'Well, it's the strangest thing, miss, but when the doctor advised Mrs Butler to seek you out, he mentioned your dear mother. He said he knew her from the war and that he had heard her play for his battalion. Well it nearly bowled me over, miss, and before I knew it I had learned that the good doctor was stationed just down the line from my good self, and that it was your mother, God rest her blessed soul, who had been the one to play for us.'

'That is quite a coincidence.'

I thought about Mother before, what I had seen from photographs and the like, when she was much younger.

'Yes, miss. I thought so too.'

The car's wheels rattled over the cattle grid and into the grounds of Millrace. When we reached the house, Mr Burrows got out. I heard his footsteps crunching gravel then the passenger door opened.

'Are you ready, miss?' He said.

I took a breath, slid across the rear seat, and placed my feet on the ground. Then I extended my hand and Mr Burrows helped me to stand. Tramp brushed against my legs.

'Hello Tramp,' I said.

'This way, miss,' Mr Burrows said and led me up.

When we reached the top of the steps, and before we entered the main hall, Mr Burrows whispered, 'This way now, miss,' and steered me to my usual spot in the drawing room. I removed my coat and hat, sat at the piano, and readied myself to play.

'That'll be all, Mr Burrows,' Pipe-smoker said.

'I shall let Mrs Butler know you're here, miss. Will that be all, sir?' Mr Burrows said.

'Yes, yes. Very good, Mr Burrows.'

'Thank you, sir,' Mr Burrows replied and I heard him go out of the room.

'Thank you for coming again. I hope your journey here was a pleasant one.'

'Yes, very!'

'I was wondering … could I trouble you to tell me your story?' Pipe-smoker said, sucking air in noisily.

'My story, I …'

'How you came to get your injuries.'

'Why?'

'I'm interested. How did it happen?'

A thought came to me about love and blindness.

'Love.'

'What was that?'

'Love is blind, and I am blinded because of love.'

*

'Do you feel well enough to take a little walk?' Matron said.

'I'm not sure. Don't you think I should wait? Maybe tomorrow! Tomorrow I'll take a walk with you.'

'You said that yesterday, and the day before.'

I wiggled my toes, moved my legs side to side, and tried to imagine taking those first few steps. It seemed like such a daunting prospect. I spent two months recuperating from my injuries. The surgeon had done his best but it wasn't good enough to save my sight. Too much damage had been done. Blood supply had been lost. Nerves and corneas beyond repair. Medical terms thrown about like leaves in an autumn wind with only the faintest hope of catching one to examine it in more detail. It was all so overwhelming.

I hadn't managed to walk any further than the lavatory at the end of the ward, and even then, it had been with the assistance of two nursing sisters, one on each side, to hold my arms, as I tested my new surroundings. I had visitors, of course.

The school principal came to see me. I had to take time to recover. The school had suffered damage in a recent bombing raid. It was unlikely to open again until things returned to normal. I asked her what she meant by normal, and after much hemming and hawing, she said, "… you know. Like it was before the war." Things would never be normal again, I had replied sourly.

Father came to visit, at first determined to take me home, but the doctors convinced him that my rehabilitation would take some time. He brought some clothes, a dressing gown and slippers, a coat, a raggedy old woollen jumper I used to wear. He visited for a few hours that day telling me that he had left Old Man Warlock to look after the farm. "You know Old Man Warlock," he said, "not very diligent about such things, but a pair of eyes to watch over things nonetheless. I expect there won't be a cow milked in all the time I've been away."

Father filled me in on the happenings in Rashleigh.

For the first time in quite some time, I had a pang of nostalgia about the place, and thought it might do me good to be out of London, to ready myself for whatever the future held for me so I promised him I would come home, to Rashleigh, when I had recovered a little more. He assured me that he would make sure my room was ready for my new circumstances.

Father left the next day, telling me that he needed to return to the farm to ensure Old Man Warlock had not burned the place down. Some days later, a police constable came to interview injured survivors of the Balham Station catastrophe. I heard the policeman making his way along the ward, asking the same questions over and over, of each person in turn, name and address and details about next of kin. In some cases, when the patient was, I presumed, unable to speak for himself or herself, I would hear one of the nursing sister's pipe in with an answer on their behalf. "Name and circumstances unknown," or "Elizabeth Burns, 23, unmarried, Edinburgh." It went on like that until I heard them approach the woman in the bed next to mine. The nursing sister said, 'Beatrice Furlong, 46, married, Clapham Common.'

'And you, miss?' the constable said.

I provided him with my name and date of birth, and information about my next of kin, and when he was finished with his questions, I took my chance and inquired after Doris. He wasn't terribly helpful. The most he could say was that several people were still to be identified, and more were listed as missing. Due to the damage caused, some bodies may never be recovered, he explained. It was too shocking to think about. One moment right there, at the tip of my fingers, the next gone, swallowed by the darkness. How random and cruel it all seemed. When he had gone, the nursing sister came to check on me.

'Your father mentioned that you play piano. We have a piano, you know?' she said enthusiastically.

'A piano?'

'Yes,' she explained, 'it's in the day ward.'

'Where's the day ward?'

'It's no more than a hop, skip and a jump from here,' she said in a sort of singsong way.

'I don't know. I mean … Perhaps tomorrow will be better.'

'They're having a recital today. Someone from the London Conservatory came to entertain us all.'

'London Conservatory …' I said, and felt my face flush.

'London Conservatory,' she replied. 'It's just a short walk. I promise we will turn around if you feel it's too much.'

'Can you help me?'

I peeled back the heavy woollen blanket and swung my legs slowly out to the side to let them dangle over the edge of the bed. My head spun a little with the sudden effort and I steadied myself by resting my hands on the firm mattress each side of me.

'Shall we get you dressed first?'

I nodded my head a few times and a moment later, I felt the weight of my dressing gown about my shoulders.

'I've placed your slippers on the ground beside you. They're just a few inches away.'

I moved one foot closer to the ground and felt the soft edge of one slipper, then the next, and slipped my feet into each one. It was such an effort to do such a trivial thing yet also a success, and for a fleeting moment, I felt emboldened to do more.

'Let's get your arms through the sleeves. There we go. Ready?'

'Yes,' I said, and pushed myself to stand.

'We've brought a cane. Let's see if we can get you to use that and I'll hold your arm for support.'

I felt the cane in my hand, wooden and functional.

'It's got a metal tip at the end. Take my arm and tap the cane to see if you can find any obstacles.'

'Won't you tell me?' I asked, nervously.

'Yes. Of course, I will. But let's see if we can build up some of your confidence.'

'Thank you.'

The muscles in my legs were heavy and unworked and I was fatigued after just a few uncertain steps.

'Let's try some deep breaths, shall we?'

'Why?'

'Because you're holding your breath, dear. You won't get very far doing that.'

I took a few deep breaths and moved forward, tapping the cane as I did. It met the metal of the bed frame and tinged noisily, then a wooden surface, a table I learned. I stepped around it, leaning every so often into the nursing sister's arm for more support.

'That's great, dear. Let's keep going.'

'Good on you, luv,' someone said.

'Thank you,' I said and gave an unconvincing smile.

'Through the door, dear,' and I heard the door swinging open on its hinges. 'And down the corridor.'

We continued like this. Small, uncertain steps, each its own little triumph, until we reached the stairwell.

'You can do it, dear. One step at a time.'

'How many?'

'Five steps on the first flight down, and then six on the next and we're on ground level. Use your cane to find the steps.'

I tapped the edge of each step and placed my foot on each one, pausing for a few moments before continuing, and with each step, I felt a newfound confidence.

'We're turning right now and down the end of this corridor. We're nearly there. You're doing splendidly.'

*

'*Gymnopédie*.'

'What was that?' Pipe-smoker said.

'Satie. He played Satie.'

'Who?'

'The man from the London Conservatory.'

'Ah!'

'Music. I couldn't live without music,' I said, and ran my fingertips across the piano keys, pressing one key after the next, gently so as not to make a sound.

'It must have been terribly difficult.'

'I suppose only you could imagine. After that first adventure to the day ward I made it my business each day to do a little more, walk a little further, learn to dress myself, tie my shoe laces and feed myself. My sense of smell and touch and hearing became more acute. I began to have very lucid dreams, almost like premonitions. Perhaps they were a function of an over-active mind. Who can tell? It was February before I could be moved to the day ward where I took to playing piano again, much to the enjoyment of the other patients, it seemed.'

'Music raised their spirits, I assume.'

'There were nights when all the patients were moved to the basement to shelter from another air raid. The staff saw fit to move the piano too, so I could play for the assembly as the bombs rained down. Even if the bombing seemed particularly heavy, people would join in, and have a little sing-along. If memory serves me, it was at the end of February that a police constable brought news that they had found Doris' body when clearing rubble from the track system. The news seemed to close another chapter in the tale of that period of my life, and open another. They told me not long after that I was going to be released from the hospital, and that arrangements had been made for a nursing sister to accompany me home, to Rashleigh, and a new life. Those first weeks were difficult, no longer surrounded by the noise and disturbances of a busy city. Rashleigh seemed so desolate by comparison.'

'And this man you spoke about …'

'Henry.'

'Yes, Henry.'

'You were in love, then?'

'Yes,' I said under my breath. 'Yes, I loved him so very much,' I said a little louder this time.

'But he had gone away.'

'He was waiting at Victoria Station that day, but then there was the bombing raid and all those terrible things …'

'He didn't come looking for you, then?'

'Well, how could he? He was married. It wouldn't have done for him to show up at the hospital. It would have looked quite suspicious, don't you think?' Anyway, I don't suppose he had time to think about it.'

Uttering the words helped create doubt in my mind.

I wondered if Henry had looked me up, and discovering the nature of my injuries decided to abandon me, or return to his family. It was just too terrible to contemplate.

'Really?'

'I didn't make it to Victoria. He probably took it as a sign,' I said, trying to convince myself that Henry would never leave me like that.

'A sign you weren't interested in his proposal?'

'Perhaps! Oh! I do hope he is all right, wherever he is. I don't care if he's decided he could never love me … like this,' I said, and felt my eyes moisten and sting.

click-click

Then the smell of pipe-smoke wafted in my direction. How soothing it had become in such a short amount of time, to inhale that sweet aroma. I wondered if it was the pipe-smoke, or simply having someone to talk to, that made the difference. I wasn't quite sure. 'I need to tell you something,' he said.

CHAPTER NINETEEN

'You remember my story? How I had been shot down and rescued by the Naga,' Pipe-smoker began.

I nodded.

'Yes.'

'Well, I haven't told you everything. You see there was the other man. He was older. He'd been wounded, shot in the leg escaping from Rangoon to be precise.'

I swallowed hard at the mention of Rangoon.

'I'm afraid the wound hadn't quite healed so he'd been left behind by his companions, and was taken into the care of the Naga. They did their best for him, of course, potions and spells, but it was no use. Gangrene had set into the wound and the only solution was to remove the leg. So they did. The Naga, used to chopping off heads, now had to chop off a leg. I was there, in the cot beside him, when they did it. He was very brave. I couldn't watch as that old Naga medicine man went at the infected limb with a machete. *Chop, chop,* and *chop,* until sure enough the leg came off, right above the knee. I thought I might have been hallucinating, or had a nightmare perhaps, but when the fugue had cleared, I saw him there, the leg now a stump, banana leaves wrapped tight around the wound, tied off with lengths of string.

He slept most of that first day, after the operation, if that is what you might call it. He slept and sometimes he would call out in his sleep.'

'The poor man.'

'It's very important that you hear the rest. You will see. We became more fully acquainted because we were both cripples then, unable to do much more than talk about old England and getting home again, though I think in truth we never truly believed we would … get home that is. We smoked too, a concoction the tribesmen made for us. It was opium, I think. It made us quite nauseous at first, dry in the mouth, that sort of thing, but then after a few days of puffing on the pipe, well, we came to demand it. You see, it took away the pain. The burns you know. The smoke kept the bloody mosquitoes at bay too. Damned mosquitoes. My companion would tell me that it took away the pain in his wounded leg, and for a while, I wondered if he had been shot in the other leg too. It was a phantom pain, I soon realised. He would point to the place where his leg used to be and say, "… it's worse today," and I would nod my head in muddled understanding. He didn't complain much, and instead, was eager to tell me about his life before the war. How he was married, unhappily it seems, until he met this girl. Well, he could not quite get her out of his head. He knew it was wrong. He had a wife, and two children, waiting for him at home. But the affair began in earnest and soon became his obsession, he explained.'

I felt my chest tighten and it was only after some time that I realised I had been holding my breath in. I exhaled and felt just a little light-headed. I was gripping the arm of the chair. I felt the blood drain back into my fingers as soon as I released my grip.

'It was almost as if he wanted to make a confession, you see. As if the love that he felt for this woman was a burden on his soul, that he knew that he would die there in that jungle, and he didn't want to, without first telling someone, even me, a total stranger, how much she meant to him. I listened as he told me about the affair, how he had deceived his wife and children, spinning tales and fabricating lies to cover his tracks. Ensuring that his wife accompanied the children to the country during the worst of the Blitz. The bombings, in a strange twist of fate, had provided an opportunity for him to continue his affair. I suppose it happens quite a bit,' Pipe-smoker said. 'It's the immediacy of it all. That fleeting chance for the newness of things, to live a life, however brief, with someone else. A tryst, or an affair to remember, whatever way it presents itself. Not to be passed up in the times we live in.'

'No,' I said.

'We were there for some time, months I should think,' Pipe-smoker continued. 'It was easy to lose track of time. The only real measure of anything was the daily ritual of food and water, the cleaning of wounds and the application of ointment, and the noises of the night and the constant battle against the mosquitoes. After some weeks, my companion felt strong enough to venture outside. One day he returned frustrated and complained of narrow tracks through the dense jungle, and nothing overhead except more of the same, and the impossibility of ever getting out of there. I remember he smoked two pipes that day. Perhaps he had lost hope. In his opium-filled stupor, he told me more of his story. How he believed that he had betrayed everyone, and that the war was a relief, an escape, and when he was posted to Rangoon it was as if he could breathe again.'

'I'm not sure I feel sorry for this man … even after all he had been through.'

'Yes, well … perhaps I should continue. You see, it was

around this time that I also felt well enough to leave the hut. I remember it was dusk. You see the jungle comes alive at night. Wild animals and birds, hunting and hiding. I found my companion sitting on the stoop. He had his service revolver and was running the barrel back and forth between his fingers, while staring wide-eyed into the distance. I asked him if he was expecting trouble, but he simply ran the barrel back and forth without answering. Back and forth. Back and forth. *Click. Click. Click.* Perhaps you should shoot me first, I told him. He looked up then and placed the revolver, almost guiltily to one side. "Keeping it clean and dry," he said, and then he went back inside. I remember it rained that day. You have to understand that when it rains in the jungle it comes down in torrents in a matter of minutes, until the jungle floor itself becomes like this thick soup. Then after the rain, there is such heat that it is unbearable until you feel as if your very skin is peeling off. I begged my companion to put me out of my misery. "We're going home," he said determinedly. It was the following morning that the villagers, normally quite placid people, became instead very agitated. There was a sudden burst of activity. Men appeared with weapons, bows, arrows, and machetes. The enemy was coming, Rama explained. The Japanese were advancing on the village. It was all quite desperate, you see. My companion could walk no further than a few yards, and I was still too weak to stand for more than a few minutes at a time. There would be no escape for the two damned Englishmen. That's why they had to leave us behind.'

'Leave you behind?'

'Yes. Rama remained with us, and some of the elders, too sick or infirm to escape. I wished then I had had my pistol. We waited and even at that last moment, as they entered the camp, I thought of salvation. "Shoot me," I begged him. However, he would not do it. Perhaps he believed that there was a glimmer of hope. Hope that we could somehow escape. They murdered Rama first. Dragged him from the hut and slaughtered him there and then.'

Pipe-smoker's story held me tight in its embrace, peeling my eyes open to see again, to see the completely horrid world in all its gory detail.

'I'm sorry but you must know this, you see. It is vital that you know the whole story. They set fire to the huts and gathered the survivors together while Rama's body twitched and twittered in the mud. They killed everyone. Can you imagine? One after the other, right there in front of our very eyes.'

'Oh, how terrible—'

'We were witness to such horrific terror that it is hard to imagine. They dragged my companion to the centre of this circle of headless bodies. It was our turn next, I thought.'

'But he had his pistol. Surely he had his pistol?'

Pipe-smoker gave a sort of sardonic laugh. 'He didn't have bullets for his damned gun after all.'

'But why would he clean it? You told me you found him cleaning it.'

'One must always keep one's weapon serviceable,' Pipe-smoker said. 'They laughed at him as he attempted to right himself to face his persecutors. The whole damned lot of them, a weirdly demonic sort of cackle. You know, I realise now how truly strange it is to require a man to kneel when he only has one leg. Ever tried it?'

'No.'

'You just keep toppling over. Simple physics really,' Pipe-smoker said matter-of-factly. Then he gave a little laugh as if he had thought of something amusing.

'I don't think it's funny at all.'

'I'm sorry. It's just the absurdity of it, you see. A one-legged man and crispy me. I expect they thought that they had won the war if that was all we could muster. Not exactly England's finest, don't you think?'

'I don't …'

'They had this ritual you see. They charged one of their officer's, a boy really, with the task. I remember that he had this wild-eyed look, as if the very act of execution was, in itself, like an intoxicant. Well, this young officer was in the act of cleaning his sword, washing the blade with water from a canteen held by one of his underlings, when a second officer appeared on the scene. This man was older, broader at the shoulders, thickset. I remember I looked at him as he strode about the circle, stepping over bodies here and there, his footsteps making this terrible squelching sound, until he caught my gaze. Suddenly, they dragged me to kneel beside my companion in the circle. We were bound at the wrists and forearms and a length of bamboo across our backs held the binds tight.'

'Tell me everything, every moment. I need to know.'

'You know I wasn't sure whether it was right and proper that you came here.'

'I don't understand—'

He hesitated for a few moments. 'Perhaps it will become evident why,' he eventually said, taking my hand and pressing something metallic into my palm.

'What's this?' I said, and rubbed my fingers around the edges of the object. 'Your cigarette lighter?'

He continued where he had left off without making any more reference to it.

'We didn't speak. What does one say when one is facing death?'

243

'Words to remember,' I said.

'Yes … or words never to be forgotten perhaps. I tilted my head to get a better look and felt this searing pain across my back. Then I felt it again. A man stood in front of me and barked something in Japanese. It was an order. "He wants you to bow your head", my companion whispered. The soldier struck him for that single utterance and he moaned with the pain of it. I remember that it started to rain then and the jungle floor became this mix of crimson and mud. In a strange way, I welcomed the rain. I could go to my god, washed clean of my sins.'

'I shouldn't think you had many sins to wash away,' I said.

'Ah,' he said. 'I'm afraid that's where you're wrong. I have committed the greatest sin of all. The older man, a colonel I think, though I cannot be certain, the rain and circumstances have clouded such detail, he went about that circle, striding back and forth, shouting and laughing like a lunatic, before coming to stand in front of us. I remember he wore calf-length riding boots, and I thought in a strange sort of way, how silly it was to go tramping through the jungle in riding boots of all things. Riding boots—'

I heard the sound of a match being struck this time and, by now, the familiar smell of pipe-smoke reached my nostrils.

'Little Tojo spat and barked another order. I felt strong hands under my arms and they forced me to stand. They released me from my binds, and then I saw the officer take his side arm from his holster and empty the chamber. He took one of the bullets in his hand and slid it into the chamber again, and then he spun the barrel several times. The junior officer came to stand beside me then. He raised his sword and placed the edge of the blade across the back of my neck. I remember the sharpness of the blade; how fragile my neck was beneath it. The older man extended his arm in my direction, and in his hand was the pistol. He grunted something and made a gesture with his hand. Then he grunted again. Rain went plink-plink off the lip of his cap and his cape. Grunt, he went, like a little pig. *Grunt! Grunt!* The blade got sharper still. He gestured with the pistol again, and I knew, I knew then what he wanted me to do. "Take it, goddamn you. Take the pistol in your hand." I looked at my companion, his head hanging limply, waiting for an end to it all. "I can't do it." "Take the pistol."'

'No,' I said under my breath.

'I held out my hand and felt the weight as the Japanese officer forced the weapon into my grip. It was a small thing, smaller than our service revolvers. I remember it had a little wooden stock with a serrated surface and something etched on one side. A Japanese symbol, I think. I ran my thumb along the barrel and felt its slick, metallic malevolence. "I can't," I said, turning to my companion. "You don't have a choice," he said in reply. The Japanese officer made that grunting sound again. The rest looked on in silent obedience and anticipation. "Remember me to her. Promise me," my companion said. Still I stood there, my arm limp by my side, the weapon heavy in my hands, getting heavier with every passing moment. "Tell me the story of the sea," he said. The rain came heavier then, so heavy on my face. "Tell me about the sea," he said. I had told him about Millrace, the sea; how the sea had shaped everything. "The sea, deep and blue," I began, and then I took an unsteady aim. I wished for it to be clean and painless, just as I hoped for myself when the time came, but at that last moment, I closed my eyes. "The sea …," the pistol kicked in my hand and I heard the Japanese yelp and howl like a pack of baying wolves. I dropped the pistol on the ground and as I did the weight of the blade disappeared, replaced instead by the force of something else. Every bone in my body screamed in pain as they started beating me. I fell to my knees with the first blow, and then slumped to the ground with the second. "Shoot me." I got my answer to my request rather quickly. They bound my hands behind my back and forced me to bow my head. You know what is coming next, but from somewhere deep inside this voice cries out that one must rage against the dying of the light. I listened to that voice and looked towards the sky, then tilted my head to one side to see what was in my executioner's eyes. It was a sort of belligerence. I have that streak in me, you see. My executioner stopped what he was doing and berated me for my insolence. The young man said something to one of the guards standing beside me. The man forced my head around with his hands, and then he took a step back.

I turned my head again and stared into the young man's eyes. "Coward," I said, and almost immediately, I felt the guard's rifle butt on the back of my head, and slumped to the ground. They dragged me back to prostrate before my executioner. "Coward," I repeated, and my executioner's features tightened in an obvious show of frustration and anger. He sheathed his sword and spat at me. I would not relent. I would not bow to him. He kicked me, a sickening blow to my stomach, followed by another, until I crumpled forward in pain. Blood streamed from my head and made a pool on the ground in front of me. When he was done, his energy sapped with the effort amidst the heat of the day, he fell to his knees beside me. I turned my head to look at him and saw not an executioner, but a boy. "Why? Why you not accept your fate?" he said in faltering English.'

'What was your answer?' I asked him.

'I was waiting,' I replied.

'Waiting for what?'

'I told him I was waiting for him to see me.'

'See you?'

'I wanted him to see me as human, and not like an animal to the slaughter. Only then could he take my head and free my soul.'

'Oh, please, I cannot hear any more.'

'But you must,' he said. 'You must hear the rest of my story.'

Pipe-smoker continued. 'The older one, who had forced the pistol into my hand, barked out an order and a few moments later I was left there in the filth and mud with only the young officer for company. He stared at me, that boy, his eyes red from the sweat of his efforts. As I knelt there, I tasted blood in my mouth and felt a hot stream pouring from my forehead into my eyes. By god, it was hot. The rain had stopped by then, and it became hotter, like a furnace. We stayed there for what seemed like an eternity. Then, without a word, he rose from where was kneeling and walked away, berating himself as he did. I slumped forward exhausted but watched, with eyes half open, as the Japanese cleared the village and melted back into the jungle. A dreadful irony revealed itself to me then. I was the only one who had survived the slaughter. All around lay the bodies of the dead. All those bodies. All those heads. All those eyes staring back at me. I could not look at them. The crumpled body of my companion lay beside me. I bowed my head and prayed. It was gibberish really. I muttered lines about salvation and the great beyond.'

I rubbed my fingers over the object in my hand again and felt the inscription etched into its metallic surface. I supposed he noticed my movements because he cleared his throat and said,

'I know this must be difficult but the story must be told. You see, it is important, so important. It has been a burden. I must share it. Only you could know the pain, and the loss.'

I believe I knew what he meant when he said that we once

held something dear but had to let it go, never to hold it again. I saw Henry's face before me. He smiled that half-smile of his, and gave me that knowing, worldly look that so entranced me right from the beginning of it all; since those first few moments underneath the lamppost and the driving rain. As if somehow reading my thoughts Pipe-smoker piped up again and continued with his story.

'The rain returned,' he said, 'A drop here and there at first, then a deluge poured from the sky, bringing the jungle alive with a cacophony of noise. It is phenomenal. Like all the thunderstorms, you have ever experienced rolled into one. I was unmoving, bent forward as I was, my neck bared, resigned and awaiting the young Japanese' return. However, he never returned, so I knelt there, the water forming huge puddles around me.

Then came the silence. Silence marked only by my shallow breaths. One, two, buckle my shoe. Three, four, knock at the door. You think of the silliest things sometimes, don't you think? Yes. A silly nursery rhyme. Five, six, pick up sticks. I went on. I don't know how long. Hours, days, repeating, one, two; buckle my shoe, until I heard the sound of voices. Naga voices. A few scouts arrived at first then what was left of the tribe. They found me, the sole survivor, and carried me into the jungle, to a new, temporary camp, and after that to a more permanent camp in the mountains. Once there, the Naga took me to a spot where they had placed many heads, and surrounded me with gifts and offerings, and all of the tribe's people prostrated before me. I did not understand then what honour they were bestowing on me, but later, when the prostrations and fire walking were complete, an elder came forward. He pointed at me, and at the sky, and spread his arms wide, then pointed at the ground, before he fell to his knees.'

'What did it mean?'

'They thought I was a god of some sort. A god who had fallen to earth and chased the enemy back into the jungle.'

I remembered my dream, the man falling from the sky, burning and screaming. How terrible it was.

'You see, there is something else which I must tell you,' Pipe-smoker said. 'It was not my father who requested that you come here to Millrace. It was I who needed to see you.'

'You—'

'I had my reasons. First among them, that you wouldn't judge me by sight alone.'

'I'd never—'

'Please … let me stop you there. Since the day they brought me home, I don't think I have left this place more than twice. Brief hospital visits so the doctors could check on my wounds and perform their tests. I daresay the young doctors and nurses were themselves shocked to see such a sight.'

'The war has maimed and wounded so many.'

'And you, of course. You carry your burden with such grace and dignity.'

'Everyone has suffered in their own way.'

'Please, there was something else I wanted to tell you. It is very important.'

Pipe-smoker returned to his story of the jungle.

Weeks after his escape a company of Indian soldiers, patrolling deep into the jungle, happened upon the Naga encampment. It took a month of trekking, Pipe-smoker being ferried in a litter, before they reached the nearest hospital, and a further three months before Pipe-smoker could be returned to England.

'You haven't asked about my companion,' he said then.

'He's dead,' I said, and felt my heart flutter in my chest.

It couldn't be. It was too much of a coincidence. It couldn't be him, I reasoned but then what he told me next dismissed all doubt.

'We are such a tiny island after all, but yet, there we were, two men tied together by such a thing as love. He loved you, but I suspect you already know that.'

I felt tears welling in my eyes again. 'I—'

'I found it later, amongst his things. Such a simple thing, but something of value I reasoned. The inscription. His initials. I thought you might want it. Did he know that you were blind?'

I shook my head side-to-side, sobbing and unable to form the words with my mouth.

'I don't think it would have changed the way he felt for you, if that makes you feel any better.'

'You don't know that. You can't say that.'

'Henry wanted you to know. He made me promise that if I survived I would bring you the whole story, in all its detail … every word of it.'

I slumped back into my seat and allowed the emotions to swallow me whole. At last, I knew the truth of it. That Henry was dead, and that his death had been swift and terrible at the same time, and the man who had borne witness to his last moments stood before me now, accomplice and victim, destined to carry the scars of his experiences forever.

'Can you forgive me?' Pipe-smoker said.

'Forgive you. What is there to forgive?'

'I had to do it. You must realise that. I had no choice.'

'That's a burden only you can carry,' I said.

'Then you do. You do forgive me.'

'Yes,' I said. 'I forgive you for your kindness because that's what it was … a kindness of a sort.'

'Yes. I suppose it was a kindness in the end. It would have been a kindness for him to do the same for me. I think of it every day, you see. Sitting here, looking out to the sea. How he wanted me, in those final moments, to tell him about the sea. Perhaps it was his way of being near you.'

'That day, at Balham Station, I took it as a sign. I was on my way to give him my answer and then the bombing started.'

'And what was your answer?'

'I was going to tell Henry that I would marry him, and we would live happily ever after. Then the world turned upside down and I was left with this,' I touched the scar below my eye with the tips of my fingers. 'But, I never did. I didn't make it.'

'I'm sorry,' Pipe-smoker said.

'It's like a terrible nightmare,' I replied, feeling the hard ridges beneath my fingertips. 'A nightmare from which I cannot escape.'

'I apologise that I needed to deceive you … Father is ill of course and I am sure he has enjoyed your daily recitals, but this was for me. You … coming here, was for my benefit. I needed to unburden myself, you see and I needed your understanding.'

I tried to distract myself with other things.

'Would you like me to play something? Don't you think they'll find it strange that I came all this way, and didn't play?'

'Do you feel up to it? I mean … after all you've heard!'

'Music is the only thing I still possess. It's my salvation from the torments of the world.'

I turned to the piano and ran my fingers along the fret. With further tears welling in my eyes, I began to play.

When I was finished he said, 'There is one other thing that I think you should know.'

'Yes. What is that?'

'They have only done what they have done for my benefit.'

251

'Who?'

'I wanted you to know. I have involved them all in my little scheme, you see. A little light smuggling, I told them. It was the only way.'

'Your contraband?'

'Yes, but it seems now, after many months, good old Mrs Butler has gotten cold feet. Something about the War Ags Committee of all things. She's afraid she might get locked up. Mr Burrows too. I tried to convince them that they were being silly, but it's no use …'

'Can't you have a doctor prescribe something to dull the pain?'

'Damned doctors. They don't understand. Do you know what it feels like? This pain. Like hell itself,' he said angrily.

'I'm sorry. I think I should go now.'

'Yes, perhaps you should. That might be for the best now that the truth is revealed.'

I got ready and walked in the direction of the door. I placed my hand around the brass knob and pulled it towards me.

'I think I'll take the boat out again,' he said, as I pulled the door behind me.

CHAPTER TWENTY

That night I had a dream. Different to all the rest. In my dream, I went to Millrace. I walked along the long, twisting drive, pausing to take an azalea in my hand, peel its petals apart with my fingers and bring it to the tip of my nose to take in its perfume-like fragrance. Instead of that familiar sweet scent, it smelled of decay. Horrified, I watched as the flower drooped and withered in my hand. I hurried away, my legs heavy, dragging one leg behind the other, just as Father did, and when I turned to see what was the cause I saw water lapping about my feet, slowing my progress, as if the sea itself was trying to convince me to go no further.

In the distance I heard the plaintiff cry of a gull, urging me to turn back but I ignored its clarion call and carried on, a sense of dread rising with every laboured step, until I came to the stone bridge, standing like an oasis in the gathering tide. I stood at its centre, relieved to be on dry land again, and surveyed all around me. In the distance, I saw a little rowing boat, blue in colour, bobbing up and down on the waves. A pair of oars hung over its sides but it otherwise appeared abandoned to its fate. A noise disturbed me. A little black and white rabbit hopped around me, then another, and another, until the bridge itself was full of rabbits, hopping around in circles, all blindly wondering where to go as the rising tide lapped at the edges of the bridge. When I looked to see where the rowing boat was, it had disappeared.

The house appeared then; Millrace, its consequences known to me now, and I was transported to the familiar gravel courtyard. The big old car stood idling, its gold-coloured paint glistening in a momentary ray of sunlight.

There was no one about, no one but Tramp. He barked and jumped around me, warning me. I looked towards the house and the noise of Tramp's bark faded away, replaced instead by a sort of scratching sound, like nails scraping across window-glass. In each of the windows of the house, a lonely figure stood staring out to the sea. I focused my gaze on one of the figures; it had a featureless face, its mouth agape, as if in a silent scream. I called out but got no reply.

I made my way up the steps, and went inside, into the main hall. All around me, I saw the trappings of a world of by-gone days; the trophy heads and suits of armour, long draping curtains and moth-eaten fabrics. I saw the crumbling plaster and chipped lead paint, the carpet worn and frayed, cracked window-glass, wall-holes patched with old newspapers, and smells reminiscent of damp caves.

I walked through the drawing room and saw a portrait of Nelson hanging at an angle, as if lifted by a wave and allowed my fingertips to run across the old velvet fabric, which covered the armchair. I walked silently, as if walking on air itself, to the piano. I saw the chipped and broken keys and the worn cloth on the seat, and let my fingers rest on it for just a moment. I pressed one key, and then another, but no note sounded.

Silence played instead, and dread was everywhere at once, then nowhere at all. I turned my head and saw the large armchair by the window, the one I had come to know only through touch and feel and reference, positioned so that whoever occupied it could have an unhindered view of the sea. I made my way to it, expecting in a strange way to find Pipe-smoker there, but instead I found it empty. I rested my hand on its back and looked through the bay window, down the long meadow, to the sea beyond. It seemed close, closer than I might have expected, swallowing everything in its path.

I stood there for an eternity, watching and listening for sounds, until a smell stirred my senses. It was an acrid and choking cloud of invisible force.

My chest tightened, my heart slowed to a single thumping eternal beat, and I became frozen to the spot. I willed myself to run, to get away as quickly as possible. Nelson eyed me from the bridge, casting a cold eye, turning my very essence to stone.

All around was the sound of frantic voices, calling out, like the screams when the water rushes into a sinking ship and its passengers clamber for salvation.

I willed myself to move again and floated through the room and into the main hall, and up the stairs, a crackling-heat building on my skin. I made my way down the stairs, but there was no one there.

Still the voices called out to me. Window-glass cracked and exploded, paint blistered and peeled from the walls, timbers overhead burned and crashed noisily to the ground.

Outside again I found myself standing, watching as the Big House, crumbled and burned, and those solitary figures still stood, their mouths wide open, screaming silently, as the sea washed over the courtyard, and up the steps, and in through the main entrance, until the house and flames and everything was washed away.

The sea has come at last, a voice whispered.

I woke to the sound of my own voice echoing words from another realm.

'The sea has come.'

I couldn't feel my face. It was numb, tingling with a strange energy. I felt paralysed for a moment until eventually I could move first my fingers and then my toes, and felt a single tear run down my face.

'The sea—'

The wireless crackling away in the kitchen disturbed me from my thoughts. The sound was unusually loud now that I had begun to recover my senses and I wondered why Father had turned the volume up so high. I rose from where I had been resting and felt the dampness of the nightdress against the skin on my back. I shook my head from side to side to clear the buzzing sound, which persisted. It was a high-pitched note, like a tiny bee buzzing in my head.

'Father,' I called out, but got no reply.

I placed my feet on the cold floorboards and stood, unsteadily at first. The buzzing sound continued as I washed and dressed. Still a little unsteady on my legs I made my way to the window and felt the warm rays of the sun on my face.

Somewhere, a gull called out. I stood there for a moment longer than usual, listening for other sounds, and heard a dog bark and yelp.

I was eventually convinced that this was not part of the dream so I took my cane in hand and made my way onto the landing and down the stairs.

I counted the steps, as was my daily ritual, until turning along the hall to make my way to the grandfather clock. I opened the little glass door and took the key from its ledge and wound it up before continuing to the kitchen.

The wireless crackled and whined noisily. I went to adjust it and heard,

'We have a treat in store for you this bright spring morning. It is a recital of poetry to liven up the spirits. First to the news from the BBC ...'

I turned down the volume, went to the table, and took my seat as I always did. There was no place set, no porridge in its pot, no warm stove, or yapping pups, just the freshness of the morning air through an open window. How strange, I thought, to find the window ajar and the kitchen as it was. I made my way to the sink and filled a pot for porridge when it dawned on me that the stove was unlit. I stood there for a few moments trying to decide what to do next, and then proceeded outside. Despite the early morning sun, the air was cool, with a hint of winter still clinging on, refusing to give in. I rubbed my arms a time or two to warm myself as I crossed the yard.

'Father. Mr Fallada. Are you there?'

Still I got no answer, so I returned to the house, and went to fetch my coat against the morning chill. It was then I heard the sound of a motor and the squeal of brakes. There was a sound of men's voices; Father and Mr Fallada's too.

'Father, is that you?'

The vehicle hissed and puffed before accelerating away and I heard the sound of footsteps crunching gravel underfoot.

'Father ... Is that you?'

'Yes, dear.'

'What's the matter?'

He came a little closer and I got the smell of wood smoke. Strange, I thought. He placed his hand on my arm and gave it a squeeze.

'I'll just wash up first,' he said. 'Why don't you go inside and I'll follow you in.'

'I'll wash too,' Mr Fallada said abruptly.

'What is it?' I said.

'I'm afraid something has happened,' Father said.

'Tell me. What is it?'

'Let's go inside,' Father said, taking me by the arm.

'Why won't you tell me?'

'You go on ahead. I'll be in shortly then I'll tell you all you need to know.'

I made my way to the kitchen table and pulled out a chair to sit down. Father came in through the pantry a few moments later and I heard Mr Fallada come in shortly after that.

'Well …?'

'There's been a fire. An accident, they say. Stray bombs. Perhaps from an aircraft returning from a bombing raid.'

'But I don't understand.'

'A terrible tragedy, *ya*!' Mr Fallada said, and took a seat at the table.

'We fought the blaze for quite some time.'

'Where … was anyone hurt?' I asked nervously.

'They're all gone. Perished.'

'Who?'

'It's Millrace, my dear. Millrace is gone. Several of the houses at the harbour and the creamery in Rashleigh. We were sent to the Big House to help put out the fire there, but it was no use.'

'Millrace …?'

'No one knows for sure how the fire started there.'

'But the bombs …'

'It doesn't appear that Millrace suffered any damage in the bombing raid itself. The police are up there now. They'll get to the bottom of it.'

'Everyone …?'

'I am afraid so, dear. Not a soul survived the fire. It is the strangest thing.'

'What, Father?'

'This,' he said, and placed something on the table. 'I picked it up as I searched through the rubble.'

I ran my hand across the table and felt something sharp and twisted. 'What is it?'

'Well it's a piece of tin. *Florida Peaches*, it reads.'

'Florida Peaches?'

'I don't expect I've ever seen anything like it. Who could have got their hands on something like this?'

I thought back to the visit from the Land Ministry. How Mr Burrows was interested at the mention of Mr Campbell's name. The strange smells that sometimes wafted through the car. Was Mr Burrows shuttling goods back and forth, using his trips to Rashleigh as a convenient excuse? It seemed like a plausible scenario. Who would notice? Not the blind woman sitting in the back seat. I imagined Mrs Butler as a co-conspirator and Daisy an unwilling accomplice. How easy it would be for someone to land black-market goods at the jetty in the dead of night.

'There's a curse on that place,' I said aloud.

'It is a run of bad luck to be sure, but curses and fairy tales … I don't have much truck with that type of thing.'

I felt the table move and Father's chair creaked.

'We still have our work to do,' Father said gruffly. 'Cut some bread and cheese and I'll follow you shortly.'

'Yes, of course,' Mr Fallada replied, and I heard him ready himself. 'If you'll excuse me now I will go and see about the pups.'

I nodded a reply and said, 'Yes, of course. Thank you … Mr Fallada.'

He did not say anything else and simply left without another word.

'Perhaps this will take your mind off things for a while,' Father said, and he increased the volume on the wireless.

A slow, melancholy tune reverberated around the kitchen.

'Another thing before I go. A letter arrived for you in the post this morning.'

'For me?'

'Aye, we passed the postman on the road,' Father said.

'Well, won't you tell me who it is from?'

'Shall I open it then?'

'Yes, yes, please. I hope it's not more bad news.'

'Now let me see,' Father said.

He sighed loudly and said, 'It's not signed.'

'What do you mean … not signed?'

'It's just one sentence.'

'Read it.'

'*And now to the sea to slip beneath the waves.*'

'Is there anything else?'

'Nothing. The strangest thing, if you don't mind me saying.'

'It's the last two lines in a poem I once heard recited.'

'I can't say I've heard it before.'

'The poem is called, *To the Sea.*'

'A sea-faring man was he, this poet?'

'I suppose he was.'

'Oh there was one other thing. It's that young Mr Charles.'

'Pipe-smoker.'

'Who?'

'Charles …'

'That's the one. Well, it seems that they haven't found his body yet.'

'I thought you said everyone perished?'

'All but him, it seems.'

I thought about Pipe-smoker again and those final words of his, "I think I'd like to take the boat out one last time."

'Take the boat out …'

'What's that, dear?'

'It's nothing … just mumbling to myself.'

'First sign of madness my dear.'

'Yes.'

'Right so,' Father said.

The door opened and closed and I was alone, with just the wireless set crackling away. I rose from my seat and made my way to the shelf where the set was perched. I turned the dial and listened to the familiar hiss and whine until eventually there was silence. I stood motionless for some time, until the grandfather clock chimed out the hour.

'Goodness is that the time?' I murmured, and willed myself to move.

I shuffled a few steps and paused, thinking what it was I needed to do now my mornings were suddenly free again. I moved through the rooms, searching for something to occupy myself, deciding eventually to go into the study and take a seat in the rocking chair by the unlit fire. I picked up my knitting needles and ran a stitch or two, squeezed the arms of the little suit, then the legs, imagining what might have been.

I was moving mechanically between stitches, remembering recent events then casting my mind back further, to happier times, before Balham, before the war, to that very first time we met. I smiled at the thought and searched for more happy moments, to remember him. I put my stitching to one side then and reached into the pocket of my skirt and retrieved the lighter. I

261

ran my fingers over the inscription. H.M., and remembered the time I had presented it to Henry. He had a look of surprise at first, which turned to happiness.

"I'll treasure it always", he said and ran his thumb over the little barrel.

Click-click it went, then a bright yellow flame.

I rose from where I was sitting and walked the short distance to the piano. A melody was already playing in my head. It came to me, naturally, and without prompt. It was Henry's favourite tune. I moved my fingers across the keys, pressing each, slowly and carefully, just as it was meant to be played, allowing in that lonely moment, for all my sorrows to be swept away.

THE END

ACKNOWLEDGMENTS

Thank you to the long standing members of the Friday Writers Group, Paul and Andrew, for their support and encouragement of my work, and the readers and reviewers of the early drafts of the novel, including; John, Maggie and Brid. Special thanks to Basya Rose for cover art design.

ABOUT THE AUTHOR

Jack D. Whelan lives in the west of Ireland where he finds much of the inspiration for his novels..

He is an avid all-year round sea swimmer and occasional gardener.